'Look not thou down, but up!'
　　　　　'Rabbi Ben Ezra', Robert Browning

Contents

PART ONE

Looking East

'The wolves have prey'd; and look, the gentle day, Before the wheels of Phoebus, round about Dapple the drowsy East with spots of grey.'

Much Ado About Nothing,
William Shakespeare

One

Confusion

'Sector Victor Alfred 13,' said the voice on the telephone. Major Max Bayley had taken the call himself. Now he said, 'Understood,' and handed the receiver to the sergeant. 'Siren,' he commanded and went outside to where his pilots were waiting, alerted by the wail of the alarm signal. Just over medium height, fair-haired, with good features and physique, he was, at only a few months over twenty-one, young for his rank; but in this spring of 1941 was already one of Nazi Germany's leading fighter aces, and had the complete loyalty and respect of his men, not only for his prowess in the air, but because they all knew of his tragic background.

'Two squadrons of Blenheims,' he said, 'aiming for Wilhelmshaven. Sector V A 13. We will use both Flights. Seven thousand metres. Gunther on the right, Horst take the left. Flight Sergeant Mohler, you'll be my wing man.'

His flight commanders saluted and hurried for their planes, their men behind them. The engines on the Messerschmitt Bf 109F-4 R1 machines were already being warmed by the mechanics. Max Bayley's crew were waiting to insert him into his parachute harness and a moment later he was taxiing out to the runway, while his flights waited to follow.

It was an overcast March morning. The cloud ceiling was at 1,000 metres, but the met report he had received earlier had indicated that it was no more than 2,000 metres thick. Yet with the sun only just above the eastern horizon, even over the flat Flanders countryside the morning was gloomy.

Airborne, Max eased the stick back to climb as rapidly as he could. The Bf 109F was certainly a better machine than the E-model he had flown the previous year in the so-called Battle of Britain, but it still climbed more slowly than either the Spitfires or the Hurricanes he had fought so fiercely over

3

south-eastern England. But those formidable fighting machines seldom came across the Channel. Even if the Battle had been called off officially some months earlier, the British did not know that, and there were still sufficient raids on English targets to keep the interceptors at home for defensive purposes.

Max had mixed feelings about that battle. He knew, although it was not policy for anyone in Germany to say so, that the Luftwaffe had been defeated. Not in the sense that they had been dangerously reduced in numbers, or driven from the sky, but that they had entirely failed to carry out their appointed mission, which was to destroy RAF Fighter Command and thus make the invasion of England feasible. That invasion had not actually been abandoned; it had been 'postponed' until the spring. But the spring was just about here, and the idea had not been revived, at least as far as he knew . . .

But Max Bayley had mixed feelings about everything British. His father had been a famous World War I ace, with the Royal Flying Corps. His half-brother was a hardly less famous ace in the modern RAF. It was an intriguing thought that had he not opted for his dead mother's nationality Max could be flying a Spitfire himself alongside his brother.

What a great deal of angst and misfortune might have been avoided had he stayed in England. But he had made his decision, and however much he might regret it, deep in the private recesses of his mind, he had no option but to live with it. Besides, it was his nature to do his duty, even if that duty was decreed by a government he had grown to detest.

He broke through the cloud into brilliantly clear air still climbing. It took him some twenty minutes to reach the prescribed height. He looked over his shoulder to see his two squadrons fanning out beneath him. Flight Sergeant Mohler was, as required, already in position just astern and to his right.

'Babies, one o'clock, twenty-plus,' said Captain Gunther Langholm. Gunther was the oldest of Max's flying companions, from the days – was it only a year ago? – that they had both been enthusiastic lieutenants, and if Max himself did not immediately spot the enemy formation, he knew that his friend had the keenest eyes in the wing.

'Sections of three,' he said into his mike. 'They are sitting ducks. But there is a sting in their tail. We want at least half of them. Going down.'

4

He began his descent, slowly at this stage. The enemy formation was now well in sight, and he had to presume that the German squadrons would also have been sighted. But he knew from experience that the British bombers would do everything within their power to carry out their mission of bombing the naval dockyard, even if it meant risking heavy casualties. He remembered too well the previous May when the Wehrmacht had begun its invasion of Belgium and France. Taken by surprise, the Allied armies had reeled back in the debacle that had led to Dunkirk and the subsequent surrender of France. The Allied air forces had been required to stop the German advance at all costs. The French opposition had been negligible, but the British had thrown in everything they possessed, regardless of the consequences. On only the second day of the invasion they had dispatched eight obsolete Fairey Battle light bombers to destroy vital bridges across the Meuse: every one had been shot down. But they had tried again the following day. His brother John had been in that battle, flying a hardly less obsolete Bolton-Paul Defiant fighter, and had also been shot down. But he had survived.

Since then John Bayley had gravitated to Spitfires, which, sadly for the British, had not been available during the Battle of France. Max knew he and John had come close to each other several times during the three tumultuous months of the Battle of Britain, but they had only actually met in combat once. Then he had proved victorious and John again had had to take to his parachute. Had he, Max, been the superior pilot? Or had he had at last the superior aircraft in his new F-model? He certainly doubted that. But on the day he had been the better pilot, simply because of the manic aggression that had overcome him at the catastrophe that had just overtaken his domestic life.

Today he was his usual calm but ruthless self. He saw the tracers rising towards him, but none reached him. The British gunners were anxious and firing too soon. Max readied his firing buttons; in addition to two nine-millimetre machine guns, he also possessed two twenty-millimetre cannon, one in each wing. Now the range was closing rapidly, but with so many small aircraft around them, the British gunners were unable to concentrate on any one target. And now *his* chosen target was filling his sights. He fired both cannon and then again, saw the explosions on the Blenheim's starboard wing and pulled back his stick to soar over the stricken bomber and fasten on the next. Even a year ago he might have followed his first victim down to make sure both of the kill and his claim to it. But with thirty-nine bars painted on his fuselage, he was no longer interested in numbers. His objective was to break up the enemy attack, not to seek glory.

'Gentlemen!' Gunther Langholm called, banging on the bar counter. The noise slowly subsided. 'I give you, Major Max Bayley, in celebration of his fortieth kill.'

'Major Bayley!' the pilots chorused, raising their steins. Max felt quite overwhelmed.

'But it is really forty-one,' Gunther said. 'That first Blenheim you attacked also went down.'

'I think Sergeant Mohler got him,' Max protested. 'I only fired two bursts.'

'But the plane went down in flames, and Mohler says he did not fire at all.'

'Well . . .'

'Forty-one,' Gunther insisted. 'Forget the beer, we'll drink champagne, Frederich!'

The barman began uncorking bottles.

Max and Gunther sat together at dinner, as they usually did. By now the evening had taken on a rosy glow. But there was every reason for the wing to celebrate: they had not lost a single plane in the day's combat. When Max recalled the squadron dinners of the previous summer, after the completion of their almost daily sorties over southern England in support of the bombers, with at least one, and more often two or three unoccupied place settings to remind them of the comrades lost during the day, it seemed like another world.

But he was not in the mood for smiling, even after several glasses of champagne. He sometimes doubted whether he would ever be in the mood for smiling again, something Gunther well understood.

'Am I allowed to say something very stupid – and probably impertinent as well?'

'You can say anything you like,' Max said, 'even if I already know what it is.'

'I was going to say that you simply have to stop brooding over Heidi. You have told me that you never loved her . . .'

'You never met her.'

'Well, no, but—'

'She was the most exciting of women. And she was my wife.'

Gunther swallowed, but Max went on speaking, totally matter-of-fact. 'I know the marriage could not have lasted. I accept entirely the Gestapo report that she had a stream of affairs in my absence. But to have her tortured by Luttmann's thugs, and then hanged, slowly . . . it curdles my blood at the same time as it makes it boil.'

Gunther hastily refilled Max's wine glass.

'You know,' Max went on, still speaking quietly, 'I even accept that one of her lovers was a British agent, and that she gave him information I had revealed about my orders. But does that not make me the guilty one?'

'It is generally accepted that a man is entitled to confide in his wife,' Gunther suggested, 'but not that his wife is entitled to pass on those confidences to a third party.'

'I don't believe that, and I don't think you do either. Field Marshal Milch virtually confessed to me that the reason I was not involved was because I was one of Germany's most famous aces, the more famous for having abandoned England in favour of the Reich. You remember the hoo-hah they made about that? To have arrested me for treason only a couple of years later would have been a propaganda disaster. And, you know, the only reason they dared arrest Heidi was because I had been reported missing, believed killed, when I came down in the North Sea. That also was given front page treatment, remember? When I suddenly turned up again—'

'—That too was given front page treatment,' Gunther agreed. '"The pirate traitor" the English called you. Your feat was the sort of thing for which the English, had you been one of theirs, would have awarded their Victoria Cross.'

'For having taken over a tiny drifter manned by three fishermen and a girl? Believe me, Gunther, it was not one of my proudest achievements. Those people fished me out of the sea and saved my life.'

'But you had no choice. You could not let them take you back to England: you would have been hanged as a traitor.

7

And did you not have their boat refuelled and send them back to England? What more could you do?'

'The point is that having blown up that "heroic" feat the Government even less could afford to have me arrested. So here I am, while Heidi . . .'

'You are here, a hero of the Third Reich, fighting for that Reich. And, it seems, determined to get yourself killed doing so. I saw the way you went into those bombers today. You hit that first Blenheim – as it happened, mortally, but you did not know that. You did not make sure of the kill, exposed yourself to its fire as you went after the next. You have their poor shooting to thank for your survival. Why? What more do you want? You have the Iron Cross, First and Second Class. You have the Gold Award for the number of missions you have flown. You are a major at the age of twenty-one. If this war lasts another couple of years, you will be a general. You just have to get through this bad psychological patch. Listen, you have got to get yourself another woman. Someone who can make you forget Heidi.'

'I have another woman.'

'Well, then . . .'

'Unfortunately, she happens to be married to someone else.'

Max slept fitfully, but this had become the norm over the past few months. He found himself wondering if it would solve his problems to persuade Erika to divorce her husband and marry him. Of course she was his second cousin, the daughter of Max von Bitterman, his mother's first cousin. But she had never let that interfere with her passions. He also knew that she was every bit as amoral and sexually insatiable as her best friend Heidi Stumpff had been, and she shared his grief over the loss of that friend. On the other hand, she had never shown the slightest interest in parting from her wealthy, and apparently totally complacent, husband in order to marry a fighter pilot who, however famous, had only his salary to live on, and who would undoubtedly one day – perhaps one day soon – die in combat.

He realized the sky was lightening, but was still surprised at the tap on his door; it was surely too early for the RAF to have arrived. 'Come in, Heinrich,' he called. 'I am awake.'

The door opened and his servant entered. 'Good morning,

Herr Major. I am sorry to disturb you, but there is a telephone call . . .'

'I am not in the mood for telephone calls, Heinrich. Certainly not at five o'clock in the morning. Who is it from?'

'It is from Aachen, Herr Major.'

'Eh?' Max sat up. Aachen was the headquarters of the Flanders Air Fleet.

'Colonel General Udet's office, sir.'

'Colonel General Udet is on the phone?' Max tumbled out of bed, and reached for his dressing gown.

'No, sir. It is a secretary. But he wishes to speak with you.'

Max ran down the stairs and seized the receiver. 'Major Bayley.'

'I am sorry to trouble you at this hour, Herr Major, but the Colonel General wishes to see you.'

'Of course. Ah . . .'

'Immediately, sir.'

Max looked out of the window at the drizzling rain and gulped. 'I will leave immediately.' He hung up. Heinrich had followed him down the stairs into the mess. 'Tell Frederich I wish to breakfast, now, and tell Captain Langholm I wish to see him.'

'Now, sir?'

'Now.'

Max returned upstairs to shave and dress. By the time he came down again his breakfast was on the table and a bleary-eyed Gunther was drinking coffee. 'What's the flap?'

'I don't know. Udet has summoned me to Aachen.'

Gunther whistled. 'At this hour? Must be something big.'

'Yes. I don't know how long I'll be gone, or even if I'll be coming back.'

'Of course you'll be coming back.'

'Just listen. I don't even know if Hartmann is aware of this, and I don't see any point in waking him up. If we are sent up today, you are in command.'

Gunther swallowed. 'Of both squadrons?'

'Yes, pending my return or confirmation of your rank. At a reasonable hour this morning, you can inform the Colonel of the situation. If he doesn't like my dispositions, tell him he can telephone Aachen.'

'Ye-es,' Gunther said. Like all the pilots he had a healthy

respect for his commanding officer. 'But look here, see that you do come back.'

Max swallowed the last of his croissant, gulped his coffee, put on his cap and stood up. 'Keep your fingers crossed.'

Within moments of leaving the ground it was lost to sight in the rain mist. But Max knew this country better than any other; he had in fact been based in Aachen for some weeks before the commencement of the Battle of Britain. Thus he flew on compass and speedometer, in clear skies at 3,000 metres, until he calculated he was in the right place, and then dropped back into the cloud. It broke at 1,000 metres and he quickly identified where he was; a few minutes later, just before seven, he was landing at Aachen.

He had radioed ahead to inform them of his imminent arrival, and mechanics were waiting for him. It was a large airfield with a considerable number of aircraft, both bombers and fighters, parked in rows, but Max was interested to note that there were several individual planes from various fighter wings, every one of them marked with the insignia of a squadron commander.

'What might be called a brass gathering,' Major Alfred Dolenz said, joining Max for the walk to the command office. 'Bit of a flap, eh? Any ideas?'

'I hope we are about to find that out.'

'By the way, congratulations on your fortieth.'

'Thank you. I reckon we're all going to have a profitable summer, if they keep coming without an escort. What's your current bag, Alfred?'

'Thirty-three. So I hope you're right about the summer; I have some catching up to do.'

They paused at the doorway of the office to allow another officer to emerge. He glanced at them. 'Major Dolenz, Major Bayley.'

'Good morning, Dieter,' Dolenz said. 'Are you leaving?'

'Yes,' Dieter Vennekers replied abruptly, and strode off toward his plane.

'Well!' Dolenz exclaimed.

'I wouldn't say he has just had good news,' Max suggested. He entered the anteroom where there were several other officers present, standing or sitting around chatting, some smoking.

Max presented himself at the desk. 'Major Max Bayley, Fighter Wing 5.'

'Thank you, Major Bayley,' said the captain, ticking the name on his list. 'The Colonel General will see you shortly.'

'Major Alfred Dolenz, Fighter Wing 6.'

'Thank you, Major Dolenz.' Another tick. 'The Colonel General will see you shortly.'

'Any idea what this is all about?'

'The Colonel General will see you in a little while, Major.'

'These goddamned staff people give me the pip,' Dolenz growled as they sat down. 'So stuffed with their own importance.'

An inner door was opened by a major. 'Colonel Lutyens!'

The Colonel rose from his chair on the far side of the room and went into the inner office.

'So we wait.' Dolenz's temper appeared to be shortening. 'Do you realize, Max, that we could still be in bed? All this immediacy stuff is a load of rubbish.'

'They'll get around to us eventually,' Max said. He was actually greatly relieved to see so many other senior officers present. To be summoned at short notice for what seemed to be a special interview with one's supreme commander was always a nerve-racking business, and for him more than most. When he had abandoned England for the glamour and projected glory of Nazi Germany as an enthusiastic eighteen-year-old, he had been received with acclamation, not only by his mother's relatives, but by their Party friends. He had been given no choice as to what he should do with his life; as the son of a famous British airman his only career had to be in the Luftwaffe. He had had no objection to that. In 1938 the Messerschmitt Bf 109E was the best interceptor in the world, and at that tender age he had had no concept that he and his comrades would ever be required to undertake aggressive action in enemy skies – certainly not that the enemy could ever be his father's country.

When the war had actually started, only a year after Max had left England, he was naturally distressed. But in those first months Great Britain had hardly seemed a participant. He had earned his early reputation in Poland, shooting down obsolete biplanes. He was not proud of that. Yet the reputation was there. So was the comradeship and the belief, and when the 'real' war had begun it had seemed the most natural thing in the world to take on the Hurricanes and then the Spitfires of the RAF.

He knew he possessed an innate and somewhat uncanny skill in the air; his speed of thought and reaction, his patience and his nerve were unequalled, even by his brother. His immediate superiors had recognized this exceptional skill. In particular he had attracted the attention of Field Marshal Erhard Milch, Deputy Commander of the Luftwaffe. Hence his decoration and rapid promotion. But he had always been aware of an undercurrent of uncertainty and even hostility amongst some of the senior officers with whom he came into contact.

He supposed this was natural. He might have had a German mother, widely regarded as the most beautiful and accomplished woman of her time, as well as one of the wealthiest, but Karolina von Bitterman, moving in reverse, as it were, had entirely abandoned Germany for her English husband, taking her wealth with her. She had died, so tragically young, of cancer, only a year after the Nazis had come to power, but she had already made her dislike for and hostility toward the new regime abundantly clear. And she had educated her son at an English public school. Could a leopard really change its spots? Could a Bayley fight for a government his parents had detested and he had been brought up to regard as a natural enemy?

From Milch's point of view, the proof of the pudding was in the eating. But then had come Heidi. The Field Marshal, Max recalled, had been against their marriage. Heidi was the daughter of a prominent industrialist, and thus, from a social perspective, was entirely suitable as a wife for a war hero. But Milch knew her to be amoral and wanton. Max had chosen to ignore the guarded warning. He had never been in love with Heidi, but as the woman he did love – and for whose love he had defected to Germany – had chosen to marry for money rather than love, he had been desperate for a woman who might just be able to give him the companionship he so anxiously needed when not in combat.

Looking back, Max supposed that he had soon been aware that faithfulness to her marriage vows was not one of Heidi's characteristics, but, seeing her as he did only every couple of weeks, he had chosen to ignore the situation. That one of her lovers should have turned out to be an English spy had to be the worst of luck; he had never had any doubts of Heidi's loyalty to Germany. But the fact remained that she was the wife of a half-English pilot: to many people that had seemed too much of a coincidence. Yet as he had said to Gunther, Max had no doubt at all that the only reason he had not been arrested too was because of Milch's influence.

He had endeavoured to repay that support, as well as perhaps expiate his guilt at being unable to save his wife from the most dreadful of fates, by throwing himself into combat with an even greater, more ruthless determination. He had actually prayed for the bullet that would bring him down in flames, but instead had gone from strength to strength, even shooting down his own brother. Then, over the winter, Milch had been, if not demoted, certainly moved sideways, away from active command to administration. It was generally accepted that this was because of Reichsmarschall Goering's jealousy; Milch had more than once suggested strategic and tactical approaches to the Battle that Goering had dismissed as impractical or unnecessary, only to have to adopt them as the contest continued. The departure of his friend had left Max feeling distinctly exposed. However, if this was a general flap . . .

'Major Bayley!'

Another six officers had entered the inner office and then left again, each without speaking to their fellows. 'Good luck,' an increasingly morose Dolenz remarked.

Max stepped into the inner room, saluted. '*Heil* Hitler!'

'*Heil*. Sit down.'

Max cast a hasty glance round the room, which was empty apart from the Colonel General and the Major. The only furniture was a desk with two straight chairs before it, but there were filing cabinets against the wall and on the walls there were several large maps, as well as an equally large painting of Hermann Goering.

The Colonel General himself was a stocky man of medium height with blunt features. Max had met him several times, but had never exchanged more than a few words. He sat down, placed his cap on his lap, and waited.

'Congratulations on your fortieth kill,' Udet said.

'Thank you, Herr Colonel General.'

'And it is now actually forty-one, is it not?'

'Yes, sir.'

'Very good. I am recommending you for the Knight's Cross.'

'Sir?' Max could not believe his ears.

'Do you not think you deserve it?'

'I think I have been very lucky, sir.'

'Agreed. Or you would not be here. But you have put your luck to better use than most.

'Now, what I have to tell you is top secret. It is not to be discussed with your fellow officers or with the pilots of your wing. You will merely carry out your orders until you are given more. Is this understood?'

'Yes, sir.'

'Very good. You will return to Ostend and tell your men, in both squadrons, to stand down for a week's leave.'

'Sir?' This was to be a deathly secret? And both squadrons, with the RAF coming over daily?

Udet continued as if Max had not spoken. 'You and your squadrons will reassemble at Munich in one week's time. There you will find your new aircraft awaiting you.'

'New aircraft, sir?'

'It will be our latest model, the 109G. We call it the Gustav. It is the last word in fighter-bombers. When you assemble in Munich you will be given further orders. These will encompass the necessary time for you and you men to become used to the new machines. Understood?'

'Yes, sir.' Max's head was spinning: none of this made any sense. No doubt the new machines included secret features that the high command was afraid to risk falling into British hands. But that made very little sense either, as all their recent fighting had taken place either over German-occupied territory or over the sea; a plane coming down would be in no danger of capture by the enemy. 'Should we remain in Ostend until our replacements arrive? The RAF comes over almost every day.'

'Your replacements are already there, Major. Your squadrons, and yourself, are being selected for this new assignment because of the exceptional capabilities you have displayed.'

'Thank you, sir. Munich . . .' About as far away from any actual fighting as it was possible to imagine. 'Would it be in order for me to take my leave at Bitterman?'

'Certainly. It is your home, is it not? Enjoy your leave, Major, and tell your men to do so as well. This may be their last leave for several months.'

'Yes, sir. Thank you, sir.'

Udet nodded. 'Very good, Major. Dismissed.'

Max followed fashion and avoided Dolenz's eye as he left the office. He was back in Ostend for lunch, to find all his planes vanished and his men in a furious, bewildered state. 'These blighters just turned up,' Gunther complained. 'Said we were grounded and they were to take our planes. Well, they were commanded by a colonel, who wouldn't argue. I went off to see Hartmann, but he'd gone too – nobody seems to know where. What a fuck-up! When I got back here, our machines were all up. Reconnoitring, the crew says.'

'There's something odd going on,' Max agreed, 'but I know very little more than you. What I can tell you is that we are all to take leave, and reassemble in Munich a week today.'

'Leave?' Gunther demanded. 'All of us? With the RAF so active?'

'Our replacements are intended to take care of the RAF.'

'But who are we supposed to fight out of Munich?' someone asked. 'We'd be out of fuel before we could even reach the Channel.'

'Do you think Switzerland is going to declare war?' asked someone else. There was a burst of derisory laughter. 'Well, it could happen,' the young man insisted.

'Speculation is a waste of time,' Max said. 'In fact, speculation outside of this room is strictly forbidden. We will get our orders in Munich. What I can tell you is that we are going to be flying the very latest 109, the Gustav.'

That brought a chorus of approval. Only Gunther remarked, as the meeting broke up, 'But we are not to fly them against Spitfires.'

'Patience, old friend. Go home and see your folks. And your girl – you do have a girl?'

'Never had the time. I'm going to Berlin and the nightspots. Are you coming?'

'I thought I'd go down to Bitterman. Do you know that what with one thing or another I haven't been there for two years?'

'And it is your home.'

'Well, sort of . . .'

Gunther saw the shadow cross Max's face and clapped him on the shoulder. 'And it is close to Munich. I will see you next Friday.'

'Max, my dear fellow, how good to see you!' Max von Bitterman embraced his cousin; they were both named after the founder of the Bitterman financial empire, his uncle and young Max's grandfather. 'And you have come to visit?'

He stood on the huge front steps of Schloss Bitterman and looked from the Munich taxi to the single small suitcase beside Max's boots. He was a big man, tall and broad, in his late forties and running to stomach, whose thinning hair was beginning to grey; he had none of the fine features that had characterized his cousin Karolina, and his cheek was marked with a livid Junkers' scar.

'Just a week – if you'll have me.'

'But of course.' Bitterman signalled the waiting butler to pick up the suitcase and escorted Max into the huge entry hall. What memories it brought back. The suit of armour with which he and John had loved to play when they were little boys, the double doors on the right opening into the grand drawing room, the curving staircase leading up to the first floor. Two floors higher up, Max recalled, were the crenellated battlements, another favourite playground, and the two turrets with their steeply sloping copper roofs, their narrow windows looking out at the distant Alps.

'Oriane!' Bitterman shouted up the stairs. 'Oriane! Come down. Max is here!' He led Max into the drawing room and to the sideboard. 'Schnapps?'

'Thank you.'

Bitterman poured two small glasses of the white liquid. '*Heil* Hitler!' He tossed the drink off.

'*Heil* Hitler!' Max followed his example.

Bitterman refilled the glasses and gestured Max to a chair. 'You did get my letter?'

'Yes. Thank you.'

'I did think of coming up myself, but . . . well, I knew you would not be long in Berlin, and it's not as if I had more than a nodding acquaintance with Stumpff. I never did meet the daughter – Heidi, was it?'

'Heidi,' Max agreed. And you had no intention, he thought, of becoming involved in a treason trial, even if it concerned your cousin.

'Those Englanders are swine,' Bitterman declared.

Max knew that he was referring to one Englishman in particular: *his* father, who as far as Bitterman was concerned had made off with Karolina's fortune, which he considered should have come to him as the closest living relative of the dead count.

'The agent was a German,' Max said mildly.

'In the pay of the English. Who seduced a German lady. He is as much a swine as his employers.'

Max realized that it was going to be a long week if he couldn't get hold of Erika. But before he could raise the subject, Oriane appeared. 'Max! Oh, it's so good to see you.' She embraced him and kissed him, with some difficulty; she was less than half the size of her husband. Small and dark, her hair also streaked with grey, she seemed in a perpetually agitated state. How this pair had produced a daughter like Erika defied the imagination. But Erika had to be a throwback to some glamorous ancestor – the same ancestor, perhaps, from whom his mother had obtained both her looks and her elegance, although he did not suppose Karolina would have appreciated the comparison, at least as regards morality.

'We were shattered when we heard the news,' Oriane gushed. 'You poor boy. You poor, poor boy.'

'I am endeavouring to forget about it,' Max said. That was the only way out.

'Of course you must do that. You are so strong, so brave.'

Her husband handed her a glass of schnapps. 'Max has a week's leave.'

'Oh, how lovely. Is it something special?'

'Ah . . . well, I have just made my fortieth kill.'

'Forty!' Bitterman shouted. 'My dear boy, that must make you Germany's leading ace.'

'I think Marseille has more,' Max said, modestly. 'And I know Molders has more, while Witz had more than fifty before he went in. But I am to get the Knight's Cross.'

'Then you are up there with the stars. Herrmann!' he bellowed. 'We will have a bottle of champagne.'

Oriane kissed him again. 'We must celebrate. Tell us what you would like to do.'

'Ah,' Max said, 'is Erika around?'

Erika and her husband actually lived in Nuremberg, only 150 kilometres away, and she promised to come over the next day. It had been a long evening, as Max really had nothing in common with his older cousins, nor was he in any position to answer their questions about the course of the War and his part in it. He was up early, having the grooms saddle one of the horses for a canter in the open country outside the grounds, and was just returning over the brow of the hill overlooking the road when he saw the little Volkswagen beneath him.

He kicked his horse and descended the slope, reaching the road just in front of the car, which braked and blew its horn. Then the door was opened as a woman stepped out. 'Max! I did not recognize you.'

He dismounted and went towards her, leading the horse. He had been able to get together with her twice since Heidi's death; but for the ability to hold her in his arms, the knowledge that he would be able to do so again, at least occasionally, he thought he might have gone mad. She was, as always, entrancing – at least to his eyes. He supposed there were people who would have said her features were a trifle too bold – even coarse – for beauty, but framed by her long black hair they were certainly compelling, especially when smiling in welcome. Her real beauty lay beneath her neck, even if today it was more than usually concealed. Not very tall, she possessed a superbly voluptuous figure that even the baggy trousers and floppy jumper worn over a loose blouse could not truly suppress; her feet were thrust into ankle boots.

He released his reins to take her in his arms and kiss her mouth, seeking her tongue. It was a peculiar feeling of combined heaven and hell that he owned this woman, when in her company, but that he could only take possession on widely spaced occasions, while the rest of the time she belonged to someone else, and, knowing her as well as he did, that she went to her husband's arms as willingly and enthusiastically as she came to his. Nor did he have any idea how many other arms she habitually visited; again, he could have no doubt that this was the case.

But right this moment she was his. 'I had a terrible fear that Hans might have come with you.'

She kissed him again. 'Hans is busy. Hans is always busy. You have a week?'

'I have five days now.'

'Then we do not have time to waste. Corsair,' she told the horse, 'be a good boy and just wait there for a while.' She held Max's hand to lead him back to the car.

'Will he obey?' Max asked.

'Probably not. But if he runs off, it will only be to go back to the *schloss*. That is his home.'

'But if we haven't got there by then, they'll think I have come off and send people to look for me.'

'You worry about trifles. I suppose it comes from being an airman.' She opened the passenger door. 'You get in first.'

Max obeyed and she followed him, straddling his knees. 'The wheel gets in the way on the other side,' she explained.

He held her close and nuzzled her neck. 'I don't see how we can do anything in this confined space with all these clothes on.'

'Of course we can. We can do anything we wish, if we are determined to do it. Have you never wanted to make love in the cockpit of your Messerschmitt?'

'As a matter of fact, no.'

'You have no imagination. I suppose that is an asset, in a fighter pilot. Every time I think of you, I imagine what it would be like to have sex with you in your cockpit – is that not an appropriate word? – especially if we were flying at the time. Now, start on my tits. Suck them. Suck them hard.'

He obeyed, pushing her jumper up to her neck, unbuttoning her blouse and sinking his face into the soft flesh, seeking the always hard nipples, more erect than ever in the chill March air. Erika never changed. He hoped she never would. After a few minutes of sighing contentment, she dismounted, unbuckled his belt and pulled off his breeches and drawers. Then she dropped her own trousers, sensuously sliding them down her splendid legs – she was not wearing underclothes – and mounted him again. 'Now,' she said as he sank into her, 'Now. We are flying at eight thousand metres. In your 109. That is close to heaven, eh?'

'If we were in my 109,' Max pointed out, 'in this position, you would be getting my stick up you ass.'

'Now, that is something to look forward to.' She began to move.

*　　*　　*

19

'Major Bayley!' Colonel Hamel shook hands. 'You are looking well.'

'Thank you, Herr Colonel.' I am feeling well, Max thought. He had never before had five days of Erika exclusively to himself. They had indeed flown close to heaven. But now he had to forget her, at least for the immediate future.

'And your men?'

'Seven are here now, sir. I expect the rest in this afternoon.'

'Excellent.' Hamel turned to the window. 'What do you think of them?'

Max had been unable to resist the temptation to inspect the machines parked neatly, wing tip to wing tip, on the apron. 'They look good.'

Hamel sat behind his desk and gestured Max to a seat. 'They do not appear so very different to the old E-model, but their performance is far superior. And their cannon are now thirty millimetre – that is the most destructive aerial weapon in existence. While you now have a two hundred and fifty kilogramme bomb-carrying capacity. That makes it the most complete fighter-bomber in existence, as well.'

'I look forward to trying this marvel, sir. Ah . . .?'

'You can take one up this afternoon – now, if you wish. And your men. You leave tomorrow morning for a fairly lengthy flight, so you will have ample time to get to know the crate. You have spoken to no one of this assignment?'

'I do not know what my assignment is, sir.'

'My orders are to instruct you to fly to Dresden.'

'Sir?' He was being sent further and further away from the War.

'As Dresden is approximately five hundred kilometres from here, and you have the new long-range tanks, you will not find it difficult. You will fly at seven thousand metres, so that you cannot be identified from the ground.'

'There is no enemy territory between Munich and Dresden, sir.' Czechoslovakia had by now been fully assimilated into the Reich.

'Nonetheless, those are your orders.'

'Yes, sir. May I have a copy of the orders, sir?'

'There is no copy available, Major, because there are no written orders.' He gazed at Max's expression. 'I received them in a coded telephone message from Luftwaffe Headquarters.'

'Yes, sir. And are we to be based at Dresden?'

'I have no idea. You will receive further orders when you reach your destination.'

'Dresden?' Gunther mused. 'Well, it is supposed to be a beautiful city. But a bit remote from the Channel . . . '

'It's the Italians,' Lieutenant Kramer suggested. 'They are having trouble with the Greeks. They are asking for help.'

'And we are sending them our latest fighter-bombers?' inquired Senior Lieutenant Horst Geiger.

'We'll be in Dresden for lunch,' Max told them, 'then we'll find out. I'll be putting you through your paces to familiarize you with the machine. But I don't want to lose any of you – or any of them – so concentrate.'

Flying the Gustav was a dream, or so it seemed. The new machine climbed far faster than the F, and turned more sharply as well. Max had an enormous desire to test it against a Spitfire. But he was going to Dresden. Or was he? 'Dresden Traffic Control calling Commander Wing 5. Come in, please, Major Bayley.'

'I am he,' Max said, more mystified than ever; this entire assignment was supposed to be top secret, including presumably the name of the Wing Commander.

'What is your position?'

Max checked his map and then looked down for confirmation. It was a beautiful spring day and from 7,000 metres it seemed that all Central Europe was displayed beneath him. 'We are approaching Leipzig. We will be with you in half an hour.'

'What is your fuel situation?'

Max checked his gauge. 'Still over half.'

'Very good. Your orders have been changed.'

'Say again?'

'You are to divert to Prague. It is no further away than Dresden. You will refuel in Prague: they are expecting you. Once refuelling is complete, you will fly on to Budapest. You are expected in Buda by 1300. There fresh orders will await you. Dresden out.'

'Did you copy that, Gunther?' Max asked.

'I did. What the shit are they playing at?'

'Looks like Kramer was right; it must be something to do with Greece. All pilots, Wing will alter course 105. Follow me.'

While the machines were being serviced, on a very crowded airfield, Max sent his pilots to the mess to grab something to eat; he had no idea when they would get lunch, if at all. He remained to see that the fuelling was proceeding satisfactorily, then followed them.

'Max!' Major Joachim Hederling had trained with him before the War, although Hederling had opted for bombers rather than fighters. Now he shook his friend's hand. 'I am hearing so much about you.' Max gave him an old-fashioned look and he hurried on. 'About your fortieth kill. The Knight's Cross!'

Max frowned. 'How do you know about that?'

'It was gazetted, a few days ago. Did you not know of it?'

'I knew I had been recommended. I've been out of touch this last week.' They went into the mess and were served a late breakfast. 'Are you stationed here?'

'God forbid – these people hate us! No, we flew in this morning, only just before you. Now we are off to Budapest.'

'Snap.'

'Good lord!'

'When did you receive your orders?'

'At dawn this morning.'

'To take your Stukas to Buda?'

'That's right. And you?'

'We were actually on our way to Dresden when we were diverted here, en route to Buda.'

'It has to be the Atakers screaming for help. They've been getting a succession of bloody noses all winter, and now the Englanders are putting troops into Greece . . . Do you know that we are moving ground forces into the Balkans as well?'

'Sounds big. Well, it'll make a change to be flying in warm sunshine instead of fog and rain.'

'But why were you going to Dresden?'

'I haven't the slightest idea, Joachim, and I was told not to speculate.' He finished his meal. 'I'll see you in Buda.'

They landed, as instructed, just before one, and Max reported to Flight Control, while he wondered if he would have any time off to inspect the famous twin cities.

'Major Bayley!' Colonel Esselmann shook his hand. 'It is a privilege to have you under my command.'

'Thank you, sir.'

'What do you think of the Gustav?'

'I am very impressed, sir. I look forward to trying it in combat. Against a worthwhile opponent.'

'You mean a Spitfire. Sit down, Major.' Esselmann moved behind his desk. 'I'm afraid that will have to wait for a little while. There are more important, and immediate, targets for the Luftwaffe.'

'In the Balkans, sir?'

'In the immediate future, yes. What you are about to do is a diversion from the task you were sent to Dresden to prepare for. Do you know anything about that?'

'No, sir.'

'Well, it's top secret. But as I say, it has been put on hold for the time being. The Italians are having a difficult time in Greece and have asked for our help. The Fuehrer has of course agreed, and we are moving an army corps down to Albania. It was assumed that there would be no problem getting there. The government of the Yugoslav regent, Prince Paul, willingly agreed to permit the passage of our troops through their country, and the Wehrmacht is already concentrated on the Hungarian border. But only two days ago there was a *coup d'état* in Belgrade. Prince Paul and all his pro-German ministers were dismissed and the country taken over by the army, in the name of King Peter. However, as he is a small boy I doubt he knows much about it. This sort of thing is of course commonplace in the Balkans; their idea of politics is perpetual anarchy. We usually ignore them completely. However, in this case, this so-called democratic government has repudiated the arrangement made by Prince Paul with us and has refused to allow any German troops on their soil.' He paused, staring at Max, awaiting a reaction.

'Well, sir,' Max suggested, 'it is their country. I suppose they have a right to decide who shall enter it . . .'

Esselmann snorted. 'They are attempting to stand in the way of the Reich's legitimate requirements. That is unacceptable. Next they will be allying themselves with the Western democracies. The Fuehrer is furious. Our orders are to take over the country by force, and treat anyone who opposes us as an enemy-under-arms. The Wehrmacht crosses the border tomorrow at dawn.'

Max nodded. If he were to start questioning the morality of his government at this late stage, he would have to resign his commission. 'Very good, sir. And we are to fly in support. Does Yugoslavia have an air force?'

'A very small one, and totally obsolete.'

'It hardly seems a task for our latest fighter-bombers.'

'It will be a good test for them. You are not flying in support of the Wehrmacht, Major. You are flying in front of it. The Fuehrer's orders are that Belgrade is to be razed to the ground.'

Two

Father's Day

'Good morning, gentlemen. Good of you to come.' Air Commodore Hargreaves was his usual courteous self: he had commanded their presence. He was a solidly built man with surprisingly delicate features and thinning pale hair who exuded good humour, although none of the twenty men standing before him – all of whom had served under him long enough to know him well – had any doubts as to either his determination or, when necessary, his ruthlessness.

They were all at least squadron leaders and thus experienced fighting airmen, and while they all knew they must have been summoned for a specific purpose, they were more interested in the man who had accompanied the Air Commodore into the room: he wore the uniform and the insignia of a colonel in the Army, and was carrying with him a large bag and, incredibly, a parachute.

'Please sit down,' Hargreaves invited, and the chairs scraped. He looked over their faces. As they knew him, so he knew them, some better than others. He picked out the dark head of his son-in-law, but gave no immediate sign of recognition. 'As you may know,' he said, 'since the German attacks on England have diminished in intensity, we have been repaying them in kind, with almost daily raids by small bomber groups on their naval bases and other military targets in France and the Low Countries. These have been universally successful, but at an increasing cost. Over the winter, while their bombers were still coming over in force, you chaps were wholly occupied in defence, as the Luftwaffe fighter arm was almost wholly occupied with escorting their bombers. That is now changing. They are devoting more time, and men and machines, to defence, and are thus shooting down too many of our bombers for comfort. But we now

25

have the fighter capacity to enable us to contemplate offensive action in defence of *our* bombers.'

There was a rustle around the room.

'Now, of course,' Hargreaves said, 'this requires us to consider
the situation from a totally different perspective than in the past.
One of our great advantages during the Battle of Britain was
that the Messerschmitt 109, our principal antagonist, only had
the fuel capacity for at most half an hour over England. This
meant that the further he had to go, as for instance, London,
his time over the target was brought down to little more than
a few minutes. Unfortunately, at this moment, our planes have
no greater capacity. That means that once we start sending your
Spitfires over France you are also going to be limited to no
more than a few minutes of combat. Obviously there can be
no question of any of our fighters penetrating German airspace.
But this brings me to my second point—' He paused to take a
drink of water from the tumbler on the table, and there was
another rustle. 'Our second big advantage, and it was very
nearly the decisive one in the Battle of Britain, was that it was
fought over Britain. You are all well aware that all the rubbish
that has been printed in the newspapers about our shooting
down four German planes for every one of ours lost is just that:
rubbish. The difference was that, again as I know you are aware,
unless our people were killed outright or badly wounded, as
they were baling out over our own territory, they were all able
to rejoin their units. But every German airman who went down
– even if he was in the best of health on landing – was out of
the War. Their losses in experienced airmen compared with ours
have been truly exceptional. But again, that situation will be
entirely reversed when we start operations over France. France
was our ally when this War started, but it is no longer. Sadly,
this also applies in a large measure to the French themselves.
Colonel Blatchford will be saying more about that in a moment.'

Heads turned to look at the Colonel, who was staring at
the ceiling.

'These are all factors which you, and your men, will have
to take into consideration,' Hargreaves said. 'I will now ask
Colonel Blatchford to address you on this subject.'

The Colonel stood up. 'Good morning, gentlemen. I am
sure none of you ever take off for combat with the expect-
ation of being brought down, but it does happen, and over

enemy territory you will be faced with flak as well as hostile aircraft. Were any of you Boy Scouts?'

Several hands went up.

'Then you'll know the motto: Be Prepared. It is my business to give you some indication of what you should be prepared for, and how to deal with it. This information you will pass on to your pilots, together with some equipment I'm going to give you.'

Heads turned to look at the bag.

'Now,' the Colonel went on, 'have any of you gentlemen been shot down in combat?'

Again several hands went up.

'And you have all survived, which proves the Air Commodore's point about the advantages of fighting over your own country. But were any of you shot down in France last May?'

Heads turned and John Bayley stood up. 'I was, sir.' He was a tall, slim young man with good shoulders, craggily attractive features and dark hair. Hargreaves beamed at him. John Bayley, the son of his old comrade from the Great War, had always been a favourite of his. He regarded him as the son he had never had, and that the youthful ace was now married to his only daughter – who was about to give him a grandchild – made his life complete.

'He's been shot down all over the place,' someone remarked, and there was a ripple of laughter.

Blatchford glanced at Hargreaves. 'Put Colonel Blatchford in the picture, Bayley,' the Air Commodore invited.

'Yes, sir. I was shot down on 12 May over Belgium, in July last year over the Channel – actually I ran out of fuel while engaging the enemy – and again in September last year. That was over England.'

'Then you are a walking example of what I am going to talk about – survival. Were you flying a Spitfire on each of these occasions?'

'No, sir. On the first I was flying a Boulton Paul Defiant two-seater. We found the 109 too good for us. The other two were in Spits, but as I said, one was a fuel failure. The other . . .' a shadow passed across his face. 'I was defeated by a better pilot.'

'Squadron Leader Bayley was shot down by his own brother,' Hargreaves said.

'Oh!' Blatchford exclaimed. 'My God! Of course, I remember reading about you and your brother. I am most terribly sorry. I did not mean to . . . well . . . I mean, to have a brother fighting on the other side . . .'

'Max is my half-brother, sir. He had a German mother. It was his decision as to which nationality he chose. The decision was made before the outbreak of war.'

'Of course. Yes. Well . . .' Blatchford was distinctly flustered.

'You were going to talk about escape and evasion,' Hargreaves reminded him, gently.

'Ah, yes. Quite.' Blatchford visibly pulled himself together. 'You were shot down, the first time, over Belgium, which was then in German hands.'

'Only some of it, sir. The invasion had only just begun.'

'But where did you come down?'

'I managed to get my machine back over the Allied lines before baling out.'

'Well done. But supposing you had come down behind German lines. What would you have done?'

John raised his eyebrows. 'I would have been taken prisoner, I suppose.'

'Had you given any thought to this? To what might happen then, what you might be able to do?'

'No, sir. As you said just now, it's very difficult to fly successfully – at any time, much less in combat – if one is anticipating coming down.'

'But as I also said, and as you have learned, it does happen. Now, gentlemen, as I am sure you know, many thousand British troops, and quite a few airmen, were forced to surrender during the Battle of France. The majority of these are now in prison camps in Germany. But a surprising number are back in England, or in Vichy France awaiting the opportunity to get home. This phenomenon, which began as a trickle, has now become a stream, and a special branch of Military Intelligence has been set up to handle it. This is MI 9, of which I am a representative.'

He had their undivided interest.

'Now, those men who are prepared to take risks to regain England in preference to spending the rest of the War behind barbed wire, are subdivided into two groups, as Air

Commodore Hargreaves has indicated: Escapers and Evaders. An Escaper, as the name suggests, is someone who falls into enemy hands and subsequently escapes. An Evader – again obviously – is a man who manages to avoid capture at all, save on a most temporary basis.

'The first thing I wish to impress upon you is the necessity of considering the possibility of being taken prisoner, and your immediate reaction to it. The key word is "immediate". If you are surprised and dismayed by your capture or having to abandon your aircraft over enemy territory, and thus allow yourself to become depressed, when you recover your spirits it may be too late. It stands to reason that it is more difficult to break out of a prison camp than it is to make a break before one even gets to that camp. But the state of mind to make that break must be present before the situation even arises.

'It often happens, when men are taken prisoner in the middle of a battle, that they find themselves in the midst of considerable confusion. They will almost certainly be passed from the front-line troops to whom they have surrendered, to support troops, who will then pass them on to base troops; it is a myth to suppose that there are Gestapo agents attached to every German regiment. These transfers will probably be made under fire, and the quality of the captors, as soldiers, will steadily decline – certainly as regards alertness and decision-making ability. That is the most profitable time to make a break. Of course there is the risk that your guards may merely shoot you. It must be your decision as to whether the opportunity is greater than the risk.

'From the points of view of airmen, the opportunities of avoiding capture altogether are excellent. If you are so unfortunate to come down in the middle of a German position, well then, you must act as a prisoner. But if you come down in the midst of a deserted countryside, well . . .' it was his turn to take a drink of water. 'It is then your business to make your way to safety. Unless you are fortunate enough and possess enough know-how to get to the coast, steal a boat and get across the Channel – and incidentally, this has been done, by more than one evader last year – your best bet is to make for Vichy France. If you are apprehended in Vichy, you will be very unlucky to be handed back to the Germans; in most instances escapers, and evaders, are sent to a prison camp in

Marseilles, which I can tell you is very loosely supervised, where you will find friends who will help you to get to Spain, Portugal or Gibraltar and thence home. But, you will be asking yourselves, how do I get to Vichy after being shot down in, say, the Pas de Calais? I am going to tell you how to do this, and you must pass on the information to your pilots.

'The first thing you need to do is get rid of your uniform, and in particular, your flying boots; they are a dead giveaway. You may find scarecrows useful, or washing lines. Rope-soled shoes, as worn by the French peasantry, will be invaluable. You must also shed any military bearing. You do not march along the road, or even walk briskly: you shamble, and you accept humiliation and contempt without question.

'Now, of course, the ideal situation is where you find a local willing to help, and you may suppose that coming down in Belgium or France, this will be an easy matter. Get that idea out of your heads. The information fed to us by our agents on the continent suggests quite the opposite. The French are divided roughly into three groups. The vast majority, while they will not be actively hostile, are people who did not wish the War in the first place, are just happy to have survived and do not wish to become involved in any way with an occupying force whose methods are, to say the least, severe. The very last thing any of these people desire is to have a downed English airman turning up on their doorstep asking for help. They may not turn you in, but they are very likely to slam the door in your face.

'The second group, and they are a large minority, are of the opinion that the British let them down, by abandoning them at Dunkirk, and the RAF in particular by not sending more squadrons for the defence of France. The truth of the matter – that they let themselves, and us, down by the incompetence of their commanders and the reluctance of their men to fight – is not acceptable to them. Approach any of these people and you will be handed over to the Germans.

'The third, and unfortunately the smallest of the groups, at least right now, are those Frenchmen, and women, who refuse to accept the fact of their defeat, are determined to reverse the situation as rapidly as possible, and recognize that their best – perhaps their only – means of accomplishing this is in partnership with Great Britain. These people will help you, but do not forget that it will be at the risk of their own lives. If you are captured, you will be sent to a prison camp. If they are caught helping you, they will be shot, regardless of age or sex.

'Now, how you locate these people has got to be your judgement, but I can give you some pointers. It may seem obvious, if you happen to come across a chateau, to expect help from such an obviously well-to-do source. Do not believe it. Our information is that the French upper classes are more fed up with this war and our part in it than anyone else. The peasantry are much more likely to be sympathetic, but that depends on how much stick they have recently taken from the Germans. Your best bet is probably the clergy, who are by definition anti-Nazi, simply because the Nazi philosophy places man above God. I'm not guaranteeing you won't strike a bad egg, but if you are, or can pretend to be, a Roman Catholic, you can at least claim the protection of the confessional.

'But when you come down to it, success or failure will depend upon yourself. Neither I, nor anyone else, can predict the circumstances in which you might find yourself, the injuries you might have suffered, the mood – either of depression or euphoria – you may be experiencing at the vital moment. What we can do is provide you with some practical assistance in implementing any plan you may form.'

He opened the suitcase and took out a cloth waist belt. 'One of these will be issued to every pilot who will be flying over France; the bomber crews already have them. It is an ordinary belt, as you can see. It will replace the one you are currently wearing, and cannot be objected to by any would-be captor or interrogator. Its secret is in the buckle.' He held it up. 'This is made of brass, and on the underside contains a tiny compass. It is very easy to become disoriented when you find yourself in strange surroundings and under perhaps an overcast sky. This will tell you which direction to take.'

He put down the belt and picked up the parachute, laying it with effort on the table. 'These new parachutes are being issued, again to every pilot or aircrew required to overfly France. It is a perfectly ordinary silk parachute, again to which no enemy can take exception. However, printed on the silk there is a map of France. Your standard procedure, on landing after you have baled out, is to get rid of the chute. However, before doing so, you will locate the map and cut it out to carry with you, making your way in the correct direction as indicated by your compass. You will see that such things as railway lines, main roads, towns and even villages are clearly marked. As you can also see, this requires a large map, but as it is printed on silk, the material will fold into a very small area, easily concealed about the person, and which, when flattened for use, will have accumulated no obstructive creases or cracks.

'However, all of these aids to reaching safety are only of use if you evade capture long enough to begin your escape or to locate someone willing and able to help you. For this reason it may be necessary for you to lie absolutely doggo, in total concealment, for some time – maybe as long as a couple of days. To enable you to do this, we have devised an escape pack.'

From the suitcase he took what could have been a tobacco tin, flat, rectangular and disconcertingly small. 'This is designed to fit comfortably into the side pocket of your flying suit.' He laid the box on the table and opened it. 'The contents are as follows.' He held the objects up one after the other. 'A packet of malted milk tablets: ready nutrition for two days. A packet of liver toffee: ditto. A box of matches. A packet of chewing gum: settles the nerves. A fishing line and hook: France is full of small rivers and streams, and these will be your prime source of fresh food. The matches will enable you to light a cooking fire if it is safe to do so. A packet of boiled sweets: again, instant nutrition. Another compass. Needle and thread: the clothes you beg, borrow or steal may need adjusting to obtain a reasonable fit. Razor and soap: personal hygiene is important. A packet of halazone tablets for purifying whatever water you need to drink; a small, flat bottle for holding the water is on the underside of the box.' He held it up. 'And a packet of Benzedrine tablets to combat any pain you may be in.' Having replaced the various items in their proper places, he closed the box with a snap. 'You will also be issued with the equivalent of twenty-five pounds in francs.' He grinned at them. 'Please note that you will be required to account for this at the conclusion of every sortie. Well, gentlemen, that is all I have to say. Thank you for listening, and good luck.'

He closed his suitcase and Hargreaves stood up. 'I am sure

we would like to show our appreciation of Colonel Blatchford's splendid lecture.'

The officers clapped, with varying degrees of enthusiasm.

'And now, dismiss. Your orders will be posted tomorrow.' His gaze flicked to John and he gave a brief nod, so that John remained seated as the other officers filed from the room.

'Any news?' the Air Commodore asked.

'Not yet. I took her in last night, when the pains started, and they said to check back this morning. I had no idea this "chat" was going to last so long. I'm going over there now. You coming?'

'I don't seriously think Joly will want her dad breathing down her neck at a moment like this. But I'd like to be kept informed the moment the little lad appears.'

'You will be, sir. But you're being a little premature as regards gender.'

'I'm easy. Just so long as it survives and Joly is all right. What did you think of Blatchford?'

'He seems to know his stuff. Is there really an MI9 department intended solely to handle escapers and evaders? I mean, is escaping an Intelligence matter?'

'I don't think it's quite as simple as that. Obviously, we want to get as many downed airmen back as is possible; it's a matter of morale as much as anything. But chaps returning from behind enemy lines are a very useful source of information as to what is actually going on behind those lines. There's also the slightly sinister fact that Jerry is undoubtedly cottoning on to what's happening – I mean that some of our people are getting out, and that to do so they are being helped by certain of the locals – but they aren't devoting all that much time to tracing these people, which is uncharacteristic. Can there be a simpler way to smuggle an agent into Britain than to have him turn up in Marseilles claiming to be a downed RAF crew member trying to get home? The MI9 boys need to be able to tell who is genuine and who is not. The point is, did that talk boost your confidence that if you did come down you'd be able to get out?'

'I'd feel better equipped to do so, certainly, sir. But I don't think I can really contemplate being shot down again. I mean, what would Oscar Wilde say? To be shot down once can be called bad luck. To be shot down twice has to be carelessness.

But to be shot down three times is surely incompetence. As for it to happen a fourth time . . .'

'Don't sell yourself short, Johnnie. The first time you were flying an inadequate machine against vastly superior numbers. The second time you ran out of fuel after pulling off that amazing rescue of Turnbull from that Belgian beach—'

'I was actually hit by that Jerry before I went in. I have an idea he punctured my fuel tank, which is why I emptied so suddenly. That counts as being shot down.'

'Well, we'll never know the truth about that, as your plane is at the bottom of the English Channel. But you were outnumbered three to one. As for the third time . . . do you seriously believe that Max is a better pilot than you?'

John grinned. 'No, I don't, actually. He took me – he took us all – by surprise. I mean, I knew it was him; I had just heard his voice on the radio. But the performance of his aircraft was superior to anything I'd previously encountered.'

Hargreaves nodded. 'The F-model. And now we believe they have developed a G-model, which is more superior yet.'

'Can't we develop something new?'

'We're working on it. The de Havilland people have something up their sleeves. But getting these things right takes time. Nothing is worse for morale than a knee-jerk reaction that doesn't work. You'll remember that disastrous decision to arm a couple of Spitfire squadrons with cannon during the Battle, in an attempt to counter the German twenty millimetres.'

John nodded. 'Well, we don't seem to be doing too badly with what we have. But there was more than the machine. Max came at us like a bat out of hell. There were six of us and he was alone. Yet he never hesitated. That surprised all of us. There were no tactics involved. He seemed to have gone berserk. I seriously thought – and so did most of the other fellows – that anyone he couldn't shoot down, he meant to ram.'

'But instead he went into the clouds and got away.'

'After shooting me down.'

'And the next time you run into him?'

'Oh, I intend to shoot *him* down for a change.'

Hargreaves studied him for several seconds. Then he asked, 'Do you hate him – Max?'

'Hate him?' John mused. 'No, I don't think I hate him . . .'

'I'm glad of that. It's pretty grim, to hate your own brother. But it's also dangerous to allow personal antagonism to come into combat. Sometimes it can interfere with your judgement. Give Joly my love, and don't forget that I want to know the moment something happens.'

John rode his Harley-Davidson, his most precious possession apart from his wife, into Tunbridge Wells. Although he knew that he should be thinking only of Jolinda and the baby, he couldn't stop himself reflecting on the morning. Blatchford's lecture, and his conversation with his father-in-law, had brought into sharp focus too many aspects of his life that he had always intended to bury in his subconscious, at least until after the War was over.

He knew that, when once in combat, one never considered the possibility of going down until it actually happened. That was a vital psychological aspect of being able to fly in the first place. And when it did happen, it usually happened so quickly that one merely responded as one had been trained to and rehearsed innumerable times. But that could not negate the post-survival feeling of horror – indeed, of fear – as one realized that one had lost control of events, that survival was a matter of luck as much as judgement.

He had never experienced the ultimate horror, that of being trapped in the cockpit of a burning aircraft. On the three occasions he had gone down he had always had what could be termed a soft landing.

In France, in May 1940, while he could still remember the feeling of angry frustration at having, for the first time in his life, been unable to overcome by sheer strength and determination, he had been too busy trying to keep his stricken Defiant flying long enough to get him home, aware always of the dead gunner in the cockpit behind him. When he had finally realized that he wasn't going to make it, as the bullet-riddled plane was about to fall apart around him, he had been back over the Allied lines.

When he had gone in to the Channel, while he was wounded, it was within four miles of the Sussex coast, and he had already been assured that an Air-Sea Rescue launch was on its way to pick him up. It had just been a matter of waiting, supported as he was by his life jacket; even the pain from his wound dulled by the coldness of the water. And when Max had brought him down, although he had sprained his ankle he had actually landed not a mile away from his own home. Talk about the luck of the Irish. But as he had no Irish blood it could not possibly last for ever.

Did he hate Max? he wondered as he swung the bike into the hospital car park. They had always been rivals, even as small boys. That was because of the circumstances of their births. He was the result of a one-night stand indulged by his father when on embarkation leave before going to France as a pilot in the spring of 1917. Although he had often felt deeply resentful of that unhappy start, and his father's part in it, over the past year – and especially since Jolinda Hargreaves had taken over his life with her cool sanity and calm understanding of other people's, and particularly his, problems – he had been able to reassess the situation.

Mark Bayley had been eighteen years old. Having lied about his age in order to join up, he was already a veteran of the Western Front before qualifying as a pilot, but he was still an utter innocent apart from the ability to fire a gun and fly an aircraft, and he had known as well as anyone that he had virtually been handed a death sentence: the life expectancy of an RFC pilot in France in 1917 was three months. So when a most attractive woman, several years older than himself, had virtually thrown herself at him, he had reacted with predictable enthusiasm; John could not remember his mother, but from what he had been able to discover about her, he had found no reason to disbelieve Mark's version of events. Patricia Pope had been wealthy and sophisticated. But she was also the widow of an officer killed in the early days of the War, and in her search for mind-numbing pleasure had become a problem to her family and friends. John could not doubt that her seduction of the young airman had been just an evening's fun for her. But the consequences . . .

Mark had known nothing of all this. He had had his night on the town and had gone off to France to do or die. And he had done a great deal. He had become an ace, with more than thirty kills to his credit, and a hero. Inevitably he had been shot down in the end, but he had survived, as a badly wounded prisoner-of-war. And while he lay in a hospital bed he had fallen in love with one of his nurses, who had reciprocated. Mark Bayley had had no idea that the beautiful young woman doing her bit for the Fatherland was actually the only daughter and sole heiress of one of Germany's richest men. But could he possibly be blamed, with his career apparently ended because of his shattered leg, for accepting the love offered him by Karolina von Bitterman, and the great wealth that had gone with it?

Meanwhile, Patricia had discovered she was pregnant. John realized that it was an example of the uncertainty of her mind that she had not immediately sought to contact her youthful and brief partner; perhaps there had been other candidates for fatherhood; perhaps she had merely rejected the idea of tying her life to a gauche boy with little education and certainly no social background. But at the same time, it had apparently never crossed her mind to have an abortion; her refusal to do so had led to a final break with her family. And when she did determine to find a father for her child, it was too late: Mark Bayley had been reported missing in action and presumed dead.

It had been months and Patricia was already a mother when she discovered that he was still alive, and then her letters had not reached him. When she had finally learned that he had returned to England, still unsuspecting of what he had left behind, it was later still: he was married and Karolina was pregnant. So, being by then definitely of unsound mind, she had to all intents and purposes laid her love child on the Bayley front steps and committed suicide.

When he considered his maternal background John sometimes had to wonder if he could be entirely sane himself. But he was a teenager before he had learned the truth. Karolina had insisted that the baby boy be brought up as her own, be legitimized, and even be officially regarded as the heir to the millions she had bestowed on Mark. That was her character. It went with her bubbling good humour, her confidence, the essential generosity of her nature – even after she had been told she had only months to live. No man could have had a better mother, or, he supposed, looking at it from his father's point of view, a better wife.

But she had also had a son of her own. As long as Karolina was alive, this had not been critical; Max had been brought up as the younger brother, and appeared happy to accept that role. But with her death, he also had learned the truth. No less than Karolina, Dad had always treated his two sons as equals, and had continued to do so after her death. But Max had been unable to stop himself considering the situation. He was the only legitimate son of his millionairess German mother. But as his mother had left everything to her husband, the only way to any of that wealth and prestige was through the goodwill of his English father, and then his English half-brother. John did not suppose that his sibling could truly be blamed for finding the companionship of his German cousins, who also felt betrayed in financial matters, preferable to that of his immediate family. Of course Max, when he had left England in 1938, had not had the slightest idea that Britain and Germany would find themselves at war in little more than a year. And John had still considered that a reconciliation could be brought about. Now, however . . .

'I'm afraid Mrs Bayley is not receiving visitors at this time,' the woman on the reception desk announced frostily.

'Is something the matter?' John demanded.

'Is that any concern of yours?'

'I'm her husband, you silly woman.'

'Oh! Ah! Why didn't you say so?'

'You didn't give me the opportunity. Has something happened to my wife?'

'We've been trying to get you all morning,' the woman accused. 'But you weren't there.'

'Well, I'm here now.'

'I'm afraid you're too late. Mrs Bayley went into the labour ward two hours ago.'

'Oh, fuck it!' John left the desk and ran for the stairs, pounded up them and the next flight, arrived on the second floor out of breath, and encountered a staff nurse. 'My wife,' he panted. 'She's in labour.'

'Would you be Squadron Leader Bayley?'

'Yes. Yes, I'm Squadron Leader Bayley.'

'Come with me.' She led him along the corridor.

'Is she all right?'

The nurse paused before a door, gave a gentle knock, and opened it. 'Your husband is here, dear. Do remember she's just given birth,' she warned John, and stepped aside.

He entered the room. 'Joly!'

Jolinda Bayley was propped against a mountain of pillows, the sheet folded across here waist. She wore the special maternity nightdress she had purchased as soon as she had discovered she was pregnant; she did not normally wear clothes in bed. Her tawny yellow hair was spread on the pillow behind her, and her exquisite features – she took after her father – wore their habitual rather sceptical expression.

'Hello, stranger.'

He advanced to the bed, stooped to kiss her forehead, and her arm went around his neck to bring his face down to hers. 'I'm not that fragile.'

'I'm so terribly sorry. I had to attend this effing lecture, which I assumed would last about an hour, and it dragged on and on. The bloody boffin had verbal diarrhoea.'

Jolinda squeezed his hand. 'I did get the idea from some- where that there was a war on. Anyway, you'd probably only have got in the way.'

'Was it . . . I mean, is it . . . well . . .?'

'It was no big deal.' Jolinda had grown up in America in the care of her divorced mother and had in fact spent two years in the WAACs before coming to England to join the WAAF and serve under her father's command; she had early learned to take life as it came. 'No more than half an hour. As for "it", I think he's coming along now.'

The door was opened again and Sister brought in the tiny scrap of humanity and placed him in his mother's arms. 'Looks like his father,' she remarked, her tone suggesting that she was not paying the child a compliment. Presumably, John thought, she was another who considered he should have been there. 'Let him suck a while. Get him into the habit for when the milk comes in.'

The tiny hand was clawing at the bodice of the nightdress and Jolinda unbuttoned and moved the material to allow the lips to close on her nipple. 'How long do I stay here?'

'If all goes well . . . the end of the week.'

'Holy shit!'

Sister raised her eyebrows. Well-bred young Englishwomen did not use that kind of language. Then she remembered that this young woman, if English-born, was American by adoption.

'And then,' Jolinda continued, 'how soon do I get back to work?'

'My dear Mrs Bayley ... what sort of work?'

Again John found the Sister's mind easy to read: this rather gorgeous, somewhat languid and entirely uninhibited young woman actually went out to *work*?

'I,' Jolinda said, coldly, 'am Section Officer Jolinda Bayley of the Women's Auxiliary Air Force. I have been given leave of absence for this business, but I'm sure they'll want me back as soon as possible. Ask him. He's my boss, from time to time.'

Sister glared at John. Now she was definitely holding him responsible for the whole thing. Well, he supposed he was – at least for the immediate situation. He grinned at her. 'I suppose that's up to you,' Sister said, with equal coldness. 'My interest, as yours should be, is the welfare of the child.'

'Well ... ow! Shit! He doesn't have teeth yet, does he?' She removed the offending mouth.

'That would be highly unlikely, Mrs Bayley.'

'Well, that sure felt as if he was trying to bite the goddamed thing off.' She stroked the injured flesh. 'OK, Sister, you've done your bit and I'm extremely grateful. Many thanks. Now Johnnie and I have things to discuss, so ...'

Sister retreated to the door. 'And the child?'

'I think he and I need to get to know each other a bit better. Come back for him in half an hour.'

Sister closed the door behind herself.

'I hope you're pleased,' Jolinda said.

'I'm over the moon.'

'He is a cutie, isn't he?' She kissed the baby's head and he began looking for her nipple again. 'OK,' she agreed. 'But take it easy. On the other hand, I guess that's the only sex I'm gonna get until next week. Now, listen. There are things to be done. Dad.'

'He's waiting for my call. I'm sure he'd like to see you. And him.'

'I'd like to see him too. Tell him to come in this afternoon. I guess you'll let your own folks know. Then there's Mom ...'

'I'm going to put an announcement in *The Times*. And *The New York Times.*'

40

'Mom lives in Los Angeles. You'll have to call her.'

'Ah. I got the distinct impression that she didn't approve of our marriage.'

'You're damned right she didn't approve of our marriage. She got the idea that it was engineered by Dad, which it was. And she went off him in a big way fifteen years ago.'

'Ah,' John said. 'I also had the distinct impression that I had something to do with it.'

'Sweetheart, I adore you! You'll have to bite the bullet and telephone her.'

John nodded, reluctantly. 'I'll do that.'

'Listen, she has to like the idea of being a grandmother.' Jolinda frowned. 'On the other hand, maybe not. Did you put that advert for a nanny in the papers?'

'Ye-es . . .'

'And?'

'There have been a couple of responses.'

'Great. We'll start interviewing the moment I get home.'

'I think we should talk about that. As Sister said, the boy must come first.'

'Are you resigning from the Air Force to be a father?'

'Well, of course not. There's a war on.'

'Right first time. You're fighting a war. So is Dad. So is everyone I know, who's able. And so am I. Baby comes first, right. *After the War.* I'm going to have Dad swing it so I can get home every night, but settling Mr Hitler comes first. That's what I came over here to do. Being fucked by you, and having you put a ring on my finger to make it legal, has been a big bonus, but it doesn't alter the facts. Right?'

'If you say so. Look, I have to be off.'

She nodded. 'You'll come in again tomorrow?'

'If I can. There's something big hanging about.'

'I get you. Well . . . see you in the funnies.'

He kissed her, and the babe, and stood up. 'A name! We haven't given him a name!'

'I think we should name him after your dad.'

'That's brilliant. He'll be tickled pink. But . . . you sure?'

'Sure I'm sure. It's time we had another Mark in the family.'

Rufus, the huge black Newfoundland, barked with his usual enthusiasm and bounded forward as the Harley swept down

41

the drive to come to a halt before the front entrance to Hillside House. John adjusted the stand, stepped off, and braced himself as the dog stood on its hind legs to place a paw on each shoulder. 'You're putting on weight,' he pointed out, disengaging himself and going to the door.

He had always had mixed feelings about this house. It was large, rambling, very comfortable and, as its name indicated, it was perched on the edge of the South Downs and commanded an exceptional view of the coast and the Channel beyond. Hillside was a beautiful home. But it was Karolina's home, bought, recreated and furnished with her money. And even seven years after her death, it remained filled with her spirit.

As with everything else, he had been a teenager before he had realized this. As was her wont, Karolina had never left anyone in doubt that Mark Bayley was the owner, as he was the dominating factor in their lives. John had a feeling that, having been born to wealth and power, but having volunteered for the nursing service during the Great War and thus come face to face with the reality of pain and suffering of humanity in extremis, she had wanted to be dominated by a man she could love. That the man she had chosen was one of those in more extremis than most, with a bullet-shattered body clinging to life by the merest of threads, had been part of her contradictory nature, as had been the fact that he was nowhere near her social class and, at that time, an enemy. Perhaps fed up with the effete arrogance of the aristocracy of the Kaiser's Germany, the class into which she had been born and bred, she had sought to create a man of her own . . . but she had wanted a man who, upon creation, would take over her life.

Well, she had succeeded, as she had succeeded in most things she had set out to do, save when faced with the disease gnawing at her vitals. But had she never considered that all of this, her creation, would one day be inherited by a man who was not of her flesh and blood, and his American wife? And not the son who *was* of her blood? Because that was what was going to happen.

Clements the butler, an old and faithful friend, had heard the sound of the motorbike and opened the door before John could use his own key. 'Mr John! Is it . . .?'

'A boy, Clements. A boy!'

Oh, sir!' Clements shook his hand. 'My very best congratulations. And Miss Jolinda?'

'In the pink. So open a couple of bottles of the Bollinger,
there's a good fellow.'

'Of course, sir.'

Clements hurried off and John faced the stairs and the
woman descending them. Helen Bayley was his second stepmother, and he was even less sure what to make of her than
he had been of Karolina. The contrast between the two women
couldn't have been greater. Where Karolina had been tall,
slender, elegant and above all, quiet, Helen was medium height,
inclined to plumpness, rather ponderous in her movements
and given to booming. She boomed now as she reached the
floor and embraced him. 'Johnnie! I heard what you said to
Clements. Is it really a boy?'

'It is indeed.'

'Oh, how marvellous! When can we see him? And Jolinda?'

'She'll be in hospital for the next few days, but I know
she'd love you to visit. Dad about?'

'In the study. He'll be pleased as punch. Come along.'

She set off through the drawing room to the library. John
reflected that if holding her naked in his arms must evoke
unflattering comparisons with Karolina in his father's mind,
there could be no doubt that she adored him and had been
very good for him.

For six years after Karolina's death Mark Bayley had been
virtually a social hermit. He had devoted himself entirely to
his career as an aeronautical consultant and designer – he had
played a part in the development of the Spitfire at Fairey
Marine – and when off duty had found comfort only in this
house and the company of his sister, Joan. He had in fact
become a remote and somewhat grim figure, even to his sons,
which John supposed had had a lot to do with Max's preference for the understanding he had known in Germany.

That situation might have endured for ever had not Joan,
herself for so long under the spell of Karolina's personality
and thus content to replace her at least as housekeeper, fallen
in love and determined to marry. Aunt Joan, not wishing
entirely to abandon her beloved brother, had brought the
recently divorced Helen Stanton into the house. The two had
been friends for years and she knew that Helen was an admirer

43

of Mark's, if only from a distance. John knew that his father had been reluctant to take on a new wife, with all that entailed, and not only because of the ever-present memory of Karolina. Mark Bayley had only saved his shattered leg from amputation by the utmost determination and the support of his nurse. But the leg remained a distorted wreck, to be seen by no one save his wife and sister. Karolina had only ever known him as a cripple, and a sister is a sister. But for a new woman, in her early forties, married for more than ten years to a perfectly healthy if apparently unpleasant man, to be confronted with it for the first time . . .

Yet it seemed to have worked out very well. Mark Bayley stood in the study doorway to greet his son. As tall as John, he was less powerfully built now, and leaned on his stick. His hair was completely white, but that had been the case almost since John's memory began, and his handshake was as firm as ever. 'Do I gather it's a boy?'

'Indeed it is.'

'Terrific. Joly all right?'

'I think it's safe to say that Joly is back to her best.'

Mark Bayley grinned; he found his daughter-in-law's extroverted personality exhilarating.

'And she's longing to see you.'

'Then she shall. This afternoon. Eh, Helen?'

'Of course, Mark.'

'So . . . Clements!'

'I have it here, sir.' Clements brought in a tray with the ice bucket and glasses and placed it on the sideboard. One of the bottles was already uncorked, and he poured.

'And take one for yourself,' Mark invited. 'Bearman. Where's Bearman?'

Jimmy Bearman had been his mechanic during the Great War and his chauffeur and faithful retainer ever since.

'He's in the village, sir.'

'Then we'll have another celebration later.' He raised his glass. 'Here's to . . .?'

'Mark.'

Mark lowered his glass. John had never seen his father quite so embarrassed.

'Joly's idea,' John assured him.

'Well . . .' he looked at Helen.

'What a lovely idea! Now, lunch,' she said, 'and then we can go to the hospital.'

'Were you there for the birth?' Helen asked over the meal.

'Unfortunately not. I got stuck in a lecture on how to survive when shot down over France.'

'Are you planning to get shot down over France?' his father inquired. 'Or are you moving from Spits to bombers?'

'Neither, if I can help it. But the brass has come to the conclusion that our bombers need to be protected. We're losing too many of them.'

'Won't that mean a fuel problem?'

Helen looked from face to face. She knew absolutely nothing about aeronautical matters.

'It gives us the same problem as Jerry's fighters face over here, yes. So it'll be a quick in and out until they can come up with a long-range fighter. Have you heard anything of what de Havillands are working on?'

'Top secret,' Mark said. 'But there is something in the pipeline. Have you heard the news today?'

'Haven't had the time.'

'Well, it seems Hitler really is set on the entire Balkans. He's just invaded Yugoslavia. Seems he's lost interest in us.'

Three

The Midnight Express

Great pillars of smoke rose above Belgrade. Beneath them, innumerable fires raged out of control, while between them the three great rivers that came together at this point proceeded with calm and incongruous majesty towards the Black Sea, flowing around the shattered bridges.

The Messerschmitt fighter-bombers ranged unchecked above the scene of devastation. They had started the fires, but now their job was done; the Stukas and Heinkels were arriving behind them to complete the task. Looking down, Max felt vaguely sick. Two years before, the Poles had proved unable to withstand the onslaught of the Wehrmacht, but they had fought with furious determination for several weeks; Warsaw had not fallen until after twenty-eight days. And the job of the Luftwaffe – at least the fighters – had been to destroy the Polish air force. Of course, in those days they had not been flying fighter-bombers. It had still been a massacre, and for that reason vaguely distasteful, but they had not been required to do any great strafing of civilians on the ground.

In France the previous year, they had been ordered from time to time to break up the great masses of refugees streaming along the roads leading south. That had been horrible, but they had been told it was part of a general strategy to shorten the war by inducing terror and panic in the civilian population. And, he supposed, it had worked. The French campaign had lasted only a few weeks longer than the Polish.

But this was plain murder. Unlike either Warsaw or Paris, Belgrade lay so close to the Hungarian border that with the war only an hour old, the German columns were already nearly there; they would have to halt until the bombers finished their work, where they could surely have just marched into the city with the Yugoslav army still only half mobilized. Nor was

46

Belgrade of any special moral significance. Yugoslavia was a federal state. Its components, Serbia itself, Croatia, Montenegro, Bosnia, and Kosovo, all had their own highly individual ethnic backgrounds and their own capital cities. In fact, the levelling of Belgrade, lying as it did on the main route for any army wishing to pass through Yugoslavia to gain Albania and Greece, was likely to hamper the movement of such an army rather than help it.

But orders were orders, and Max and his men had carried out theirs. 'Time to go home,' he said into his mike. 'Gunther, Horst.'

'Understood,' Gunther said.

'Understood,' Horst added. 'Holy shit!'

Max turned his head to see Horst's machine engulfed in flames. He couldn't believe his eyes. There had been no aerial opposition whatsoever, and although there had been some anti-aircraft fire at the beginning of the raid, it had been ineffec-tual and had now entirely ceased. 'What's happened?' he demanded.

'I don't know.' Horst's voice was high with fear. 'I must get out.'

'Yes,' Max agreed, and looked down again. They were still over the burning city, and to the north the Heinkels, preceded by the Stukas, were now clearly visible. He looked at Horst again, saw the explosion of white silk as his parachute opened. He was going down to be bombed by his own people. Worse than that, he was dropping into the midst of a population who had to be frenzied with hate and fear. 'Good luck,' he muttered.

'What the shit could have happened?' Gunther asked as they left their machines after landing at Buda.

'Something must have hit him,' Kramer suggested.

Max didn't join in the conversation, but went straight into the Control Office.

'You lost one?' Major Willems asked incredulously. 'Our information was that there was no anti-aircraft defence.'

'There wasn't much, and we'd settled that before Horst went down. Something happened to his machine.'

'But these are brand new machines – the very best we have.'

'I know,' Max agreed grimly.

He assembled the ground crew and stayed with them while

they carried out a meticulous inspection of the engine of each aircraft in the Wing. The engines were perfect, while the flight there and back had been so brief the fuel tanks were still nearly half full.

'I don't know what to say, Herr Major,' said Sergeant Steiger.

'Neither do I.' Max shook his head.

It was a long day. The Wing was kept on standby in case it was needed for another attack, but there was no call, and that afternoon Max was summoned to Colonel Dorff's office, where he found Major Hederling waiting for him. 'Heard you lost a man,' Hederling said.

'Yes, and you?'

'No, no. That sort of target could have been specially manufactured for my 87s. Damned bad luck on your fellow.'

'Gentlemen,' Dorff said, 'you will be pleased to know that General Simonovic has asked for an armistice.'

'So now we go on to Greece?' Hederling asked.

'Your Stukas do, yes. Major Bayley, you will take your Messerschmitts back to your original destination, Dresden. You will leave tomorrow.'

'Yes, sir. May I ask if our troops have occupied Belgrade?'

'They are in the process of doing so. But despite Simonovic's request for a ceasefire, they are encountering sporadic resistance. I'm afraid the Yugoslav army does not possess either homogeneity or discipline. So it may be a day or two before the city is secure.'

'I was wondering if we could obtain any information on the pilot I lost: Senior Lieutenant Horst Geiger.'

'He went down into the city?'

'I'm afraid so.'

'Hmm. I'll certainly get in touch with the army commander. You know your man is likely to have been killed on sight by the Yugoslavs?'

'Lynched, you mean,' Hederling growled. 'Those bastards.'

You're wrong, Max thought. *We* are the bastards. But he said, 'We must hope for the best.'

'I'll let you know as soon as I get a report,' Dorff said. 'Dismissed.'

Dinner was a sombre affair. Being shot down over England or France had not involved any personal danger once one reached the ground – except, Max thought wryly, in his case,

48

as the English considered him a turncoat. But to be seized and hanged, or worse, by a rampant mob – the very idea made the blood curdle. The meal over, Max stood up, glass in hand. 'To Horst.'

The other officers also rose. 'Horst!'

'I'll drink to that,' Horst said from the doorway.

'Horst!' they shouted, crowding round to offer him drinks. 'What happened?'

The young officer certainly looked the worse for wear. His uniform was both torn and dirty and he had lost his cap. But he appeared perfectly fit. 'It was a little tricky. I came down in a back yard, which was being used as a chicken run. They set up one hell of a squawking, but there was so much noise it was some time before anyone came to investigate. Then they were mainly women. I chased them off by brandishing my pistol, but they came back soon enough, accompanied by their menfolk, one of whom was in uniform and carried a rifle.'

'What did you do?' Gunther asked.

'I had no choice. I shot him.'

The officers looked at one another. Although it was their business to shoot down enemy aircraft and strafe people on the ground when ordered to do so, none of them, save Max himself, had ever fired at a recognizable human being on the ground. And while Max had had to use his Luger to take control of that North Sea drifter last September, he had not actually fired *at* any of the crew, merely to warn them to do as he commanded. 'Did you kill him?'

'Well, I had no choice,' Horst repeated. 'He was pointing his gun at me, and shouting. I don't know exactly what he was saying, but he was obviously telling me to surrender.'

'And what happened then?' Gunther asked.

'The women and the other man ran off. One of them tried to pick up the rifle, but I fired at her too.'

'And?'

'I hit her, but she wasn't killed. She went off howling and streaming blood. There was nothing else I could do, Max.'

'Of course.'

'Did they not come back, with more soldiers?' Gunther asked.

'Before they could, a bomb fell on the house. It just disintegrated. I was thrown to the ground by the blast, so I stayed there, on the ground, until some of our soldiers arrived. I must have lain there for several hours. There were bombs falling all about me. I have never had an experience like that.' He peered at Max. 'There was nothing else I could do.'

He was clearly highly distressed. Max clasped his shoulder. 'You did what you had to do. And you survived. Well done.'

'What do you think of the Gustav?' Colonel Albrecht inquired.

Max chose his words with care. The Wing had arrived in Dresden only an hour previously, after an uneventful flight, but he could tell that his pilots had been in a state of some apprehension; they were certainly in no condition to engage an enemy. 'It's a brilliant machine, sir.'

Albrecht was a well-built man, completely bald, although Max did not suppose he was much over thirty. Now he gazed at his subordinate for several seconds. Then he said, 'I feel there was a "but" at the end of that remark, Herr Major. Would that have anything to do with the plane you lost? It was not shot down, was it?'

'No, it wasn't. Its engine caught fire for no apparent reason.'

Albrecht nodded. 'But you recovered the pilot. That is good.'

'Actually, sir, the pilot recovered himself, with great determination.'

'As I would have expected, from a man in your Wing, Herr Major. I have to tell you that yours is not the first Gustav we have lost.'

'What? Where?'

'A few days ago, in the North African desert. A squadron of Gustavs was assigned to the Afrika Corps.'

'And one of them was shot down by the RAF?'

'No. The RAF has very few planes operating in Libya, and almost no top pilots. His engine caught fire, without being hit.'

Max stared at him.

'Exactly,' Albrecht said. 'This must be between you and me, Max. If there's a fundamental fault with the engine, it will be found. But the suggestion that such a fault might exist must not be made. There are Gustavs coming off the production lines every day. To have their pilots wondering when their engines may blow up would be disastrous for morale. I'm sure you agree with me.'

'Yes, sir.' Max couldn't be sure whether he was telling the truth or not.

'Now, are your men settled in?'

'They're doing so now, sir.'

'Excellent. Your visit here was to be a brief one, but it has been extended. So you have a few weeks for your people, both on the ground and in the air, to familiarize themselves with their machines. I think you should work them as hard as you can.' He smiled. 'But have them look at Dresden. It is really a fabulous city, if you are the least interested in culture and architecture.'

'Thank you, sir.' Max hesitated. 'May I ask exactly why we are here? My men are all very experienced pilots. They really do not require more than a day or two to familiarize themselves with any aircraft . . .'

'I'm not in a position to answer that question, Herr Major, because I do not know. You will remain here until I, and you, receive further orders.'

'Did you know,' Gunther asked at lunch, 'that there is a Wing of Junkers 88s here as well, and that they're expecting Hederling's Stukas to be back in a few days after they've blown the hell out of the Greeks?'

Max drank some wine. 'It certainly seems an outsize concentration. All for training, which we don't need?'

'Ah,' Senior Lieutenant Rech interjected, 'I've been talking to an 88 pilot, and he says we're on our way to India.'

Everyone round the table stared at him. 'From Dresden?' Gunther exclaimed scathingly. 'What do we do, tow fuel tanks behind us?'

'And won't the Ivans object?' Horst asked.

'This chap says the High Command is doing a deal with the Ivans, to let us pass through and over their territory to gain Persia.'

'What do you think of that, Max?' Gunther asked.

'Sounds a little far-fetched to me,' Max said. But they had to be there for a reason, and he simply could not think of one. Except for the unthinkable. England might be no longer of any great importance, but she hadn't made peace, and she had an army, albeit a small one, in that North African desert, which

51

was being outfought by the Afrika Corps. He didn't suppose that the Greeks, even with British support, were going to be able to hold out against the Wehrmacht for very much longer. This seemed to indicate that, Britain apart, all of Europe would be under the Nazi aegis by the end of the summer; Franco might be reluctant to get involved in any more shooting, with Spain still devastated by its civil war, but he was certainly of the same mind as Hitler and Mussolini. That left only Soviet Russia. But to go to war against Russia seemed entirely unnecessary. The Soviets were faithfully fulfilling the terms of the 1939 agreement and dutifully sending vast amounts of grain, meat, oil and important minerals to the Fatherland every year.

On the other hand, he had, as every German was required to do, read *Mein Kampf*, with its claim that Germany had to expand to the east to cater for its future population growth. It would be a tremendous affair. According to his information, Russia had an army of several million men, and an air force of at least 9,000 machines. Of course, he didn't doubt that the Wehrmacht and the Luftwaffe were superior to any other military force in the world – except possibly the RAF – but the odds still seemed tremendous.

The meal over, Max left the mess and wandered along the aprons towards the exit road, hands in his pockets. The airfield was only part of a vast military encampment, much of it recent, he estimated. And there were clearly a great number of ground troops in residence, as well as a large tank park; at least two Panzer divisions. Add to that the several aircraft wings, and he reckoned he was in the midst of an army corps.

His reverie was interrupted when to his surprise a motorbike stopped beside him. 'May I be of assistance, sir?'

Max gawked at the rider. She wore uniform, and while her black skirt was neatly tucked beneath and around her, her stockinged legs were exposed and extremely attractive. As was the rest of her. She wore a black tunic over a white shirt with a black tie, and her yellow hair, confined in a bun behind her head, was topped by a black side cap. Her features were a trifle large, but certainly handsome; her eyes were blue. She wore a captain's insignia on her tunic, but was definitely several years the elder.

'I was considering having a look at Dresden,' he told her.

'I am going into Dresden,' she said. 'I could give you a lift.'

'On the back of that machine?'

'It will be perfectly safe.'

Max considered for a moment. But why not? 'I'll have to hold on to you,' he pointed out.

'I can stand it if you can.'

He swung his leg over the pillion seat and clasped his arms around her waist. The engine had been ticking over, and now she put it in gear and moved away, not fast enough to cause any inconvenient wind.

His face was close to the back of her neck, and she smelt delightful. 'Do you not think we should introduce ourselves?' he shouted.

'You are Major Max Bayley,' she called over her shoulder.

'How do you know that? I only arrived here this morning.'

The bike slowed to a stop before the barrier, but the guard could recognize two officers and saluted before raising the bar. The young woman rode through and the bar fell into place behind them.

'Everyone knows of Major Max Bayley,' she said. 'Are you not one of our leading fighter aces?'

'It seems that I am. But how on earth did you know I was coming here? It's supposed to be secret.'

'I am General Clausen's secretary.'

'And he knew of my arrival?'

'General Clausen knows everything. He is the Commanding Officer of the Dresden garrison.'

'And your name is?'

'I am Captain Hildegarde Gruner.'

'Well,' he said, 'I think I would like to talk some more with you.'

The motorbike increased speed, and conversation became difficult.

Hildegarde Gruner found a pavement café, in the New City on the north bank of the Elbe. 'Over there,' she explained, 'is the Old City.' She pointed across the river to the south bank. 'Actually, this is the older city; it was built by the Slavs, when the new old city, if you're still with me, was just a crossing point.'

They sipped Pilsners. 'Have you been here long?' Max asked.

'Only two weeks. It was all very rushed. And very hush-hush.' She gazed at him. 'So no questions, please.'

'I think I'm beginning to work out the answers, even if I don't believe it. Do you get into the city often?'

'Oh yes. There's not a great deal to be done at the moment.'

'Save keep track of top secret troop movements,' Max suggested. 'Would you be in trouble if it were known you had told me that you knew who I was and when I was coming?'

Hildegarde gave a rather delightful chuckle. 'The general would probably spank my bottom.'

'But nothing more serious than that. Does he often spank your bottom?'

Another chuckle. 'It is something he likes to do.'

'And?'

She shrugged. 'He never hurts me, really. And if it keeps him happy . . .'

'I see you are in a privileged position.'

Another gurgle of laughter. 'So some would say. Some of the time.'

'So can you tell me why I and my men – and, I would say, some fifty thousand others – have been concentrated in such haste in this delightfully quaint, but rather unimportant backwater? And why have we now been told we are to sit here for several weeks?'

'Now that *is* secret. And Dresden is not a backwater, really. It is the rail centre for all south-east Germany. From here you could go anywhere.'

'My people do not normally travel by train.'

'Good point. But you cannot operate without ground support.'

'And we are going to operate? Somewhere, some time?'

'You will be moving on from here quite soon.'

'I'll take that as a promise. Will you be moving on too, in the same direction?'

'Where General Clausen goes, so do I.'

'May I ask another top secret question?'

'I don't have to answer it.'

'Would you be more than a secretary, by any chance? I mean, apart from providing your undoubtedly delightful bottom for his pleasure.'

'Would you care?'

'I think I might, if encouraged to do so.'

She finished her beer and stood up. 'What time do you have to be back at camp, Herr Major?'

'Whenever I choose. I am in command of the Wing.'

'In that case, let me show you something of the city across the bridge. And then we could have dinner before returning.'

It was absurd to suppose that he was being unfaithful to Erika: Erika had never been faithful to him. Well, then, to the memory of Heidi? But that too was an absurdity: Heidi had been a catastrophe. The main reason, he knew, for his sudden attack of conscience was that while he wanted to become seriously involved with a woman – it was his nature – to get too close to Hildegarde really was criminal as it could hardly last: he was way past his allotted span as a fighter pilot.

But Hildegarde was a delightful companion. She was as sexually liberated as either Heidi or Erika, and even more earthy. He supposed that was something to do with having belonged to the female half of the Hitler Youth, with their camps in the woods, their uninhibited behaviour, their nude bathing in the rivers; but if that made her an impossible consideration as a wife, at least to him, it made her all the more irresistible.

She held a most responsible post, but didn't let that interfere with her enjoyment of life, and no matter how much she drank, she didn't ever seem in the least likely to betray any secrets. Unlike poor Heidi, she was totally confident, and if she enjoyed sex even more, he understood early on that to her men were a pleasure, as much as her next glass of champagne, but not in any way a necessity.

So notwithstanding his reservations, Max found himself, during the several weeks the Wing spent in Dresden, thinking more and more of permanency, despite knowing almost nothing about her. She never revealed anything of her background or domestic situation – whether she had a man, or had ever had a man on any kind of permanent basis; he didn't even know why she had picked him up so immediately after his arrival, unless she was a romantic who felt that the bed of an air ace had to be better than any other.

They rented a room in the city where they could be sure of privacy, and went there as often as possible. His officers, and her fellows, undoubtedly knew of the liaison, but they were both too senior for criticism.

Hildegarde lay with her head on Max's shoulder, her leg thrown across his. 'Are you happy?' she asked.

Women were always asking questions like that, despite the

fact that in the middle of a war they were impossible to answer. He kissed her forehead. 'I am happy now.'

'But you will not be when you leave this bed.'

He sat up. 'There's a war on. Now, I am in bed with a lovely woman.'

'You mean you would rather be flying your airplane than here with me?'

'I would rather be here with you, had I not the airplane to fly for the Fatherland. We've now been here six weeks, just sitting around.'

'You've been exercising your men, and their machines, every day of those six weeks. You must be the most highly trained fighter Wing in the Luftwaffe.'

'There comes a time when too much training is counter-productive. One grows stale.'

She sat up as well, arms clasped around her knees. 'You should have been in action by now.'

'Eh?'

Hildegarde swung her legs out of bed and went to the wash-stand. 'It was to be May 19, which was yesterday. But it was put back a month to clean up this Balkan business.' She turned to face him while using the towel. 'There, you see, I have broken my oath of secrecy.'

He got out of bed as well, went to her. 'But it will be in a month?'

'You, me, all of us, are moving out next week.'

'To go where?'

Her mouth twisted. 'You do realize that if anyone, *anyone*, were to know what I'm telling you, I would be hanged?'

Had Heidi ever considered this when sharing a bed with her treacherous boyfriend? She hung like a vast shadow over his life. 'I shall never betray you.'

She kissed him, rubbed her breasts against his chest. 'We are moving to Warsaw.'

'Bandits, two o'clock, twenty plus,' said Flight Lieutenant Newman.

John turned his head. He and Newman had flown together since Dunkirk, had lasted the Battle of Britain, during which almost every other member of the original squadron had been killed or seriously wounded. Today they were flying at 25,000 feet, some 10,000 above the two squadrons of Blenheims below them, and they were just crossing the Dutch coast. He had never flown over Holland before. Now he looked down at what seemed to be a great deal of water enclosed by an arc of islands: the Dutch Frisians, which would link up a few miles further north with the German Frisians. He wondered fleetingly how well Colonel Blatchford's evader equipment would cope with coming down in that watery mess.

But he didn't really have that in mind. The Messerschmitts were flying at 20,000 feet, closing on the bombers from the north-east and apparently oblivious of the Spitfires hovering above them. 'Here we go,' he said into his mike. 'This is what we came for.'

He put his machine into a steep dive, setting his firing mechanism as he did so, and at the same time casting a quick glance over his various gauges. The fuel needle hovered at just over half, so there wasn't too much time to play with if he was going to get home again.

The range was now closing very fast, when suddenly there was an explosion of German chatter over the radio, which he well understood from his youthful holidays in that country. 'Spitfires!' someone was shouting. The Messerschmitts hastily abandoned their attack and began to climb, scattering as they did so.

'One apiece,' John said, fixing on the enemy leader and frowning as he saw that while the aircraft carried the insignia of a Flight Commander, it had only three bars painted on the fuselage. The pilot was certainly not a happy man as he saw the Spitfire racing at him. He opened fire at something like 1,000 yards, and the flickering red lights of the tracers disappeared long before they reached John's machine. The German pilot then put his aircraft into a steep climb well before there was any risk of a collision. In doing so he presented his underbelly to John's eight machine guns at a range of not more than 300 feet. John fired a ten-second burst into the huge target and the Messerschmitt seemed to fall apart. The pilot was not killed and dropped past John before his parachute opened. He was presumably falling into friendly hands.

There was no time to see him go in. Another German aircraft was already in John's sights and he was firing then twisting his machine to get on the enemy's tail before opening fire again. This aircraft burst into flames and its pilot did not get out. John went down with it for several thousand feet and saw it disappear into the water.

The German squadron was dispersed and the seven survivors were heading for home; not a single Spitfire had been lost and the bombers were continuing placidly on their way, now only in danger from the flak, which was rising but exploding mostly beneath them.

'Good shooting,' said the bomber Squadron Leader.

'We have to go home now,' John said, 'but we'll be replaced for your homeward journey. Come along, lads.'

'Piece of cake,' said Pilot Officer Renfrew. He was the newest and youngest member of the squadron, all pink cheeks and excited eyes; this had been his first sortie.

'Did you get one?' asked Flying Officer Singleton, on the desk.

'Well, no. I don't think so . . . I shot at a couple but I didn't seem to hit any of them . . .'

'You were firing too soon,' Newman said. 'But it seemed to frighten them.'

'How many?' Singleton asked.

'Five out of twelve.'

'You got one,' Renfrew said admiringly.

'And the skipper got two,' said Pilot Officer Hassell, another newcomer.

Singleton looked at John who was, as was his custom, allowing his junior pilots to give rein to their exuberance before filing his own report. 'They really weren't very good,' he said. 'Is the boss in?'

'Waiting for you.'

John knocked on the door of the inner office.

'Come. John!' Wing Commander Browne was a chunky man with thinning fair hair. 'Seems you had a cakewalk.'

John sat before the desk. 'Yes. Rather odd. Last month the Blenheim crews were being attacked by very experienced pilots: today there was not one machine with more than three kills painted on its fuselage, and he was the Flight Commander. What's happened to that whole lot of very experienced pilots Jerry has, chaps who've survived the Battle of Britain?'

'Including your brother. You don't suppose he's been shot down?'

'We would surely have heard. We heard about Luther last week, and as far as I know, he didn't have as many kills as Max.'

'Well, he must be on leave. Even Jerry gives his pilots leave, from time to time.'

'He and his entire squadron? And all the other veteran squadrons that we know they have, at a time when we're going over just about every day?'

'We've only recently started using a fighter escort. Maybe he's surprised.'

'Maybe . . .'

'But you don't believe that.'

'I can only say, sir, that if the best pilots in the Luftwaffe are no longer defending their North Sea coasts, then they must be doing something else.'

'Such as?'

'I have no idea, but it must be worth putting to the brass.'

Browne grinned. 'Our immediate brass is your father-in-law. I suggest you put it to him yourself.'

'Interesting,' Hargreaves said, pouring two whiskies. 'But I think we know where they've gone. It was reported that a Messerschmitt wing took part in the blitz on Belgrade.'

'A whole wing? Didn't they use bombers?'

'Oh, they did. Stukas, followed by Heinkels. It was really rather brutal. The Yugoslavs had virtually no air defences.'

'So why did they need fighter protection?'

'Hmm, they may have been simply trying out this new machine of theirs, the so-called Gustav.'

'With respect, sir, would the Luftwaffe have sent their latest machines and their most experienced pilots halfway across Europe to try them out against a virtually defenceless target? I would have thought they'd be anxious to put them up against us. And in any event, Belgrade fell six weeks ago. What have they been doing since?'

'That is an interesting point. I'm seeing Douglas in a few days. I'll mention it to him. Now tell me, how is the boy doing? And the girl?'

John made a face. 'The boy is doing very well. The girl is proving increasingly difficult. She wants to be back in uniform. She seems to feel that without her presence, Jerry could invade at any moment. Perhaps you could have a word with her?'

Hargreaves refilled their glasses. 'I'll go across tomorrow. But . . .'

'She is the most enchanting creature,' John said, 'just as Little Mark is the best son a man could have. I just want them both to prosper.'

The Army Corps moved out on May 20 as Hildegarde had forecast. The infantry, even by train, took some ten days to reassemble on the east bank of the Vistula. The Panzers were there far sooner, as was the headquarters staff. The Luftwaffe was there in four hours.

'So now we know,' Gunther said. 'I suppose you've known all along.'

'Let's say that I guessed some time ago.'

Gunther looked to the east across the seemingly unending Polish plain. 'Is it like this on the other side of Brest-Litovsk?'

'I believe it is. For a good distance.'

'Didn't you fly over it in 1939?'

'The deal was that the Russians would occupy that half of the country. Anyway, our business was to knock out the Polish air force, such as it was. We did that inside a week and were then sent home. The Stukas did the rest.'

He remembered those days so well, the enthusiasm, the élan, the total confidence in themselves and their machines. Well, he still had total confidence in himself, if not entirely in his machine. But the enthusiasm was gone. Perhaps he had simply been in the killing business too long. But that surely went for every soldier in the Wehrmacht, much less the Luftwaffe.

They still had a job to do. He just wanted it finished as rapidly as possible.

'Is it true,' Gunther asked, 'that the Ivans have more than nine thousand planes?'

'So they claim. But they don't have any Messerschmitts, and I don't think they have any combat experience, either. You scared?'

Gunther grinned. 'I was thinking that it will be a good opportunity to catch up with you. Although I suppose you'll be shooting them down as fast as I can. Will they be waiting for us?'

Max reckoned that his oldest living friend *was* actually a

little apprehensive. 'There's no evidence of it. I believe there are large troop concentrations just inside the border, but they've been there since 1939.'

'But haven't our reconnaissance planes been overflying their territory for the past couple of months? Surely they must have realized we were more interested than we should be? I mean to say, what would we do if a Russian machine suddenly appeared over Warsaw?'

'I imagine one of us would be ordered up to bring him down. Don't ask me how Ivan thinks. It seems that every commander is terrified of the man above him all the way up to Stalin himself. You remember all those thousands of officers, including half a dozen generals, who were shot in 1937.'

'An incredible business. What has he got left?'

'I have an idea,' Max said, 'that that is what we are about to find out.'

Over the next week the rest of the troops arrived. Max naturally sought out Hildegarde at the first opportunity. She continued to grow on him. Their first meeting had been so abrupt and unexpected, and yet by that first evening they had known they were going to be lovers. But his experiences over the previous two years had left him profoundly suspicious of female motivations, and nothing could have been more suspicious than the way she had picked him up. He had supposed she was merely looking for sex, and where better to start than an air ace, even if he was several years the younger and had a somewhat scandalous background? But she had given her all, without reservation, and had continued to do so throughout the month they had spent in Dresden. Perhaps she was actually fond of him. Certainly, now was not the time to talk of love.

As always, she seemed very pleased to see him, and got off duty as rapidly as she could. Her motorbike had been brought up in one of the transporters and they rode into Warsaw for a look. 'Have you been here before?' she asked.

'No.'

'But you must have flown over it during the *Blitzkrieg*?'

'I never got this far east.'

'I was told it was a most beautiful city.' They rode past the huge sloping bank of red and white roses at the foot of which was the Poniatowski Palace. 'That is certainly beautiful,' Hildegarde remarked.

But the same could not be said of the city where, even very nearly two years after its capitulation, many of the houses were still shattered wrecks and there were still craters in the roads. The people cast surreptitious glances at the man and woman in uniform, but offered no greetings.

They stopped at a café for a beer and were served in silence. Max would have felt uneasy, but for the presence of large numbers of German soldiers, though it was still uncomfortable.

Hildegarde felt it too. 'Let's get out of here,' she said.

They returned to the encampment. 'Do you think any German city will ever look like that?' she asked.

'Not unless the Luftwaffe stops flying.'

'But the English have bombed Berlin.'

'Have you been there recently?'

'I haven't been there this year. I was there the night of the first raid.' They had parked the bike and were strolling towards the barracks.

'Why, so was I!'

'Were you? On duty?'

'I was on leave. I was staying at the house of Herr Stumpff, my father-in-law.'

'Oh,' she said. 'Yes.'

'You must know of that?'

'Some. You don't have to talk about it if you don't wish to.'

'Do you not suppose it haunts me?'

'You mustn't let it – certainly not when about to go into battle.'

'I've been in battle several times since Heidi's death, and I don't think it has affected my performance.' He smiled. 'It's in between battles that the ghosts crowd round. That's why having someone like you to share my time with is so important.'

'You mean there's no girl waiting for you in Germany?'

'I don't think she is *waiting* for me . . .'

'But she is there?'

He stopped walking and turned to face her. 'I would prefer to think that she was right here.'

Hildegarde gazed at him for several seconds.

'Or do you have a man waiting for you?'

She pouted. 'I will wait for you here, until this operation is completed. When one is at war, it is best to let the future take care of itself.'

She hadn't actually answered his question.

'Gentlemen,' said General Clausen, looking over the faces of the officers gathered in front of him. As far as the Wehrmacht was concerned, they were all at least colonels. From the Luftwaffe, they were the various wing commanders; Max sat next to Hederling, who had flown in with his Stukas a few days previously.

Clausen stood at a long desk. Seated to either side of him were several other senior officers, as well as, at the end, Hildegarde. 'I imagine you have all by now deduced why you are here. I can now tell you exactly what is going to happen. Beginning tomorrow morning, the Panzers and the infantry will move up to the Russian border. The Luftwaffe will remain here, but all planes must be ready to take off at 0300 the day after tomorrow, Sunday June 22. The operation is code-named Barbarossa. It has become necessary for us to destroy the ability of Soviet Russia to wage war upon Germany, because our information is that they are preparing to do this. We know they have a very large number of men concentrated just over the border. It is our initial purpose to annihilate these troops. To accomplish this, OKW is employing more than two million men. Once the enemy armies are destroyed or scattered, we will then proceed to occupy all of European Russia – that is, to the Urals.

'In the first instance, there are three army groups involved, with three separate objectives. The Southern Group, commanded by Field Marshal von Runstedt, will drive on Kiev, absorb the Ukraine, cross the Don Basin and head for the oilfields of the Caucasus. Field Marshal von Leeb's Northern Group will drive on Leningrad. And the Centre Group, of which we are part, commanded by Field Marshal von Bock, will drive on Smolensk and Moscow.' He smiled. 'What might be called the traditional route, the one followed by Napoleon.

'But all this depends upon the complete defeat of the frontier army. You might agree with me that it is a strategic mistake to place so many troops so close to the border, where they

63

necessarily lack room to manoeuvre except backwards. But they are there, and it is our business to see that they cannot escape to safety. Captain Gruner.'

Hildegarde got up and pulled down a huge map of European Russia that hung behind the General, then stood to one side.

Clausen touched the map with his wand. 'This very large area just beyond the border is, as it appears on the map, a huge morass, known as the Pripet Marshes. It is impenetrable to wheeled vehicles and even tanks. It has only one or two poor roads so infantry would also find it slow going. We therefore intend to ignore it. In fact, it makes a boundary between Army Group Centre and Army Group South. South of the marsh, General von Kleist's Panzers will drive behind the Russian Ukrainian Army, and isolate it. North of the marsh the same duty will be undertaken by General Guderian's two Panzer Divisions, one to each side of the Russian position. They will seek at the earliest opportunity to swing towards each other and link up so as to surround the enemy. The task of the infantry will be to advance frontally and complete the business.'

He looked at the air force officers. 'The Luftwaffe's task is twofold. The fighters are required to ensure there is no Russian interference from the air with our Panzers. You will fly continuous sorties until the encirclement has been completed. The bombers will attack the Russian forces on the ground, inducing as much confusion and panic as possible. If by any chance the Russian air force is easily dispersed or does not appear at all, the fighter-bombers will also turn their attention to the ground forces. Certain squadrons will be designated to attack the Russian airfields, which are clearly marked on your maps. With the element of total surprise, which you will have, it should be possible to destroy a large number of the enemy machines before they can get airborne.' He paused and looked over their faces. 'I am confident that every officer here will carry out his duty in the best traditions of the Wehrmacht, and will see that his men do so as well. *Heil Hitler!*'

'Tell me something,' Gunther asked over dinner, 'are we going in without a declaration of war?'

'Does that bother you?' Max raised an eyebrow.

'Yes, it does.'

'Well, stop worrying. There will be a declaration of war.

64

It'll probably be delivered some time in the early hours of Sunday morning. That's the way things are done nowadays. If the Russians aren't prepared for it, they need their heads examined.'

Max spent the next day making sure that every machine in the Wing was fuelled, armed and ready to go; that his men were mentally prepared.

'You must not be overconfident,' he told them, 'but I would say it will certainly be an easier job than taking on the Spitfires – save in the matter of numbers. There will be a great deal of them, but –' he grinned at them all – 'it will also be a great opportunity to add to your scores. However, keep your eye on your fuel gauges at all times, and make sure you get back here in time to refuel. You do not wish to come down in the midst of the Russian army. Now, I recommend that you have an early night. You are on duty at 0200.'

He also visited the ground crew's mess to speak with them and remind them that the aircraft would be back every hour and a half for refuelling and rearming, and that this had to be completed in each case in fifteen minutes.

That evening he was visited by Hederling. 'All ready to go?'

'Indeed. And you?'

'I can hardly wait,' Hederling said. 'I regard my people as the spearhead of victory.'

Max grinned. 'Providing we keep the Ivans off your back.'

'I have absolute confidence in you, Max. We shall meet tomorrow night and celebrate our victory.'

'If there are truly a few hundred thousand Russians out there, I think you're perhaps being a little previous. But I will have a drink with you tomorrow night.'

Although Max knew he was breaking his own orders, he did not go to bed: his brain was too active. It was not that he was the least apprehensive of the morrow, either personally or for the German army, but he had a strange feeling that he was about to witness an unforeseeable event, the opening of a gigantic Pandora's Box, with an eventual outcome that was impossible to calculate. Fighting the British or the French, for all the horror and brutality involved, was a conflict between essentially civilized nations, with a common heritage, a common culture, a common belief in the value of Christianity. On the other side of that border there was pagan nihilism.

He was standing at the end of the runway, looking up at the stars sparkling in the night sky. It was just past eleven.

He heard a sound behind him, and turned. 'I tried your quarters,' Hildegarde said, 'and your man, Heinrich, said you had not come in. He's quite worried, but I had an idea where you might be.'

He took her in his arms to kiss her, and then they sat together on the grass. 'How I wish I could be flying with you tomorrow,' Hildegarde said.

Max hugged her. 'It is very nearly today.'

'And you are so calm. But you have done this before.'

'Taken off at dawn to engage the enemy? Yes, I have done this quite a few times.'

'And you never feel afraid?'

'It's a mistake to think ahead when about to go into battle. Oh, we, and the generals, make our plans, our dispositions, based partly on what knowledge we have gained of the enemy's positions and partly on our experience, but this is done days, often months, in advance, with only an allowance for any change in circumstance. My men all know what is required of them, and I know they will follow me wherever I lead them. I never think further ahead than that.'

She hugged him in turn. 'To have such certainty, such confidence, that must be marvellous.' She half turned her head. 'Listen!'

'What the shit . . .? It's only just midnight!'

The night was split by a tremendous wailing sound, almost like a huge air raid siren.

'Can the Russians have learned our plans?'

'That sound guarantees that they know nothing of our plans,' Hildegarde assured him. 'That is the Berlin–Moscow Express passing through Warsaw right on schedule, as if nothing at all was going to happen.'

PART TWO

Perdition

'Him the Almighty Power Hurled
headlong flaming from th'ethereal sky
With hideous ruin and combustion down
To bottomless perdition . . .'

'Paradise Lost', John Milton

Four

Going In

'Midsummer's Day,' Gunther said, standing beside Max as their engines were warmed up. 'It'll go on until after ten tonight, is that not true?'

'So they say,' Max agreed. At half past two in the morning, the eastern sky was already lightening. 'We should be able to get in at least ten sorties before nightfall.'

'When do we go?' Horst asked, as highly strung as ever.

'When the guns commence,' Max told him.

A dark shape loomed out of the gloom. 'I couldn't let you go without saying goodbye,' Hildegarde said. She had only left his arms an hour before.

'We'll be back for breakfast,' Max assured her. 'In fact, twice before breakfast. Join us.'

'I'll do that.' She hugged him and kissed him and then did the same to Gunther and Horst. Then she faded into the darkness.

'That,' Gunther said, 'is what we are fighting for.'

'At the very least,' Max agreed. 'To your planes, gentlemen.'

Sergeant Steiger adjusted his belts, saw him into the cockpit and made sure all his straps were securely fastened. Max looked at his watch: 0259. He raised his head and saw the Verey pistol cartridge arcing through the darkness. At the same moment the night seemed to explode. Max knew the guns were a good twenty miles away, but the noise was ear-shattering, and the entire eastern sky seemed to burst into flame.

He released the brakes and his Gustav rolled down the runway. Behind him the Wing rose together, and behind them Hederling's Stukas were already forming up.

'Seven thousand metres,' Max said, and the Messerschmitts soared into the sky, into relative daylight: it was going to be a beautiful morning. Below them, the land was still shrouded in darkness, save for the flashes of the guns, and these were all coming from the German side of the border. He checked his map and his references. 'Sector B Z 42,' he said. 'Should be ten minutes.'

They flew on in comparative peace, leaving the guns behind them. The sun was just peeping above the horizon, and a few minutes later the ground was clearly visible. Max caught his breath. In the far distance he could see an area of immense forest, but below him there was a continuation of the Polish plain, open country through which there seemed to be only one or two roads. But it was also suggestive of a disturbed ant heap. Even from his height he could see movement: vehicles, and no doubt people, rushing to and fro. But they were not his concern. Ahead of him now he could make out the airfield marked on his map. It was quite a large field and there were a great number of planes on the ground. Some looked reasonably modern, but others . . .

'Biplanes!' Gunther shouted. 'Do we get credit for planes destroyed on the ground?'

'No we do not,' Max said. 'Attack.'

He put his machine into a steep dive. Again he watched panic-stricken activity beneath him. The response was surprisingly quick. There was a ring of anti-aircraft guns around the airfield, and one or two of these actually opened fire. 'Take those guns out, Horst,' Max ordered. His target was the ranks of parked planes, some of which were starting to move. He carried beneath his fuselage five fifty-kilogramme bombs. Their weight appreciably reduced his speed, so getting rid of them was his first priority.

At 1,000 feet he released his first bomb, at one end of the parking apron. There was time to release another in the midst of the planes before he overshot. Then he came round in a tight turn, casting a glance to his left to see the rest of the squadron also dropping their bombs in the midst of a huge upheaval of earth, and metal, and men, all tinged with red flame.

He turned back into thick smoke now, but he knew that wherever he dropped his load it was going to hit a target. When the fifth bomb was gone he climbed into open air, checking his fuel gauge as he did so: just over half full. Below him he saw several aircraft getting off the ground, and again dived.

'What are those things?' inquired Kramer.

'Yakovlev fighters,' Max told him. 'They're not very fast, but they're well armed.'

But speed was what mattered. He tore into the Russian planes. Speed and experience, he thought, as he watched the tracers being fired at a hopelessly long range. Then he was within one hundred metres and opening up with his two thirty-millimetre canon. The plane in his sights disintegrated, but was immediately replaced by another, which also exploded in a red fireball.

Then he was through into clear air, looking down at the shambles beneath him, the huge number of burning aircraft, the dismounted anti-aircraft guns and the blazing wooden buildings. 'Home,' he said.

'At least two hundred,' Gunther declared.

Major Voertz, on the dispatch desk, raised his head. 'Are you serious?'

'They were on the ground, all lined up. Ask the skipper.'

Voertz looked at Max.

'I'd say that estimate is about right,' Max agreed. 'They were absolute sitting ducks.'

'Anti-aircraft fire?'

'Limited. And we quickly snuffed them out.'

'And none of their machines got up?'

'Oh yes. About twenty. But they weren't really any opposition. They lasted about ten minutes.'

'Your own casualties?'

'We did not lose anybody.'

'None of our machines were even hit,' Gunther announced.

'That is tremendous,' Voertz commented. 'When will you be ready to go again?'

'As soon as our planes are refuelled and rearmed,' Max told him, 'and we have had a cup of coffee. When we come back this time, we shall want breakfast.'

'And you shall have it!' Voertz promised.

The sun was now rising rapidly, and the landscape was depicted before them as on a relief map. The Messerschmitts looked down on a column of Panzers racing across the endless sun-baked plain towards the forest, accompanied by huge plumes of dust; they did not appear to be meeting any opposition, or even firing their guns. Several miles to their right the Russian army could be seen almost visibly disintegrating, with quite considerable numbers of men appearing to move independently, but always away from the border, while others seemed to be huddled together in an inanimate mass. Amongst them artillery shells were busting in continuous profusion.

To the west the German forces could be seen advancing, followed by their mobile artillery; which continued to explode without cessation. And in the far distance to the south Max could make out more dust plumes to indicate the presence of the other Panzer wing completing the encirclement of the enemy forces.

'What do we attack?' Horst asked.

Max considered for a moment. They had now overflown the main Russian forces, which were in any event clearly on the verge of destruction, and his prime duty was the protection of the Panzers from air attack. To waste fuel and bullets shooting up an unresisting enemy would be a dereliction of duty if, at the moment they had to turn for home for replenishment, a flight of Ilyushin bombers was to appear. 'Be patient. We will continue east for a few minutes.'

'Good God!' Mark Bayley laid down *The Times*. 'Hitler has invaded Russia!'

'Holy shit!' Jolinda exclaimed. 'Can he do that?'

Helen, on the far side of the breakfast table, looked pained. Jolinda's language always left her breathless.

'Well, he's done it,' Mark pointed out.

'But why? Aren't they buddy-buddies?'

'Never buddy-buddies. Uncertain bedfellows, perhaps. But he always had his mind on Russia.'

'It's going to be some scrap.'

'It already is some scrap, according to this. The Germans are claiming to have advanced twenty-five miles on the first day, to have destroyed at least two divisions of Soviet troops and collected God knows how many tanks and guns, and to have destroyed over five hundred planes.'

'Wow! You reckon Max will be involved?' Jolinda could hardly remember the boy she had played with as a child; he had been three years younger than her and had seemed no more than a baby. As for what he might look like now . . . there was not a single photograph of him in the house. But she had heard enough about him.

'It says here that most of the planes were destroyed on the ground, but I have no doubt that Max is there. You remember John was wondering last month where all the top German fighter pilots had gone. Now we know.'

'But what will it mean to us?' Helen asked.

'I would say it has to be good news,' Mark said. 'Jerry may have got off to a flying start, but that's principally because he's taken everyone by surprise, as usual. But I think he's going to find the Russians a bit tougher than the Poles – or the French, for that matter.'

'They're supposed to have the most powerful army and air force in the world,' Jolinda said.

'That's right.'

'The Germans must be nuts to take that lot on.'

'Perhaps not entirely. Don't let's forget that Stalin shot all his top brass in 1937, and that the Russians weren't too successful against the Finns the winter before last. It's one thing to have more men and more materiel than the other fellow, but it takes time to train the officers to lead them. And if the Luftwaffe is really destroying five hundred planes a day, the two sides may soon be evenly matched, at least numerically. I'd say it could be a protracted business, and as long as Hitler is committed to Russia he can't be planning anything very big against us.'

'It all sounds terrible.' Helen shook her head.

'Well—' Jolinda said, then looked at the doorway. 'Yes, Alice?'

The nurse was a buxom, pink-cheeked young woman who was always nervous when in the presence of Mark. Now she said, 'Excuse me, ma'am, it's time for Baby's feed.'

'Right.' Jolinda stood up. 'But starting this afternoon we're getting him on to the bottle.'

'Oh Joly,' Helen protested, 'he's only three months old. And you've still lots of milk.'

'So has the cow. If I don't get back into uniform pretty damn quick, I'm going to go stark raving bonkers.'

'Gentlemen,' General Clausen beamed at his officers, 'I have to tell you that this morning General Guderian's Panzers entered Minsk. That is to say, in under a month they have advanced nearly five hundred kilometres. The Russian armies opposed to us are completely surrounded and are surrendering in droves. It has been estimated that we will have taken very nearly three hundred thousand prisoners. In addition, the Russian air force has, certainly in our sector, been utterly destroyed. This is perhaps the greatest victory ever achieved by any army in history. I congratulate you all.

'We shall now move this headquarters on to Minsk for the second phase thrust and encircling movement; our next target is Smolensk.' He grinned at them. 'And after that will be Moscow. If we maintain this rate of advance, we will be in the Kremlin by the end of September, as per schedule. Our air wing will also advance to operate out of the captured Russian airfields. We move up tomorrow.'

'Isn't it tremendous?' Hildegarde asked when they left the conference hall. 'At this rate the war will be over by the end of the year.'

'And what will you do then?' Max asked.

'I haven't thought of it, but I would like to spend some time in Berlin with you. Do you have a home there?'

'Ah,' Max said. He had that very morning received a letter from Erika, filled with her usual enthusiastic terms of adoration. Would he have to make a choice? Hildegarde was certainly the more reliable, at least while they were campaigning in company. But that was about to end. 'I should like that very much as well,' he said. 'But I don't actually have a home there.' I don't have a home anywhere, he thought sombrely. 'I usually stay at the Hotel Albert.'

'You have expensive tastes.'

'I think I was badly brought up. I would love to spend some time there with you. But you do realize that until the campaign is over we are going to be separated, if I am taking the Wing to some isolated Russian airbase?'

'And you're leaving tomorrow morning,' she murmured thoughtfully. 'But we do have tonight.'

'It all sounds a bit grim,' Wing Commander Browne remarked. 'The Russians appear to be even less capable of fighting than the French.'

'Well,' John said, 'we'll just have to go on making hay until his big boys come back to us.'

'Absolutely. Am I right, that you now have thirty-six?'

'I think so. There was some doubt about that 110 the day before yesterday. He definitely was on fire, but he dropped into cloud and I never actually saw him go down.'

'One of the bomber crews did. Do you realize you are now only one short of your dad?'

'Hell, I'd forgotten that. He'll be tickled pink.'

'You'd better take this evening off to remind him of it. Come to think of it, take tomorrow off as well. You'll be up again on Thursday; maybe you'll bag number thirty-seven.'

John hurried across to the WAAF office. 'Guess what? I have a thirty-six-hour pass. When are you off?'

'As I am the boss lady,' Jolinda said, 'I can come when I like. I suppose you're going by bike?'

'It beats walking.'

Jolinda placed various papers in their appropriate trays and led him into the outer office. 'I'm off, Betty. I'll be in, ah . . .' she looked at John.

'Thursday morning. Unless there's a flap.'

'Yes, sir.' Jolinda and Betty spoke together.

'I feel very guilty,' Jolinda said as she settled herself on the pillion, her arms around his waist.

'There's not a lot going on at the moment,' he pointed out. 'And what's the use in having an Air Commodore as a father if you don't use it?'

'Air Vice Marshal,' she corrected.

'You're kidding?'

'He telephoned this morning. He was coming over to see your dad and celebrate this evening.'

'That's perfect. We'll have a party, and you can officially ask him for a thirty-six-hour pass. But does that mean he's going to be moving on to bigger things?'

'I guess so.'

'Then you'd better make the most of it until he leaves. The next bloke may not be so cooperative.'

'Hmm,' she said thoughtfully. 'Anyway, if the weather holds fine I think we should take little Mark for a spin tomorrow: your dad seems to have a lot of spare petrol coupons.'

'Tomorrow afternoon,' John corrected.

'What's happening tomorrow morning?'

'We are spending tomorrow morning in bed. I think it's time we started serious work on Mark mark two, if you follow me.'

'Hmm,' she said again. 'You do realize that I'm still inclined to trickle?'

'And they're just about twice their normal size. If I don't get you home soon we'll be arrested for indecent behaviour on the public highway.'

'You are going in at a tighter angle than usual,' Singleton told the pilots assembled before him. 'There's an aircraft factory at Amiens which the brass wants taken out. There'll be a flight of twenty-four Wellingtons, and we'll put up two squadrons of Spitfires. If all goes well you should be able to make the round trip in company. However, watch your gauges, and be sure you all come back.'

'Amiens is actually closer than northern Holland, isn't it?' Bowman asked as they left Dispersal in an unseasonably chill drizzle.

'I think that's what he was getting at,' John agreed. 'But as he said, there's still no room for carelessness.'

'And you'll be looking for that number thirty-seven, sir,' suggested Hassell with his usual enthusiasm.

'If it comes along,' John said. 'I think we've a while to go yet.' He settled into his cockpit and a few moments later was airborne, disappearing into cloud almost immediately. 'Twenty-five thousand feet,' he said into his mike; the bombers would have left some half an hour previously.

He was aware of feeling perhaps dangerously relaxed. Yesterday morning had been one of the most memorable of his sexual life, and Joly was always memorable. He supposed that was because they had never actually had the opportunity to live together on a day-in, day-out basis, but had had to be content with the (if they were lucky) one night a week he had been able to escape duty.

And yesterday morning had followed quite a wild party. The two old gentlemen – rather a liberty, he supposed, as neither was yet forty-five – had been in a celebratory mood, and even Helen had got tight, while Joly was always happy to let her hair down. But now he was back to business.

Domestic bliss had to be forgotten in the search for total commitment.

He found himself thinking about Max. In view of the news coming out of Russia there could be no doubt that Max, and all his veteran pilots, were now in that theatre – again, if the reports were the least accurate – having the time of their lives against negligible opposition. Max would soon be in the hundred-plus bracket, a total achieved by no other fighter pilot of any nationality, except for the almost legendary Marseille, so far as he knew.

From 25,000 feet the Channel was calm, briefly. Then they were over the Pas de Calais. They had overtaken the bombers, who were some 10,000 feet beneath them, and were now within a few miles of their target. The weather was clear up here, but there was still considerable heavy cloud below them blocking the sun from the ground. At his height, however – 12,000 feet above the cloud ceiling – it seemed that he could see for ever.

And there they were. 'Bandits, one o'clock,' he told his pilots. 'Twenty plus. Maintain your height until they close in.'

The bombers had certainly seen the approaching Messerschmitts as well, but held their course, placing their confidence in their fighter protection. 'Going down,' John said, when he reckoned the enemy planes were too close to escape an engagement, and put his machine into a steep dive. He didn't have to look around him to be sure his squadron was following.

Now the Germans had seen them. Roughly half of them rose to intercept; the rest began their attack on the bombers.

'They've got guts,' John said. 'Take those buggers out, Bobby.'

Newman peeled off with two flights. John and their remaining four flights were now very close to the enemy. Tracers filled the air, but he had a sublime confidence that his nerve and therefore his aim were better than that of any German, save perhaps Max himself.

He ignored the flying bullets, and even the exploding cannon, concentrating on the German flight leader. At one hundred yards the Messerschmitt sought to take evasive action to avoid a collision, as John had known he would. He loosed a five second burst into the enemy cockpit. He was so close he could clearly see the man's body jerking beneath the impact of the bullets. Then the plane was spiralling down, and he could fasten on to his next victim even as he registered: number thirty-seven. Now to get ahead.

Another plane was in his sights and another burst saw flames coming from the Messerschmitt's engine. John turned his head to make sure he was going down and was suddenly lost in a damp mist.

His first supposition was that he had flown into cloud, but the clouds were still several thousand feet beneath him. Then he realized that the damp was *inside* the cockpit rather than out, and both from the smell and the taste of the liquid enveloping him, it was glycol, his coolant.

'Shit!' he muttered. But there was as yet no flame or smell of burning. And if the engine must have been hit, it was still working. He wondered how long, lacking coolant, it would take to seize up, put the stick forward and dived into the cloud, considering the situation.

'You all right, Johnnie?' Newman asked.

'Probably not,' John said. 'Take command.'

His engine was now making an odd clanking sound, and at last he could smell scorching metal as various moving parts ground against each other; he was reminded of the famous lines Shakespeare had put into the mouth of Richard III, something like: 'Whence comes that knocking?' And also recalled that the beleaguered king had cried, 'A horse, a horse! My kingdom for a horse!'

He did not suppose a horse was going to do him a lot of good at that moment. He dropped through the cloud at 8,000 feet and could look around him. To his right, perhaps ten miles away, he could see the columns of smoke rising above Amiens. The bombers had done their work and were now hurrying for home; he did not know if they had lost any, but one or two anti-aircraft guns were still firing, he could see the bursts of flak.

There was in fact no other aircraft visible; all the action, if it was still continuing, was 10,000 feet above him, beyond the clouds. Decision time. Between the city and himself there was a small wood and then what looked like some open country. He turned towards it, endeavouring to control his machine. But trying to put it down without power would be too risky, especially as the Spitfire was now starting to drop very fast. So, it will be a fourth time after all, he thought, and this time with a prison camp at the end of it. Bloody hell!

He pushed back the canopy.

'The skipper?' Singleton demanded, incredulously. 'You saw him go in?'

'I know he was hit,' Hassell said. 'He suddenly dropped out, and his cockpit was a mass of liquid.'

'But no fire?' Singleton asked.

'I spoke with him immediately after,' Newman said. 'He suggested he was going down and told me to take command. We were still engaging so there was no time for a chat, but he didn't sound as if he, personally, was hit. I tried again later but he must either have gone in or baled out.'

The inner door opened. Browne looked over the tense faces in front of him. 'What's happened?'

'Bayley's gone in, sir,' Singleton explained.

Browne stared at him, then at Newman.

'He got two of the bastards,' Hassell said, 'but he didn't seem to see the third. I got him, but by then the skipper had been hit.'

'And?'

'He was alive; I spoke with him,' Newman put in.

'When you spoke with him,' Browne commented. 'Fuck, fuck, fuck! I'll call the Air Vice Marshal. He'd better tell Mark Bayley himself. But . . . Ah . . .'

'I'll do it,' Newman volunteered; he had been John's closest friend for over a year and best man at his wedding.

Newman walked slowly across the station to the WAAF office. Jolinda was standing in the doorway. He knew she always counted the planes as they came in, just as he knew she could identify most of them by the number of swastikas painted on the fuselages. Only he and John had more than twenty.

He halted at the foot of the steps, and they gazed at each other.

'Tell me?'

'He's alive, Joly. I'm sure of it. I spoke with him.'

'But he went in? Over France?'

'Just north of Amiens. This Jerry sneaked up on him—'

'And you saw him bale out?'

'Ah . . .'

'So you don't know?'

'There was heavy cloud beneath us. He dropped into that. We were still engaged in combat, and there was no time to follow him down before we had to come home. But he was alive, and so far as I could judge, unhurt.'

'When you spoke with him.'

She turned and went back into her office.

Air Vice Marshal Hargreaves got out of his car and patted Rufus on the head; he had been coming to this house so often the two were old friends. Then he squared his shoulders and went to the door. A commanding officer from WingCo up had to become accustomed to writing letters of condolence to surviving relatives. It was a grim task, but it was also once removed from the grief the message would induce. In all his long years of service he had never personally had to inform a father that his son might be lost. As for his own daughter . . .

Clements opened the door. 'Mr Hargreaves, how good to see you.' His tone was uncertain; he was not used to receiving military callers in the middle of the afternoon.

'Good afternoon Clements. Mr Bayley in?'

'He's in Southampton, sir. At the marina.'

'You expect him back today?'

'Oh yes, sir. He's always back by evening.'

'Ah. Well . . .'

'Cecil! How good of you to call.' Helen emerged from the garden, pulling off her weeding gloves.

'Helen!' He held her hands.

Helen frowned. The Air Vice Marshal was not usually a demonstrative man. 'What's happened? Mark . . .?'

Still holding her hand, Hargreaves drew her into the drawing room. 'Johnnie's gone in.'

'Johnnie . . .' Helen sank into a chair.

Hargreaves also sat. 'I only heard the news an hour ago.'

'You mean he was shot down?'

'His plane was hit, yes, and he went down. But he sank into cloud and was not seen again.'

'Oh my God! He's dead!'

'We don't know that. Bob Newman spoke with him as he disappeared and got the impression that he was not hurt. Everything depends on whether or not he managed to bale out. There was no time, you see, for any of the other pilots to go down and see what had happened; they were at the very end of their fuel range.'

Helen's shoulders were hunched. 'Mark, he'll be shattered . . .'

'He survived,' Hargreaves pointed out, 'and he didn't have a parachute. And always remember that Johnnie has come down three times already and is still around.'

'Different times, different people, different planes,' Helen muttered.

Rufus was barking again. They heard the sound of a car engine, and a moment later the front door was opening. The car drove away again.

Hargreaves stood up to face the doorway. Clements had not spoken and stood inadequately in the hall; he had overheard the conversation. Jolinda stepped past him and looked at her father. Then she came to him and he took her in his arms. 'He'll survive,' he promised. 'Bayleys always do.'

She released him and he saw that her eyes were dry. Helen was also on her feet, but managed to resist the temptation to gush as she was prone to do. Instead, she held Jolinda's hand and drew her forward for a kiss on the cheek.

'Does Mark know?' Jolinda asked.

'Not as yet,' her father said. 'It's not the sort of thing I can say over the telephone. And to tell him to come home because I had urgent news would be the same thing.'

Jolinda nodded.

'Tea,' Helen announced. 'Clements!'

'At once, Mrs Bayley.'

'Mr Browne gave me the afternoon off,' Jolinda said. 'I'll just go up to my room and dump this uniform, see how Baby is.'

Hargreaves caught her hand as she turned for the door. 'Joly . . .'

'I'm all right, Dad. I'll be all right.'

He let her go, watched her climb the stairs with sombre eyes.

Jolinda closed the bedroom door behind her, kicked off her

shoes, threw her skirt and tunic on a chair and lay on her stomach across the bed. Thirty-six hours ago she had lain here with John on top of her. Thirty-six hours.

She rolled onto her back and gazed at the ceiling. Now the tears were coming fast.

Theirs had been an unusual relationship. She had not come back to England looking for a romance; nothing could have been further from her mind. Her parents had divorced when she was eight years old, and her mother had gone to live with her sister in California, taking her small daughter with her. She had grown up in the laissez-faire atmosphere of that most laissez-faire of states, and by her mid-teens England had become nothing more than a memory of rather stuffy people and even stuffier conventions and behaviour. She had gone to college, danced at proms, necked violently, without a care in the world or any idea what she wanted to do with her life.

But the fact that she had an air force background had never deserted her, even if it was a subject her mother had never wished to discuss. Mom had in fact been scandalized when her only daughter had announced her intention of joining the Women's Army Air Corps; with her background, and a college degree, a commission had been hers for the asking. She had thoroughly enjoyed wearing the starched white summer uniform, the training, the camaraderie, and most of all the individual freedom when off duty. She had lost her virginity as a matter of course, as had most of her friends. Life had been one long, enthusiastic party, but with a sufficiently serious undertone to make it worthwhile.

That had all changed on 3 September 1939. Like most Americans, she had not been the least interested in European politics over the previous half-dozen years. But suddenly she had become very conscious of the fact that although she was an American citizen, she was British by birth, and her father was one of those fighting for that birthright. She had known instinctively that her place was at his side.

It had taken a while to arrange, and Mom had very nearly exited into space, but she had never been one to be easily deterred from any plan of action and Dad had, of course, pulled strings to have her accepted into the WAAF, and then, after a brief period, to have her commissioned. She had naturally gravitated towards the Bayleys because of her father's long-standing friendship with Mark; and besides, she had known both him and the two boys when they were children together. They had not kept in touch, but her father had filled her in on the family's doubly tragic background: the death of Karolina and the defection of Max. If her memories of Max were vague, Karolina was not a woman easily forgotten, even after sixteen years. This had made Joly wary of getting too close, but then she had found herself posted to the same station as Johnnie. She now knew there had been no coincidence about this. Her father had always wanted John Bayley as a son-in-law, and she was his only daughter.

She remembered being resentful of this back then, when John had come on heavy, always encouraged by her dad. Perhaps the combination had proved too strong for her to resist, but she did not really believe that. John Bayley was a strange mixture of formidable fighting man and somewhat diffident youth. She had never experienced the fighting man. But she did know that he had broken his engagement to another woman to pursue her, and he had done that with a mixture of charm and determination, however often rebuffed, that *had* eventually proved irresistible.

Thus, for just over a year she had been the happiest of women, at one in her job and in her love life. Just over a year! She sat up and dried her eyes. He will survive, no matter what, she told herself; he will survive! His father had survived being shot down and badly wounded. But then she remembered that it had been while in a German hospital that Mark Bayley had met Karolina . . .

She dressed, washed her face, applied make-up and went to the nursery. At least she had her son.

Helen invited Hargreaves to stay for dinner; he clearly felt it was his duty to break the news himself.

Jolinda joined them for an aperitif, and they were in the library when they heard the sound of the Rolls. All three stood up to face the door, but one look at Mark's face told them that the news was stale.

'Wing Commander Browne telephoned the office,' he said.

They waited. It was only a couple of hours' drive from Southampton to Hillside, and it was now six o'clock. The squadron had returned from its mission just after ten. Browne would hardly have waited more than six hours to make the call, once he had determined to do so after all, instead of leaving it to Hargreaves.

'Is that whisky you're drinking?' Mark asked.

'I'll pour,' Jolinda said.

'Oh, Mark!' Helen was in his arms.

He reached past her to shake Hargreaves' waiting hand then took the drink from Jolinda, retaining her hand to squeeze the fingers. 'I have no doubt at all that Jerry will let us know if he's dead. Until then, he's alive. And Browne tells me that he had two kills before being hit. That's thirty-eight; one more than I ever achieved. Clements!'

'Sir?'

'The Bollinger. Two bottles. We'll drink to Johnnie's success.'

Despite the alcohol, he did not sleep, and at about midnight got up and limped downstairs to the library. He had spent some of the happiest moments of his life in this room, with Karo, and then with the two boys while they had been growing up. He had taught them everything he knew about flying, and now they had both surpassed him. He was certain John was alive. But when he would see him again, and in what condition, he could not estimate. So all he could do was wait, and hope. After Karolina, he was not too good at praying.

The door opened. The room was in darkness but she knew where he was sitting, and sat beside him, their fingers locked together.

'How's the boy?'

'Sleeping like a baby – well, he should be.'

'You know, this is your home, now and always.'

'I'm not going anywhere. I have to be here for when John comes home.'

They sat together until dawn.

The day was suddenly amazingly peaceful, although shrouded in a persistent drizzle. Amiens had vanished from sight by the time John dropped through the clouds; the smoke pall merely appeared as an additional heavy cloud – there was no wind to disperse it. Nearer at hand, to his right, was the wood. He would have preferred to come down closer to it because of the chance of immediate concealment, but as he was drifting slowly but inexorably to the north, he didn't think he was going to achieve that ambition. In front of him the pasture stretched for a good way, broken up by hedges and narrow lanes; he could not see any people. Instead, he saw the burning wreckage of his Spitfire, several hundred yards away. Odd, he thought; he had not heard the noise of the explosion as it had hit the ground, but it was acting as a beacon for anyone who might be looking for him. In the distance, at the limit of his visibility, perhaps three miles, he thought he could make out a group of buildings, one of which was fairly large.

Now he was very close to the ground. He remembered landing awkwardly the previous September and spraining his ankle. That was not something he could afford today. He tensed himself, and in fact timed it perfectly, striking the earth while running. Unfortunately, what had appeared as almost a lawn from even twenty feet up, turned out to be both soft and uneven, and after a few steps he fell headlong, being promptly covered in mud.

Winded, he lay still for a few minutes, then rose to his knees and slowly gathered in the parachute while the drizzle settled on his flying helmet and shoulders and smudged his goggles. These he now took off, leaving them draped round his neck.

As far as he could tell, he was unhurt. And, for the moment, undetected on enemy territory, but the burning plane would certainly attract attention. He began hunting through the parachute, turning over fold after fold, until he came to the map. He drew his knife and cut out the large square of material, but reading it was intensely difficult in the wet. He needed shelter, and there was only the wood, now a dark blur some three quarters of a mile behind him.

He folded the map and thrust it inside his tunic. Then he gathered the parachute, rolled it up and scooped it into his arms like a large bundle of washing. It was surprisingly light. Then he set off towards the wood, moving very slowly as he splashed through puddles and stepped into unexpected holes.

Concentration was difficult, as his mind kept drifting back to the recent engagement and his own criminal negligence in not seeing the Messerschmitt closing on him; he had been too euphoric about his thirty-eighth kill. But he simply had to remember what Blatchford had told him. At this moment it all seemed absurdly hypothetical: he was extremely unlikely to come across a washing line full of suitable clothing, even supposing any housewife would dream of hanging out her washing in the rain. The only railway line in the vicinity would be in and out of Amiens, and he did not suppose he would get very far walking the streets of a city in an RAF flying suit. Nor had he seen the least sign of one of the streams, teeming with fish desperate to be caught, that the Colonel had promised. Not that he would have been able to light a fire and cook anything in these conditions; he had never been partial to raw fish.

So it seemed the only bit of advice that he could follow was to lie doggo for a day or so and see what might turn up: at that moment he could not envisage anything worthwhile doing so. Still, the shelter of the wood remained his number one priority. Supposing he ever got there.

The drone of an aircraft engine was suddenly very loud. He knew from the sound that it was not a fighter, but probably a reconnaissance plane, and now he saw it, skimming over the distant treetops and coming straight at him.

He fell to his face, with the parachute cuddled beneath him; the white silk would be easily visible from a few hundred feet.

The plane dipped lower yet as it passed over him, then it soared upwards and towards the still burning wreckage of the Spitfire. He gave a sigh of relief, rose to his feet and heard it again; it had turned and was coming back. There could be no doubt that it had seen him. Trying to conceal the parachute was now a waste of time. He threw it to one side and began running: the trees, more than ever, seemed his only hope of evasion.

The aircraft climbed away again. He reached shelter, panting and staggering, tripped and fell to his knees, got up and ran some more, before collapsing, utterly exhausted. He regarded himself as being as fit as the next man, but the heavy flying-suit and boots had never been designed with cross-country running in mind.

He rolled over and lay on his back gazing up at the tree canopy. The drizzle was having difficulty penetrating this, but it was gathering on leaves and branches and every so often delivering a deluge. Slowly, he got his breathing under control and was then aware of an immense thirst. He used his cupped hands to collect enough water for some relief, but it took time;

when he looked at his watch he discovered it was eleven thirty. He had been on the ground for well over an hour and was still within a mile of where he had come down. He didn't suppose Colonel Blatchford would approve of that.

He reached into his pocket and pulled out the tin, opened it, and selected a malted milk tablet to suck. Then he peered at the map. It was of course an extremely small scale, and seemed smaller because of the wealth of detail it contained, but there was a considerable key in the left hand margin. As far as he could make out, if he could get through the wood he reckoned he might be able to find the railway track that led to the east. But it was a hell of a long way to the Vichy border. A change of clothes was essential. By referring to the key, he deduced that the suggestion of houses to the north was actually a chateau, no doubt surrounded by its outbuildings. According to Blatchford, to try that would be extremely risky. His best bet was a village and a church, and there was one about three miles on the other side of the wood, but the wood itself was some two miles across, supposing he went in the right direction.

He checked the compass. The malted milk tablet having been consumed, he replaced it with a boiled sweet, folded away his map and pocketed the tin, got up and began to make his way through the undergrowth.

He walked, or stumbled, for half an hour before coming to a track running through the wood. He was tempted to follow it, but it was roughly at right angles to the direction in which he wanted to go. He was still considering his options when he heard the sound of a car engine. He darted back into the bushes beside the track and crouched there, watching a tourer, with its roof up, coming slowly towards him. It contained four soldiers, the driver and three men armed with rifles.

To his consternation, however, the car stopped opposite his hiding place. Being fluent in German, John had no difficulty in understanding what they were saying. 'You are mistaken,' said one of the men, obviously the most senior.

'Those bushes moved,' insisted the second man. 'And there is no wind.'

The four men peered into the trees. 'He will have a gun,' suggested the driver.

John had in fact instinctively unbuttoned the flap for his

revolver, but like most RAF fighter pilots, he wore the gun more as a macho accessory than with any intention of ever shooting at anybody. Fortunately, the Germans were not aware of this, and even more fortunately he was realizing that they were Landwehr troops and not front line soldiers: they looked neither fit enough nor smart enough to be regulars, and they handled their weapons more with apprehension than confidence. He supposed they had far less experience of shooting at people than he did, and certainly of being shot at.

'If he's in there,' decided the senior soldier, 'he's not going anywhere. They intend to surround the wood as soon as the company comes out from Amiens. That will be by tomorrow morning, when they intend to sweep the whole area with dogs. By then, he'll be soaked to the skin, starving and probably freezing cold. He won't be any trouble. We'll just check the chateau.'

'You won't get much out of that old bitch,' remarked the other soldier. 'She hates us. And that daughter of hers . . .'

'We'll just have a word. Let's go, Oscar.'

The car moved off down the track.

John remained absolutely still until it was out of sight, then he retired a little further into the trees and sat down to consider his position.

He was already soaked to the skin; the mud clinging to his uniform was extremely unpleasant. But if by tomorrow morning the whole area was going to be crawling with men and dogs, he had to do something today, or at least tonight. Or simply surrender. And be carted off to Germany for the foreseeable future. He was damned if he would accept that.

The soldiers had seemed to suggest that contrary to Blatchford's warning, whoever lived in the chateau did not readily cooperate with the Germans. It would be an enormous risk, but there did not seem an alternative. And he would have tried.

Obviously there was nothing he could do until nightfall, which was still several hours away. He could only hope the soldiers had been accurately delineating the situation and the active search would not begin until tomorrow.

He retraced his steps to the north side of the wood, and there crouched in the rain. He had the malted milk tablets and the boiled sweets and the liver toffee to keep him going, but as the drizzle turned to rain and grew steadily heavier, there was very little protection from the elements, and as the German soldier had suggested might be the case, he was growing colder by the minute as the rain penetrated.

He heard the drone of the airplane again as it circled the wood and swooped over the pasture. Then it also disappeared as the rain grew yet heavier. The burning Spitfire was now just a mass of twisted, blackened metal. It was a tremendous temptation to chance his arm and cross the fields, especially after the car came rumbling back, now travelling quite fast; the soldiers were clearly in a hurry to get out of the wet. But he made himself be patient, until by six o'clock the evening was growing very gloomy, although there were still some hours of daylight left.

He stood up, slowly and painfully; every muscle seemed to have fused into its neighbour. He jumped up and down a few times to restore circulation and then set out.

Visibility was now very poor; the clouds were low and the rain seemed to be heavier than ever as he left the shelter of the trees. He could not make out the chateau; there was not even a light to be seen – presumably because of the British air raids, the Germans were enforcing a blackout. In the gloom it was difficult even to read his tiny compass. On the other hand, the track apparently led to the chateau. He knew it was some distance to his right, so he moved in that direction, round the northern edge of the wood. This took some time with the inevitable stumbling over rabbit holes, and it was past seven before he came across the more even surface.

He could now walk quite fast. The sudden easiness of his progress relaxed his concentration and he was taken by surprise at the sound of an engine behind him. He turned and saw a pair of headlights coming towards him and alarmingly close.

Shit! he thought. Hastily he jumped off the track as the lights, hitherto dimmed, suddenly assumed full beam. He crouched beside the slight parapet but had clearly been seen, and the car, having drawn level with him, stopped. 'I see you, Englander,' a voice said in English, but John had no doubt that the speaker was German.

This was confirmed a moment later when the door was opened and a man in uniform stepped down. He wore a greatcoat, but from his high-peaked cap John deduced that he was an officer. He advanced to the edge of the track and shone a flashlight, at the same time drawing his Luger pistol. 'If you do not surrender, I will shoot you,' he announced.

The flashlight beam was not actually shining on him, and John realized that the officer did not know exactly where he was. On the other hand, he was very soon going to find out. The big decision. But he had already made the decision by not surrendering to the soldiers that morning. He drew his revolver, at the same time standing up, feeling rather foolishly like some Wild West hero on the streets of Dodge City facing the man in the black hat.

The beam picked him up. 'Ah,' said the German, levelling his pistol. 'Raise your hands.'

John had done his required share of shooting practice, but he had never been all that accurate. Now he raised his gun and fired, twice. To his amazement the officer gave a grunt and fell to his knees, but as he did so he also fired. John felt the impact without, at the moment, experiencing any pain. But he also was on his knees. He stayed there, while the officer fell to his face.

John struggled back up and advanced, very cautiously, but the German never moved. John crouched beside him and searched for a pulse, but there was none. Both bullets had entered his chest and John reckoned he must have died instantly.

Five

Allies

It was the first time John had ever looked on the face of a man he had killed. He felt vaguely sick, but was also aware of the dangers of his position. He was no longer merely an Evader: he had killed a German officer, and would, no doubt, be shot on sight. And he was wounded. He took the flashlight from the dead man's fingers and played it over himself. The blood was seeping from the left thigh of his flying suit, but as he could move quite freely he felt sure the wound was superficial. On the other hand, if he was leaking blood he would very easily be traced – certainly by any competent bloodhound. He took off the flying suit and left it on the ground, transferring his survival tin to the side pocket of his tunic. Then he wrapped the parachute map around his thigh. He had to cut the material with his knife to make a couple of ends to secure the rough bandage, but he did not think the map was going to be of any great use to him now: if he couldn't find help he was a dead duck. He took a couple of steps away from where he had been hit and shone the flashlight on the ground; there was no trace of blood. He replaced the revolver in its holster and re-buckled the belt. Then he considered the situation.

He might not be badly hurt, but he was hurt, and if the wound was not attended to it could well fester. He was also now a wanted murderer, at least in German eyes. The chateau, which could not now be very distant, was his only hope. But even if they were disposed to help him, he could not risk leading his pursuers up to their front door, and his flying boots would be very easy to follow. He switched off the car headlights and hunted through the interior. He found what he wanted: a pair of blankets lying on the back seat. He cut one of these into halves and then again into strips and tied them around his boots. Then he took the other blanket and the half remaining from the first and spread them in front of him, taking them up one after the other as he made his way along the track, again feeling like some Wild West hero as he recalled reading this was a method used by frontier scouts to hide their tracks from Indians.

It was a very slow business, and his leg was becoming increasingly painful, but at least the exertion warmed him up. The continuous slow movement required so much concentration that when suddenly a dog barked quite close, and he looked at his watch, he saw that it was ten o'clock. Now he realized that he was exhausted and had a tremendous thirst. But at least he was on a hard surface. He staggered forward and came to a gate. This was latched but not locked. He pushed it open and the dog became very loud, although apparently it could not access the yard in which he found himself.

There were buildings all around him, the one in front high and large, obviously being the chateau. As he was now on a firm surface, he scooped up the blankets and carried them in his arms. Thus far he had still seen no lights, but as he crossed the yard the door at the top of the steps opened to reveal a pale orange glimmer. 'Who's there?' a woman's voice asked, in French.

John took a deep breath, and in his best schoolboy French said, 'I am Squadron Leader John Bayley of the RAF. I need your help.'

He had been advancing all the while and had now reached the foot of the steps, and could see not one but two women standing above him. The dog continued to bark, but was still not visible. 'Are you mad,' one of the women asked, 'coming here?'

This was a different voice from the first. 'I am wounded,' John said.

'We want no part of you,' said the second voice. 'Go away.'

'Nathalie,' said the first voice, 'if he is hurt . . .'

'He is still no concern of ours, Mama. He will bring trouble. Those soldiers said they would be searching the entire area tomorrow morning. They will certainly track him here.'

'We must help him,' the mother said. 'Think of Henri.'

'I am thinking of Henri,' the younger woman replied.

'I am wounded,' John said again. 'If I could just bandage

92

it up properly, and if you could spare me a change of clothing, I will be gone by morning. I used these blankets to disguise my footprints and to hide my tracks. They should not be able to trace me – certainly if it keeps on raining.'

'You come in,' the grey-haired woman said, 'and we will attend to you.'

John limped up the steps and into the light. Quite a lot of the mud had penetrated through the flying suit to his uniform; the blanket strips around his boots were caked; he was hatless and knew his hair was plastered to his head. 'I suppose I look a sight,' he suggested.

The two women were peering at him with equal interest. The mother, he guessed, was in her sixties, but her grey hair still retained dark streaks and her face indicated that once upon a time she might have been quite a beauty. She was not very tall, and the thinness of her body was accentuated by her black gown, but the material was excellent. The daughter, who he put in her late thirties or early forties, was altogether taller and larger, her features handsome rather than pretty. She also wore black. She now said, 'You are a mess, Monsieur Bayley.'

'You have come from the wood,' the mother said. 'The Boche told us they thought you were in the wood. They did not think you could possibly come here.'

'But they warned us, anyway,' the daughter added. 'And they said that Captain Schultz would probably come to see us this evening. You are fortunate that he seems to have changed his mind, or you might have encountered him. Or did you come across the field?'

'I encountered him,' John said.

'But . . .?'

'I'm afraid I shot him.'

The women stared at him in consternation.

'He threatened me with his pistol,' John explained, 'and told me to surrender. But I did not wish to be a prisoner.'

'Now you are a criminal,' the daughter pointed out. 'You will be hanged. If we help you, we will be hanged. Mama . . .'

'Oh, be quiet, Nathalie,' her mother snapped. 'He has killed a Boche. How many Boche do you think Henri killed before he died?'

'This is madness,' Nathalie declared. 'What do you propose to do? Conceal him?'

'Until he is well enough to travel, yes.'

'And when Dufour comes in?'

'He will not betray us.'

'Madame . . .' John ventured.

'My name is Lafarge, but you may call me Aimee.'

'I am most terribly grateful. But I do not wish to put you at risk.'

'You have already done that,' Nathalie reminded him.

'First thing,' Aimee Lafarge announced, 'we must get you out of those wet things and see to your wound.'

John was shivering again. The house was not heated. 'If I could have something to drink . . .'

'But of course. I am a thoughtless old woman. And food. You must be starving. Nathalie, take Monsieur Bayley into the cloakroom and help him out of his clothes.'

'Mama!' Nathalie protested.

'For heaven's sake, you are a married woman. Do it. I will prepare a supper.'

Nathalie hesitated for a moment, then said, 'You will come with me, monsieur.'

She escorted John along a corridor into a cloakroom. He kept apprehending a meeting with the dog, but it seemed to be locked away somewhere, and now it had even stopped barking.

'Take off your clothes,' Nathalie commanded.

John took off his tunic, while she knelt, nose wrinkling, and untied the blanket strips from round his boots. 'Why are you wearing these?'

'To hide the distinctive soles of my boots.'

'You are a thoughtful man. Sit.' She indicated the single chair. John sank on to this; he was starting to feel dizzy. Nathalie tugged off his boots, then turned her attention to unwrapping the parachute bandage. The door opened and Aimee came in carrying a tray on which there were two glasses of red wine and a tumbler of water. 'Drink the wine,' she commanded, 'then the water, then the second wine.'

John gratefully obeyed, while the women peered at the torn pants. 'These must come off,' Aimee determined.

Nathalie grunted, helped her mother release the belt and drag the pants down. Aimee bent over the bloody flesh and probed it with her fingers; John had to make an effort to keep still. 'At least the bullet has come out. But it is not good,' Aimee commented. 'It must be cleaned and disinfected.' She raised her head. 'You understand?'

John understood very well, but the glass of wine on an empty stomach and in his exhausted condition had sent him into a pleasant daze, just as the water had slaked his thirst. He picked up the second glass of wine. 'I am yours to command, madame.'

Nathalie snorted, but her mother went to the cupboard over the handbasin and took out various medications. John preferred not to look at what they were doing. It was certainly painful, as the gash in his thigh was swabbed, and then what he gathered from the smell was iodine, added. He could not prevent a groan and an involuntary jerk of the leg. 'Fetch some more wine, Nathalie,' Aimee ordered. 'Bring the bottle. It will be all right now, monsieur.'

John opened his eyes and watched her deft fingers applying a roll of bandage. 'Are you a nurse?' he asked.

'I was a nurse in the Great War,' she explained. 'That seems so long ago.' She stood up and took a heavy overcoat from the hook behind the door. 'Put this on and come and eat. You will feel better.'

The two women sat one on either side of John while he ate. 'Where did you encounter Captain Schultz?' Aimee asked.

'Something like a mile along the track.'

'He was driving his car?'

'Yes. He saw me before I could get far enough off the track.'

'And he shot you then you shot him with your revolver? It is an English revolver, is it not?'

'Yes.'

'Then they cannot possibly suppose he was shot by a Frenchman; they will be able to identify the bullet. Therefore they will know that it was you.'

'They will be able to track him here,' Nathalie said.

'I told you, I used the blankets to hide my tracks,' John explained. 'And if by morning I am gone, even if they come here, if you hide my clothes they cannot suspect you.'

'You are being absurd,' Aimee said. 'Leave here before morning? With a bullet wound, and the countryside crawling with soldiers? You must remain here, until you are strong again and until we have made the necessary arrangements to get you away.'

'But madame – Aimee – the risk. Your servants . . .'

'Servants,' Aimee said sadly. 'Do you know, John – you do not mind if I call you John? – two years ago I had eighteen servants in this house. Now there is only Nathalie and myself.'

'You spoke of someone named Dufour.'

'Dufour is an old retainer. He comes out on his bicycle three times a week from Amiens and does whatever heavy work is required. As I said, he will not betray us.'

'I still feel the risk is unacceptable.'

'My husband was killed by the Boche in 1917.'

'My father was shot down by the Germans in 1917. Not far from here.' He decided it would be better not to mention what happened after that.

Aimee clapped her hands. 'But he survived! As will you. So you see, I have been a widow for twenty-four years. I took solace from Nathalie, here, and her husband, Henri. But he was killed by the Germans in May of last year.'

'I was shot down in May of last year, again not far from here.'

'And like your father you survived.' Aimee kissed his cheek. 'It is fate. The Germans owe me, owe Nathalie, two lives. Yours will be one of them.'

John looked at Nathalie, who shrugged. 'My mother is a romantic, Monsieur Bayley, but she is my mother.'

John's plate was empty and he had had the best part of a bottle of Burgundy. He could not prevent a yawn. 'Now you must go to bed,' Aimee decided. 'I do not think the Germans will come looking for Captain Schultz before daybreak. He often stays late when he visits us: he likes my wine cellar. Tomorrow morning we will have to conceal you for perhaps twenty-four hours. But they will not find you. My husband's great-great-great-grandmother was concealed in this house for over a month during the Terror in 1793. So you see, we have done this sort of thing before.'

John slept heavily and was woken at first light by Nathalie, wearing a brocade dressing gown and with her hair in pigtails. 'They are coming now,' she said, and gestured toward the window.

The bedroom was on the third floor of the chateau and faced south. John got up with some difficulty as his leg had stiffened. He looked out over the meadow and the track and saw several vehicles and motorcycles and men and dogs casting about.

'Come.' With his discarded clothes and boots in her arms, Nathalie led him along a corridor to another bedroom. Here there was a large fireplace, empty of any kindling. She moved one of the bricks and the wall swung in to reveal a very small room, just wide enough for a cot bed. 'You will be safe here. You see this vent opens into the fireplace.' She smiled. 'You will be safer than my ancestress, because it can be uncomfortable here when the fire is lit, or indeed any of the ones below that share this chimney. But we have very little firewood and even less coal, so we only light a fire on the very coldest days.' She dropped the clothes on the floor and left him for a few moments, returning with a tray that she also deposited on the floor. 'There is cheese and wine. It will sustain you until I can come back for you. Now I must go and make your bed –' another smile – 'remove all trace of you.' She went to the door and turned back. 'When you come out I will give you a razor, and you will have a bath. Then everything will look much brighter.'

She closed the door and the wall clicked back into place. It occurred to John that if by any chance there was a trace of him to be found in the house and the two women were carted off to a concentration camp, someone in perhaps two hundred years' time, when renovating the chateau or perhaps pulling it down, would be able at last to work out what had happened to Squadron Leader John Bayley, who had mysteriously disappeared in 1941. He wondered which of his, or Jolinda's, descendants there would be by then, and if their name would still be Bayley.

But that was the least of his worries. Just a glimmer of light came through the vent, but it was sufficient for him to locate the tray and pour himself a glass of wine.

Then he listened. Very little sound got up to this floor for some time, but eventually the tramping of boots became apparent, and shortly afterwards there were obviously several people in the room. But only briefly. Then he heard feet overhead in the attics. Soon all was quiet, but as no one came to release him, he supposed the Germans were still around.

In the middle of the morning he ate some cheese and drank some more wine. He found himself thinking of a great many things. He seemed to have fallen on his feet, and if these people were prepared to outfit him, he felt he could make some progress. Whether he could get to Marseilles was another matter; it was a very long way.

And then, an even longer way across Spain to either Lisbon or Gibraltar. Unless he could find a passage on a ship. And all the while the War would be going on without him. Of course, his presence would make no difference either to what was happening or to the eventual outcome, but it was galling to think that there might be something big looming in which he would be unable to play a part.

Far more distressing was the thought that Joly and his dad would not know what had happened to him. His squadron would obviously report that he had gone down, but as he had seen none of them after baling out, none of them could have seen him. Joly! Only the day before yesterday they had wrestled naked in each other's arms in glorious mutual ecstasy. Would he ever hold her in his arms again? Or the boy?

This was the longest day of his life. He was still very tired, and had lost a lot of blood, so that he dozed off from time to time, always to awake with a start. And as the afternoon dragged on and the faint light from the vent faded, he could not prevent himself experiencing a slight panic. The remote possibility he had briefly considered that morning – that he would wind up a skeleton in this abandoned priest's hole – suddenly seemed very likely indeed: he had been there for twelve hours!

And then he heard a sound on the other side of the wall.

As the Hurricane touched down, the ground crews sprang to attention; they recognized the aircraft. Singleton, looking out of his window, also spotted the arrival and went to the inner door.

'Yes?' Browne asked in response to the knock.

'The Air Vice Marshal has just landed, sir.'

'Eh?' Browne emerged from his office, buttoning his tunic, and hurried on to the apron. The Hurricane had now halted and Hargreaves was climbing down. Browne moved toward him. 'Sir?'

Hargreaves' face was grim. 'Not good news, Wing Commander.'

'Confirmed, sir?'

'It may as well be. I'll be with you in a moment. Section Officer Bayley about?'

'In her office, sir.'

Hargreaves nodded and strode across the tarmac, acknowledging the salutes of both the pilots and the ground crews as he passed. Jolinda had of course seen him land and was waiting in the doorway of the little building. She also saluted. 'Sir?'

'We'll go into your office,' Hargreaves said, and followed her past the two WAAF secretaries standing to attention. He closed the door. 'You'd better sit down.'

Jolinda sank into her chair. 'He's dead.'

'That is not confirmed. His plane went in, certainly, and a British pilot, who can only have been John as we did not lose any other aircraft on that sortie, was seen from the air, apparently seeking shelter in a wood. However, he has not actually been seen since, apparently.'

'Well, then . . .'

'Unfortunately, on the same evening that he went in, a German officer driving along a track out of that wood was shot and killed, and beside his body was found a discarded RAF flying suit and helmet.'

Jolinda clasped both hands to her throat. 'Doesn't that mean John got away?'

'In that instance, yes. But the Germans are naturally treating the incident as murder. We understand they are instructing their people in the Amiens area to shoot to kill. So he will not be captured.'

Jolinda gazed at him for several seconds. 'But he could still be alive.'

'At this moment, perhaps yes. I felt you should know that the odds aren't good.'

'He's had bad odds before. Until we have definite confirmation that he is dead, I am going to believe that he is alive and on his way home.' Her tone was fierce.

Hargreaves went round the desk and kissed the top of her head.

*　　*　　*

'I think,' Aimee said, 'that in another week you will be able to travel.'

'Another *week?*' John cried. But he knew she was right. Although he exercised every day, walking round and round the paddock in the company of the dog, a large animal of indeterminate breed that went by the patriotic name of Roland, he was not yet capable of staying on his feet for more than half an hour at a time.

'Why are you in such a hurry? Are you not comfortable here?'

John looked around the room. He gathered this was the winter parlour; Madame Lafarge no longer used the drawing room, except to 'entertain the Boche', as she put it. This was indeed a very comfortable room, even if the empty grate in the huge fireplace suggested that it, like all the rest of the chateau, was going to be distinctly cold in a few months' time. 'I am most comfortable here, Aimee, but when I think of the danger . . . suppose the Germans come back?'

'They have no reason to do that. They searched us so thoroughly last week and found absolutely nothing. No, no. You are safer here than anywhere else in France. But I understand that you wish to get home to your wife and child.' John had shown her the photograph of Jolinda and little Mark that he carried in his wallet. 'You will only accomplish that by the most careful preparation. We have been arranging this. Ah, Nathalie, are they finished?'

Nathalie had just entered the room carrying a pile of clothing, which she laid on the table. 'I think so, but we must try them on.'

Aimee clapped her hands. 'We will have a fashion show. John?'

John took off his uniform, which had been laundered the day after the Germans had searched the chateau while he had soaked in the most luxurious hot bath he had ever known, even if the understanding that they were delving into their limited store of fuel to make him so comfortable was another prick to his conscience. As for undressing before them, he had become so intimate with these two women that he almost regarded them as the mother he had lost and the sister he had never had. Now Nathalie fussed around him, first of all trying on the shirts she had altered, and then inserting him into each of the two suits, frowning and making adjustments with pins. 'They will be ready tomorrow.' She placed a blue beret on his head, adjusted the angle. '*Voilà!*'

Again Aimee clapped her hands. 'You look more French than a Frenchman.'

'And you are happy to let me have your husband's . . . your son-in-law's, clothes?'

'Henri will never use them again. Now, the underclothes. You will try them on in your room, eh?'

'Is that really necessary?'

'Of course. We cannot tell what lies ahead of you, when you may have to undress before other men; you must be French from the skin out. The socks should not be a problem, but the shoes; I am afraid they will be a little large. Henri had big feet. We will put some paper in the toes, but you must wear two pairs of socks.'

'Now,' Aimee said, 'arrangements. You will travel as Henri Dufresne, using his passport. How did the photograph come out?'

Nathalie showed them the passport, in which she had replaced her husband's photograph with the snap of John she had taken with her box camera; this she had had developed in Amiens by an apparently trustworthy professional photographer. 'I think it is very good. You'll see I have scribbled a signature over it. Sadly we do not have a stamp, but most of these people only flip the cover open and glance at the photo. Are you concerned about this?'

'No, but I don't think I'm going to do very well with my French . . .'

'You will not have to,' Aimee said. 'Nathalie will come with you.'

'Eh?'

'You are her husband, Henri Dufresne. It is natural for you to travel together.'

John looked at Nathalie. She smiled. 'I know, I will have to try to look younger and we shall have to make you look older, but the Germans will merely think that I am a lucky woman to be married to a much younger man.'

'Don't the Germans know that Henri is dead?'

'Some Germans know, the ones who came here. But we are not likely to encounter any of them. We will walk into

Amiens and take the train to Paris. In Paris, we will go to the house of my daughter. She will know where you can hide until it can be arranged to move you to the south, and I will return here.'

'Your daughter will agree to do this?'

'Of course. She is with the Resistance.'

'What is the Resistance?'

'They are people who will not accept the Boche as their masters. They wait for the day that you British return to drive the Boche away.'

John wondered how much Blatchford and his MI9 knew about this. 'And the Germans do not know of it?'

Nathalie shrugged. 'If they do not at least guess then they are more stupid than we suppose. Oh, they make arrests, and I believe one or two people have been shot, but we are at war.'

Again John had to reflect at the calm, matter-of-fact way she spoke; it was the life of her daughter, not to mention her mother and herself, that she was putting at risk. 'Where do I carry this?' He took the revolver from its holster; there were still four bullets left.

'You do not carry it anywhere,' Aimee said, 'you leave it here with me, and your uniform. It will be waiting for you when you come back, victorious.' She smiled at him. 'Do not be afraid. It will be all right.'

'Aimee, when one is surrounded by so much courage, how can one be afraid?'

Yet he had to admit, if only to himself, that he felt distinctly apprehensive as he and Nathalie set off the following Monday. This was something completely outside his experience and anything he had ever anticipated. He had gone direct from school to Cranwell, the son of a famous airman. His path, he knew, had been made as easy as possible, and then as a qualified pilot he had known only the Service, with its camaraderie, its *esprit de corps*, and above all, in the air, its openness. One flew against an enemy who was roughly of an equal strength when it came down to machine versus machine – at least once he had graduated to Spitfires. You identified him, and he identified you. The closest one came to subterfuge in the air, was in trying always to have superior height, to have the sun at one's back, and in seeking the protection of a cloudbank when out-numbered or in trouble.

Now he was walking along a road in borrowed clothing and with a borrowed identity. With a borrowed wife. The only thing left of him was his uniform jacket, with its medal ribbons and his revolver, which Aimee was stubbornly keeping for him 'to collect when the War was over'. Even the photograph of Jolinda and little Mark was there: he should not have had it with him in the first place.

His leg was still sore, but had regained most of its strength. Even so, Nathalie insisted on stopping for a rest after every mile or so. She was an excellent companion, curious about his life in England, his family and child, less so about his wife. If she felt bitter over the loss of her husband and the manner in which her obviously once wealthy family had been reduced to near penury, she did not reveal it. He gained the impression that as long as she felt she was doing something for France she had no time for brooding.

'You must forgive me for being reluctant to help you when you first came to us,' she said. 'If Mama and I were to be arrested and handed to the Gestapo . . . you know about this?'

John knew that his Aunt Joan had become entangled with the German State Police before the War when she had gone to Germany to try to persuade Max to come home, and been arrested as a spy. She had never spoken of it to him, but that it had clearly been an unpleasant experience could not be doubted. Although he supposed that for any well-to-do Englishwoman to be exposed to the humiliation of arrest and imprisonment, even if only for a brief period and even if the arrest had been made by the British police, would be considered a most unpleasant business.

'It could be nasty,' he suggested.

Nathalie glanced at him. 'You do not understand. They employ torture of a most brutal nature. And for a woman . . .'

'You're not serious? This is Europe, in the twentieth century.'

'The Nazi Regime is rooted in the Dark Ages, John. Has not your own Mr Churchill said this? What I mean is, were Mama and I to be subjected to physical torture, I cannot say what we would reveal. And what it might entail for Severine and her associates.'

'Yet you are risking everything now. You are a very brave woman, Nathalie.'

'Mama made me understand what we had to do. It may be years before the Boche are driven back across the Rhine. You, the RAF, flying over our skies, are the symbol of the victory which will come one day.'

It took them several hours to walk into Amiens. Nathalie was provided with a large shoulder bag, in which she carried bread, cheese and wine. But they were exhausted when they reached the city. 'We must hurry,' Nathalie said. 'There is a curfew.'

'Will there be a train at this hour?'

'No, no. The train will be in the morning. We will spend the night here in the city.'

'Where?'

Nathalie gave one of her smiles. 'We have friends.'

The streets were very busy. It was past five and everyone had to be home by dusk. 'This is good for us,' Nathalie said.

John hoped she was right. There were also a large number of German soldiers to be seen. But none paid them any attention, and he reminded himself that it was now ten days since he had crashed and the hue and cry had to have moved further afield. Although he had a very nasty turn when he saw, pasted on the wall of a building, a large notice offering a reward of 1,000 francs for information leading to the capture of the Englishman wanted for the murder of a German officer. But they could provide no description of him.

Nathalie saw it too and squeezed his hand. She led him down a side street and to one of a row of houses. On the way they passed a considerable amount of bomb damage. 'Do you resent this?' he asked.

'I do not live in the city. I am sure a lot of people wish the bombers were more accurate. I assume they were aiming for the factory.'

'Bombing is a sadly inaccurate business,' he pointed out.

They went up the steps and she rang the bell. The door was opened by a middle-aged woman. 'Nathalie! It's good to see you.' Then she looked past her friend and the pleasure disappeared from her expression.

'This is a friend,' Nathalie said. 'We need a bed for the night. We will be gone tomorrow.'

The woman hesitated, then stepped back and allowed them into the hall. She closed and locked the door. 'You risk everything.'

'For one night, Mimi.'

Mimi sighed. 'What do we call him?'

'Henri,' Nathalie said.

Mimi gave her an old-fashioned look, but did not comment. She led the way along the hall to a small sitting room. A large man who wore a moustache rose to his feet. 'Nathalie?' He did not appear as pleased as his wife had been to see her.

'Nathalie has brought a friend, Henri, to see us. They wish to spend the night.'

The man looked from Nathalie to John and back again. 'You are the pilot,' he announced.

John held his breath.

'He is my friend,' Nathalie said, 'and therefore he is your friend, and he is the friend of France. One night, and you will not see him again. Or me, if that is what you wish.'

'Oh, Nathalie!' Mimi said. 'Of course that is not what we wish.' She looked at her husband.

'They will have to share the room,' he declared.

'That will be perfectly acceptable,' Nathalie agreed.

'Well,' Mimi said, 'I will prepare something to eat. And you, Jacques, pour these poor people a drink. They look exhausted.' She hurried from the room.

'There is only Pernod,' Jacques remarked.

'I would say that will be ideal,' Nathalie agreed.

Mimi opened the door of the spare bedroom, holding the candle above her head. 'There is only the one bed,' she explained apologetically.

'We are both so tired I don't think it will make any difference,' Nathalie said.

'Well, when would you like to be called?'

'What time is the first train to Paris?'

'Seven o'clock.'

'Then if you will rouse us at six, we will cease being a nuisance to you.'

'I will leave you the candle.' She placed the holder on the mantelpiece, said goodnight and closed the door.

Nathalie and John looked at each other and grinned, then undressed down to their underwear. Nathalie doused the candle and got into bed. 'I am sorry about the facilities,' she remarked. 'We will be in Paris by lunchtime tomorrow and you will be able to wash and clean your teeth.'

'And have a shave,' John suggested.

'Of course.'

'You make it sound as if we are going to a hotel.'

'We are going to my daughter's apartment.'

They lay still on the sagging, feather-down mattress in silence for some minutes, then she said, 'Do you know that it is nearly two years since I have slept in the same bed as a man? Henri was called up the day war was declared, in September of 1939, and I never saw him again.'

Hell, John thought. Apart from the stark horror of what she had just said, he had a sudden premonition of what was coming next. And he owed this woman his life, while even if she was getting on for double his age, she was still both earthy and attractive. But right this minute, apart from being exhausted, he had no desire to have sex with anyone except Jolinda. 'That's really bad luck,' he ventured.

She sighed. 'Luck! Is there such a thing? In war, one must make the best of what one has, not brood on what one *had*.'

Her hand touched his.

'Nathalie,' he said, 'I owe you my life, and my eternal gratitude—'

'But I am old enough to be your mother and you have a beautiful and loving wife waiting for you in England.'

'I have a beautiful and loving wife,' John agreed, choosing his words with care.

She sighed again. 'Perhaps there is such a thing as luck, after all.'

Her hand moved away.

As Nathalie had promised, despite various delays they reached the Gare du Nord just after eleven. It had been a fairly traumatic journey for John, although the woman exuded confidence. The train stopped several times, and at each stop it was boarded by armed policemen, who wandered up and down the corridors shouting, 'Papers! Papers!'

Everyone produced some kind of document. Not all were examined, but John and Nathalie had to present theirs three times, and each time his throat was dry.

As she had promised before leaving the chateau, most of the glances were cursory, just establishing that he was the same man as the photograph. But at the Paris station there was a longer inspection. Henri had been born in 1897, and Nathalie had with great care managed to delete the eight and insert a one between the nine and the seven, which was only the year before John's actual birthday. The alteration was fairly obvious, but she had then dipped the bottom half of the passport in a bowl of water, causing much of the ink to run, just enough: both words and figures were perfectly legible. The policeman on the platform flicked the pages and looked up. 'I know,' Nathalie said. 'My husband was caught out in a rainstorm.'

'This passport should be renewed, monsieur,' the policeman admonished, but he handed it back and waved them through the barrier.

'Phew!' John muttered, as they gained the street.

'They are just doing a boring job,' Nathalie said. 'To make something of a smudged passport would involve taking you to the police station and filling out various forms, and would undoubtedly make him late for lunch.'

Again John had to marvel at her utter confidence.

He did not know Paris at all well. When travelling to Germany with his father and Karolina and Max, they had invariably spent a night here, but had seldom moved beyond the comfort of the Ritz. Nathalie took him along a succession of streets, none of them at all damaged and all of them sparsely populated, until they came to an apartment building. She and the concierge were apparently friends, and the old woman did not seem the least surprised that Nathalie should be accompanied by a man obviously quite a few years younger than herself. 'Mademoiselle Severine is at Madame Constance's,' she explained.

'So early?' Nathalie asked.

'It is where she said she was going, madame.' The concierge held out the key. 'I know she will not object to your using the apartment.'

'Hmm,' Nathalie said, but she took the key and escorted John to the stairs.

'Is something wrong?' he asked in a low voice as they went up.

'It's just that she may be late coming back, and we can do nothing until she does.'

'But she must be back by dark. What about the curfew?'

Nathalie pouted. 'There are those who have to worry about the curfew, and those who do not.'

On the third floor she unlocked the door to a very comfortable, if small, apartment. The living-cum-dining area was tastefully furnished, and when Nathalie led him down a short corridor to the single bedroom, he found himself looking at an extremely large and comfortable bed. Beyond, there was a deliciously clean bathroom. 'If you wish to bathe and shave, do so,' she invited.

'Severine will not mind?'

'She will not mind at all. I will prepare some lunch.'

She apparently had the complete run of the apartment, and when half an hour later, John emerged feeling a new man, at least externally, he found a splendid meal of bread, cold meats and cheese, as well as a bottle of good wine, waiting to take care of his interior as well.

'Severine seems to be a successful woman,' he remarked.

'In war,' Nathalie said again, 'a woman needs to be very strong, very –' another moue – 'able to consider moral values in an unprejudiced light. It also helps,' she added thoughtfully, 'if one is attractive to men. Severine is all of those things.' She stared at him. 'Does this disturb you?'

'Not in the least,' he lied. If the suggestion that she made her money by selling her favours, very probably to German officers, did not actually disturb him morally, it certainly made him somewhat apprehensive, and also a little bewildered. Again he chose his words with care. 'Your mother knows of this situation?'

'Mama knows.'

'Forgive me, but I could not help gaining the impression that you, well, had fallen on hard times since the conquest of France.'

'This is true.'

'But this . . .' he looked around the apartment.

'It is complicated,' Nathalie conceded. 'Severine has become a prostitute. This hurts me but I understand she must do the best she can. And it is a cloak for her activities in the Resistance. I honour her for this, for her courage and her strength, for the risks she runs almost daily. Mama also honours her for this. But she will not accept a penny of Severine's money, both because it is earned by the sale of her body, and because it is essentially German money.'

'What do you think will happen after the War?' John asked. 'I mean between your mother and your daughter?'

'Let us get to the end of the War first, and worry about our relationships then.'

The afternoon passed slowly. They were both very tired after their long walk of the previous day and the trauma of the entire journey. John was well aware that Nathalie, a lonely woman who was yet perhaps closely connected, at least at second hand, with the seamy side of life through the activities of her daughter, still had the possibilities of sex in mind. But quite apart from having not the least desire to cheat on Jolinda, he was still simply too exhausted. Thus he refused her invitation again to share the bed and after she retired for a siesta, dozed on the settee in the lounge.

When she arose, she made tea and then they sat together, very like an old married couple – or more accurately, a mother and son. 'Will your family be very distressed when your death is reported?' she asked.

'I suppose they will be.'

'But when you reappear they will be overjoyed,' she suggested.

'If they don't suffer a collective heart attack.'

'Your parents are in good health?'

'My mother is dead.'

'Oh, I am so sorry. But you are a young man. She can't have been very old.'

'She would have been just past fifty,' John explained, 'but she died twenty years ago.'

'Oh, my Lord!' she gazed at him, waiting for further explanation, but John had no intention of going into his somewhat murky family history.

'I now have a stepmother. And my father is in good health, yes.'

'But you have a wife to get home to . . .'

'And a son.' He frowned. 'Supposing all goes reasonably well, how long do you think it will be before I get home?'

Nathalie gave one of her moues and shrugged. 'It is impossible to say. You will have to travel the length of France and then cross the Pyrenees.'

'Wouldn't it be quicker, and safer, for me to go to Vichy and thence to Marseilles?'

'You will go to Vichy, but not to Marseilles. Mademoiselle de Gruchy does not trust the Vichy set-up.'

'Mademoiselle de Gruchy?'

'Have you not heard of her?'

'I'm afraid not.'

'But you have drunk de Gruchy wine?'

John frowned. The name was familiar when connected with wine; he remembered that Karolina had served it at her dinner parties, but then he had been too young to indulge in it himself. 'I think I've heard the name. And this woman is connected to the wine people?'

'Mademoiselle de Gruchy is the daughter of the house – well, one of them.'

'Then what has she got to do with me getting out of France?'

'Mademoiselle de Gruchy,' Nathalie said reverently, 'is a leader of the Resistance. To the Germans she is the most wanted woman in France: she once cut the throat of a German officer who had raped her.'

'And she will get me out of France?' John wasn't sure whether surrendering his future to a throat-cutting Frenchwoman was really a good idea.

'Her people will.'

'And your daughter, Severine, is one of her people?'

'Of course.'

'But you still have no idea how long it will take?'

'It is a lengthy business. You will have to have proper documentation, proper clothes, arrangements will have to be made for you to be escorted – your French is not good enough to avoid suspicion – from safe house to safe house, and for you to be met at the Spanish border. As I have said, these things take time. It is not just a matter of picking up a telephone. If all goes absolutely as it should they will be able to get you to Spain in about four weeks. Things should be easier then, but it will probably be another month before you get home.'

John brooded. He had not dared allow himself to think about Jolinda's reactions. He knew she loved him, but he also knew how pragmatic she was, as well as how attractive. If he had been reported dead, as had most probably happened in view of the fact that he had disappeared, while he had no doubt she would mourn him deeply and sincerely, would she be able to resist thinking in terms of another man, and of a possible replacement father for little Mark, for a period of what seemed likely to be more than two months?

'It is not so long,' Nathalie pointed out. 'You must not let the prospect depress you.'

'I suppose not,' John said.

Nathalie poured him a Pernod and took one for herself. She wanted to talk, but thankfully did not probe into his affairs any further. Instead, she reminisced about the life she and her Henri had lived before the War. Then she cooked dinner, and after they had eaten regarded him quizzically. 'Do you wish to sleep on the settee?'

'I think I should,' John said.

She sighed but shrugged. 'I will fetch a blanket.'

He was still very tired, and just beginning to relax in the apparent safety of this apartment and the suggestion that he was going to be looked after. He fell into a deep sleep and awoke with a start as the front door opened.

He sat up and the light was switched on. He blinked at the two women standing there. One was young, hardly older than himself, handsome rather than pretty, and very definitely Nathalie's daughter. The other was clearly several years older, perhaps in her early thirties, and was quite the loveliest woman he had ever seen, her perfectly chiselled features rather disappointingly framed in her mop of red hair. But she was at that moment pulling off the wig, to reveal that the hair was actually shoulder-length and yellow, thus redoubling her beauty.

But the features were cold, and he realized that she was pointing a Luger automatic pistol at his chest.

Six

The House

'The call is for you, personally, Herr Major,' said Captain Schmitt.

Max raised his eyebrows, but took the phone. 'Bayley.'

'Max!' Hildegarde's voice was breathless.

'Hilde? Where are you calling from?' Over the past month the various components of the German Army had become widely dispersed as it had driven ever deeper into Russia, gaining victory after victory.

'Corps HQ.'

'Oh, I had thought you might be somewhere near.'

'In thoughts, my darling Max. I am telephoning because I have news of your brother.'

Max frowned. 'What's he been doing now?'

'I am sorry to say that he appears to be dead.'

Max stared at the telephone.

'Are you there, Max?'

'Yes. Tell me.'

'He was on a sweep over north-western France and was shot down.'

'And killed? In his machine?'

'No. He baled out and was spotted on the ground, apparently unhurt. They sent people to pick him up and he shot one of them, an officer named Schultz.'

'And was then killed himself?'

'Not then, although apparently he was wounded. Schultz's gun had been fired, once, and there was blood on the ground and on the discarded flying suit. As you may imagine, there was a tremendous search mounted, but nothing has been seen or heard of him since. That was twelve days ago, so it is assumed that he died, either from loss of blood or because his wound became infected.'

'But they don't *know* . . .'

'They have not yet found his body, but as I say, there has been no evidence of him alive either, so they have drawn the logical conclusion. The body will surely turn up sooner or later. Max? Does this upset you?'

'He was an enemy of the Reich,' Max said.

'But still your brother.'

'Yes. And once we were close. But we could never be close again, no matter how the War turns out. I shot him down, once, and had every intention of killing him then. Now it is over. I am sorry for my father.'

'Did you know that your brother was married, and had a child?'

'No, I did not know that. It's very good of you to call, Hilde. I appreciate it. When will I see you again?'

'I will meet you in Moscow. The General says we should be there in about three weeks. The matter is so certain that half of our Panzers have been sent south to aid in the thrust for the Caucasus.'

'Is that a fact? Well, sweetheart, I will see you in Moscow. I am actually going there this morning, but I don't intend to land until after you get there. Love.'

He hung up and handed the telephone back to Schmitt, who was trying to look as if he had not been listening. John, dead? He pushed the matter from his mind.

He hoped that OKW had not been premature. On the other hand they had only recently completed another gigantic encirclement of Russian troops at Smolensk. Apparently another several hundred thousand had been taken prisoner. It hardly seemed that there could be many of even the Russian hordes left.

But John! He had not supposed *he* would survive the War, had rather welcomed the prospect of a hopefully glorious death going in with all guns blazing. Now that looked increasingly unlikely ever to happen: the Russian Air Force had still not put up the slightest worthwhile opposition to the Luftwaffe. So, with absolutely nothing to live for save the comradeship of his pilots and the comfort of his Gustav, and the occasional arms of Hildegarde or Erika, he seemed destined for an endlessly upward progress. While John, with an undoubtedly faithful English wife and now a son, not to mention Dad's millions and Hillside House, had had it all. And now, no more.

'There it is!' Gunther said. 'It always gives me a thrill.'

Max peered into the heat haze and could just make out the towers of the Kremlin. This was indeed the highlight of every recent sortie. It was incredibly boring, escorting Hederling's Stukas over miles of Russian wasteland, mostly as empty as the sky above. The Stukas only flew at 250 kilometres per hour, well under half the cruising speed of a Messerschmitt 109. Thus they also had to proceed relatively slowly, and while this greatly extended their range, their super-sensitive machines needed a lot of handling at such a substandard speed. They prayed for an intervention by enemy aircraft, and this was a regular enough diversion, but with the Gustav's superior speed and armament it was never a true contest.

So they droned onwards, looking down on occasional clouds of dust which denoted either a Panzer column or an infantry brigade rumbling onwards in its trucks. Sometimes the men and the machines were clearly visible, as they had halted to wait for their fuel supplies to catch them up; the delay was seldom much longer than a few hours.

But even the immense German Army was not sufficient to fill the even more immense Russian landscape. There *were* civilians down there. They flew over villages and towns and farms and even factory complexes. But these had been battered and sometimes were still burning. What had happened to the people who had lived in the houses and the workers in the factories he had no idea. And even these evidences of a pre-war civilization were widely separated by huge areas of prairie and forest.

Thus the daily glimpse of the Kremlin was a treat. And they had been given permission to do some attacking themselves, ahead of the more accurate dive-bombers. So . . . 'We go in now,' he told his pilots. 'Good hunting, Joachim.'

'And to you, Max,' Hederling replied.

The Messerschmitts raced away and a few minutes later were over the city. The anti-aircraft defences opened up but to very little avail, while the half-dozen Tupulov fighters that rose to oppose them were quickly disposed of.

'That is your eightieth,' Gunther shouted as an enemy machine plunged into the Moscow River.

'Marseille has over a hundred,' Max reminded him. 'Attack!'

They went in low, dropping their bombs, and then rose steeply to get out of the way of the Stukas behind them. Moscow burned, and now there were more red and black explosions as the dive-bombers swooped. Max checked his fuel gauge; he was just on half, so there should be no problem in getting back, as the Stukas only carried one heavy bomb each. The raid was completed in five minutes and then the Germans were streaming for home. The fighter pilots were, as always, elated at their easy triumph, swapping excited observations and exchanging claims as to who shot down what. But no one attempted to claim the kill made by their revered commander.

Max let them get on with it, concentrating on course and speed. He supposed that he should also be elated, because he was now behind only Marseille and Molders, and as the Russians still seemed prepared to sacrifice machines with total abandon – when they had any to sacrifice – there was every probability that he would reach the hundred figure. He wondered what his dad would make of that . . .

It happened so suddenly that he was taken completely by surprise. In front of him there was a sudden gush of flame, which almost immediately seemed to engulf the cockpit. This was exactly what had happened to Horst in May, over Belgrade. But so much else had happened since then that the incident, so disturbing at the time, had almost been forgotten, and there had been no other sudden engine failures since – at least, not in his Wing. But if he quite seriously hoped to die in combat, he had no desire to be burned alive in his own machine, and besides, this was not combat. He released his belts and threw back the canopy in almost the same moment, pushing himself upwards to be swept away from the aircraft, which was still travelling at nearly 500 kilometres an hour. Even so, his gloves and jacket were scorched and one of his goggles was cracked.

He allowed himself to fall for several hundred feet, to make sure he was clear of the following planes before releasing his parachute. Gunther dropped out of the formation to descend and circle him. He gave the thumbs-up sign and his friend waggled his wings, circling twice more to make sure he could identify the exact position where Max would land, then raced off again. He would be using his radio to alert the necessary rescuers. Max reflected that he was at least a couple of hundred kilometres behind the German spearheads. He would have preferred to come down within sight of his own people, but the ground looked even less populated than usual as he fell closer to it. How odd, he thought, that he and his brother should come down within a fortnight of each other. He wondered how Mark would react, if he would be at all concerned about his younger son. But Max had no intention of being killed.

He saw a column of smoke in the distance, which indicated perhaps a burning village, but the ground beneath him was fairly densely wooded. This did not suggest that he would make an easy landing. He looked left and right, straining his eyes, and thought he could make out one of those telltale plumes of dust, but it was very far away.

His attention was caught by his plane going in some distance in front of him. It smacked into the trees with a crackling sound, clearly audible even at half a kilometre. The trees at the point of impact immediately caught fire. All of this was distinctly discouraging, but desperately as he pulled on his cords in an attempt to direct his descent, the forest was simply too large, and there was no wind. He would have to make the best of it and hope he could get down without breaking a bone, and with his genitals intact.

In this respect the absence of wind was a help. Horizontally, he was moving very slowly. Nor was he dropping very fast. He remembered the previous occasion he had had to jump. That had been over the North Sea and he had thought that the prospect beneath him was the least attractive he had ever seen. At least this time he would be in no danger of drowning.

Now the trees seemed to be reaching for him. He brought his legs tightly together and drew up his knees just before impact. Initially, it all went very well. He plunged through the leafy foliage, breaking off various small branches, and had dropped some six metres before cannoning into a trunk with a force that left him breathless. His legs relaxed, and he fell a few more metres before being brought up by a sudden jerk as severe as when he had first opened his parachute. It was again the parachute, which had lodged in branches above his head.

It was a pine forest, and he realized that he had never taken sufficient interest in arboreal matters to understand how high pine trees could grow. The ground seemed a very long way beneath him.

He considered the situation. He had a sheath knife, but if he released the belt and went straight down he would almost certainly break something – or indeed several things. He began to swing himself, slowly at first, but gaining momentum. The nearest tree trunk, with the sort of branch which would support him, was some three metres away, and his first grab at it proved abortive. Still, he had now worked up a considerable swing and was sure he would make it the next time, when there was a tearing sound and he was dropping again.

Once more he was brought up short as the remnants of the torn parachute again lodged. Now he was hanging about four metres above the ground, but there were fewer branches to be grabbed at down here, so it was a choice between attempting to launch himself at a virtually bare tree trunk or releasing the straps and dropping.

He decided to drop and fumbled at the buckle. As he did so, he heard a sound, and looking down found himself gazing at five people.

There were two men and three women. The men wore what might once have been uniforms, but were now both torn and unkempt. The women were clad in trousers and blouses, with their hair bound up in large kerchiefs. They were all very young: he thought one of the women might have been thirty-odd; the other two he put as teenage girls. None of them was particularly attractive. The men were definitely younger than the older woman.

More important than their dress, or appearance, the men both carried rifles, and the women were also armed, two with knives and the senior with an axe. He gazed at them, and they gazed at him. He had no idea what to do. As they were Russians he was their enemy. Their appearance indicated that they were not members of any disciplined force, and he and his people were the invaders of their country. He also knew that Soviet Russia had never signed the Geneva Convention on the treatment of prisoners-of-war. But to draw his Luger would almost certainly provoke a contest that he could not win at such odds.

And now one of the men sighted his rifle. Max drew a deep breath; this was not the death he had anticipated. Like John, he doubted his body would ever be found. But the man was checked by the older woman before he could fire. They engaged in animated conversation for several minutes, the others joining in with much gesticulating. But the woman was clearly the dominant personality, and gradually the others fell sulkily silent.

'*Du!*' the woman said.

The fact she spoke at least some German was slightly encouraging. 'I am a German officer,' he replied, speaking slowly and as clearly as he could.

'Pistol,' she said. 'Throw down.'

He considered. But both men had now levelled their rifles, and even more certainly he did not think he could shoot them both before being hit himself. Carefully, he unbuttoned the flap of his holster.

'You shoot, we kill,' she warned.

'I am your prisoner,' Max acknowledged. Using only his thumb and forefinger he drew the pistol. There was a rustle of movement from beneath him, but the woman held out her arm. Max dropped the pistol at her feet and she picked it up with some satisfaction.

'Come down,' she ordered.

So it had to be a drop after all. Slowly he unbuckled his belt and a moment later also landed at her feet; the ground was softer than he had anticipated and he fell to his knees. Instantly he was surrounded, the woman removing his knife, the men ripping open his flying suit, while the girls tugged at his decorations, tearing the Iron Crosses from his tunic, all the while chattering happily. Max kept his gaze fixed upon the woman, who was definitely the commander. 'Listen,' he said, 'if you take me to the nearest German unit you will be rewarded.'

Her lip curled. 'Germans rape and burn. My father, my mother, my brother. They hang. We kill all Germans.'

'They will not hang you,' he promised. 'I will see to that. I am a senior officer. And . . .' he changed his mind about revealing that he was also a leading air ace; very possibly he and his Wing had shot up these people's village.

She regarded him for several moments, then said, 'You come.'

She tucked his pistol and his knife into her waistband and

jerked her head towards the south. Immediately her companions began arguing again, casting glances at him that varied from contempt to an almost lascivious leer. The woman replied as vehemently as ever, and after a lengthy exchange they seemed to accept her decision.

Again she jerked her head, and one of the girls pushed him in the back. He stumbled forward and they followed him, the woman walking beside him. 'They want to kill you,' she said. 'Now. The men want to hang you. And the girls – how you say . . .' she made a slicing movement with her hand.

'They would like to cut my throat?' Max suggested.

The woman smiled, not entirely reassuringly. 'Not your throat.'

Max swallowed. 'But you would like to keep me alive,' he said optimistically. 'And in one piece.' Even more optimistically.

'I think of it.'

The situation was clearly desperate, as he could not tell what she had in mind. He could not believe she felt the least compassion for his predicament; it was certainly possible that, in view of what she said had happened to her family, she had an even more gruesome fate in mind for him than hanging or castration.

In front of them the Messerschmitt blazed, surrounded by burning trees. The fire did not appear to be spreading, but the aircraft could not be approached. This was apparently disappointing to the Russians, who engaged in their usual argument. 'Your plane no good,' the woman said, unnecessarily.

'How so?'

'I wish I knew,' Max replied. 'The engine caught fire.'

'Kaput,' she agreed.

They resumed walking, keeping away from the fire, and the trees began to thin. Max watched the sky with some anxiety. Gunther would have reported what had happened by now and they would surely be looking for him. But if a low-flying aircraft were suddenly to appear, these people would probably shoot him out of hand. The woman remained his only possible hope. 'My name is Max,' he told her. 'What is yours?'

'I am Galina.' She glanced at him. 'You have woman?'

An opportunity, perhaps. 'I had a wife.'

Again she glanced at him. 'Had?'

'She was killed.'

'In the War?'

'Yes.' Which was not true in the sense that she meant it, but was not altogether a lie.

'War is terrible,' Galina observed. 'It is sad.'

Had he made progress? But a moment later they came out from the trees and faced a ruined village. There was not a house that was more than a pile of blackened timber, and there was not a living creature to be seen.

'Our village,' Galina explained.

'Were many killed?'

A mistake. Her eyes became lumps of ice. 'All were killed. We five alone are left. We not here when the soldiers came.'

Max swallowed. 'As you have said, war is sad. I am sorry.'

The five survivors had made their home in the burned-out shell of the schoolhouse; Max reckoned that the event could only have taken place a couple of weeks ago. The stench of death had gone – presumably they had buried the bodies – but the smell of burnt wood still hung in the air. The fields around the village had, however, been virtually untouched, and if there was no meat there was a very good meal of potatoes and turnips soon created by the two girls.

'There is no vodka,' Galina said regretfully, 'but there is this.' She held out a bottle of schnapps, and when he raised his eyebrows, explained, 'From a German. We killed three Germans last week.' She peered at him. 'You not have schnapps?'

'I'm afraid not.' He shook his head.

'Well, drink.'

Her tone suggested he might need the support of the alcohol. He drank from the neck and then it was passed round the group. The men had become quite cheerful, but the two girls continued to stare at him like a pair of vultures, anxious to get on with what they wanted to do.

The meal over, they seemed disposed to go to sleep. 'You come,' Galina ordered, getting up.

Max obeyed. One of the men apparently objected, but she silenced him with a few words and led Max away from them and beyond several of the burned-out houses, before choosing a spot and sitting down. 'They think you will attack me, and try to get away. If you do this I will shoot you. In the balls.'

Max sat opposite her, as indicated. He could not help but wonder if he *could* take her on and get away. But the evidence suggested that she was more accustomed to killing people in what could be termed face-to-face combat than him. It would certainly be necessary to lull her into a false confidence. 'You have never been married,' he observed.

Her nose wrinkled. 'I have never found a man I liked enough.'

'But now, your comrades . . .'

She snorted. 'They have the girls. They are all smelly beasts. You smell of perfume. Do you smell like that all over?'

'I think you are smelling my aftershave lotion. That is only on my chin.'

'I think I could like you. I would like to have sex with you.'

Certainly an opportunity. 'Well, I am your prisoner.'

She gazed at him for several seconds, then she said, 'You are thinking that when I am in passion I will let you get free. If we are to have sex I must tie you up.'

That did not sound so promising. And what might happen if, as was extremely likely in his circumstances, he was unable to erect, he did not care to think. However . . . 'And what would happen after? Would you return me to my people?'

'Perhaps.' She grinned. 'Perhaps I would give you to the girls.' She sighed. 'There is so much I would like to do. So much I wanted to do. I was to go to Moscow. I have an uncle in Moscow. Will I ever get to Moscow?'

Now, this *was* an opportunity. 'Help me,' he said, 'and I will personally take you to Moscow.'

'You?'

'I am going there. We are all going there, next month.'

'And you would take me?'

'I give you my word, as a German officer.'

She gazed at him for some seconds and he had a slow, creeping feeling of exhilaration: he was winning. But then they heard a rumble of sound, followed by a shout from the others. Galina leapt to her feet, the Luger in her hand. Max also stood, to watch the three armoured cars bouncing along the uneven track towards them.

There were several shots and someone gave a scream of pain. 'Tell them to stop shooting,' Max snapped. 'I will intercede for you.'

Galina glanced at him, then slowly lowered the pistol. She knew that resistance was hopeless: the cars had stopped and at least twenty men had got out, armed with automatic rifles, forming a circle around the charred remains of the village. The soldiers wore black uniforms, and on the cap of the commanding lieutenant there was a death's head badge.

Like all Luftwaffe officers, and the majority of the Wehrmacht, Max had never come into contact with the SS. He knew they had begun as Hitler's personal bodyguard, and he also knew that they had been expanded into a considerable elitist fighting force. What they were doing looking for him was a mystery, but a gratifying one. 'You had better give me the gun,' he told Galina.

She hesitated. 'You promised to take me to Moscow.'

'I will do that.'

She handed him the weapon. As she did so, several more shots rang out, to the accompaniment of more screams. Max stepped away from the houses. 'Stop shooting,' he commanded.

The firing ceased and the officer came towards him, followed by several of his men; the others continued to level their rifles at the houses. 'Major Bayley,' he said, 'thank God you are all right, sir. Did these people—'

'They fed me and have cared for me,' Max interrupted. 'What have you done with them?'

'We shot them. They are partisans, guerrillas. Only two are dead. We will hang the others.' He looked at Galina. 'And this one.'

'Did they fire on you?'

'A shot was fired. None of my people was hit.'

'Then they surrendered but you shot them anyway.'

'That is my duty, Herr Major.'

'Your duty? To shoot people who have surrendered? You are soldiers.'

'We are *Einsatzgruppen*,' the officer said proudly. 'We eliminate the vermin that lurk behind our lines.' His expression assumed a faintly contemptuous sneer. 'You are Luftwaffe, Herr Major. You do not come into contact with these scum. You do not have to watch. My men will take you to our headquarters.'

Max felt vaguely sick. These were German soldiers? On the other hand, the partisans would have killed him but for

122

Galina. 'Very good,' he said, 'I shall of course make a full report of this incident to your superior.'

'I am carrying out the orders of my superior, sir.'

Max nodded. 'Come along, Galina. I am most terribly sorry that this has happened.'

'You have brought this upon us,' Galina said.

'Inadvertently. And as I have said, I regret it. Now come.'

'With respect, Herr Major, this woman is also a partisan,' the lieutenant said.

'She is a partisan who saved my life and to whom I have given safe conduct.'

'No one is permitted to give safe conduct to a partisan, Herr Major.'

'I think you need to remember that I am your senior officer,' Max pointed out.

'Herr Major, what you need to remember is that I am SS, and not subject to general military discipline. The SS has its own discipline, its own code of conduct. The only rule that matters is that we carry out our orders to the letter and without question. I have been ordered to recover you, alive and unharmed, if that is possible, and to execute on the spot any partisans with whom I may come into contact. Now, sir, if you attempt to interfere with my duty, I shall have to assume that you are temporarily deranged by the misfortune of losing your aircraft and can no longer be considered capable of exercising rational judgement. I shall therefore have to place you under restraint until you can be seen by a psychiatrist.'

Max stared at him, aware of a slowly growing fury, the more intense because he knew it was going to be impotent. He had felt this way before, in Colonel Luttmann's office, when the Gestapo officer had calmly informed him that his wife had that day been executed for treason. Now . . . he looked at Galina.

She had been listening to the conversation, and had certainly gained the gist of what had been said. Now she stared at him, her lip curling. Then she turned and ran for the trees. Several shots rang out.

'Up!' the blonde woman said. 'Close the door, Severine.'

John was on his feet, relieved that his deduction of their identity had been accurate. 'Would you be Mademoiselle de Gruchy?' he ventured.

'How did you get in?' the blonde woman asked, not replying to his question.

'I came with Madame Dufresne.'

Severine had locked the door. 'Mama! She is here?'

'In the bedroom.'

'Wake her up,' the blonde woman said, and Severine hurried down the corridor to the bedroom. 'Madame Dufresne told you of me?'

'Yes, she did.'

'And you knew of me?'

'No, but from what she said, I am pleased to make your acquaintance.'

Liane de Gruchy went to the sideboard and poured herself a glass of cognac without pocketing the gun. 'For you?'

'Thank you.'

She poured another glass then moved away from the sideboard and gestured at it. He picked it up and she said, 'Your health. You are not French.'

It was not a question. 'I am English.'

'Ah. Pound sent you?'

'No one sent me, deliberately. I am an RAF officer.'

Liane put down her empty glass. 'The man who killed a German officer!'

'Something I believe we have in common,' John suggested.

'Nathalie *has* been tattling,' Liane remarked, and looked at the corridor. 'You brought him here? Are you mad?'

'I wished to help him,' Nathalie said. She had clearly dressed in a hurry. 'It was Mama's wish,' she added, obviously assuming this would carry more weight. 'Besides, he is a British pilot. Are we not assisting them to get out of the country?'

At last Liane pocketed the pistol and took off her raincoat. Her calves matched the rest of her. 'RAF officers who are necessarily incognito,' she pointed out. She sat down and crossed her knees. 'Not who are known by name to every Gestapo agent in Northern France and who are wanted for murder.'

John looked from face to face, aware that his fate was being decided. But he had to ask, 'How do they know my name?'

'Because your people in England named you. They're upset at losing you. The Nazis will no doubt soon have a photograph of you.'

Nathalie came into the room, followed by Severine. 'We came here from Amiens with no trouble.'

'Which does not mean that you, or he, will be able to leave Paris without trouble.'

'Look,' John said, 'if I'm going to be a problem, or a danger, I'll just leave and take my chances.'

'Are all Englishmen determinedly gallant idiots?' Liane inquired, suddenly speaking English with perfect fluency and without any accent. 'Yes, you are a problem, and a risk, but by coming here you have become *our* problem and *our* risk. Without guidance and adequate papers you would be picked up within ten minutes of leaving this apartment. And when the Gestapo got around to interrogating you, you would tell them all about us within another ten minutes. You must understand that they no longer have any reason to treat you as a prisoner-of-war. You have become a common criminal.'

Again John looked from face to face. The three women were all solemn enough, but he did not think there was any longer any hostility. He attempted to lighten the atmosphere. 'Perhaps it would be best for all if you were just to shoot me.'

'Someone might hear the shot,' Liane said, apparently seriously. 'And it would be difficult to get rid of your body.' She looked at her watch. 'There is nothing to be done tonight. Any man found on the street at this hour would be arrested. You will have to remain here until tomorrow morning, when we will get you to the house. How long you will have to remain there I do not at this moment know.'

'You mean you'll help me?'

Liane shrugged, a delightful gesture. 'Life is full of difficulties.' She switched back to French. 'I am very tired. What are your sleeping arrangements, Severine?'

'Well, I told you, Liane, there is only the one bed.' Her face assumed a piquant expression.

'I don't think I am any longer in the mood for sharing a bed,' Liane said. 'You sleep with your mother. I will sleep on the settee, which seems ready for me.'

'Ah . . .' John ventured.

'You – Mr . . . Bayley, is it? You will sleep on the floor. I am sure Severine can provide another blanket.'

It was difficult to be unaware of the woman. She turned off the light before taking off her clothes, but he knew that

125

she was undressing and he could not stop himself wondering just how much she was taking off. In addition, he had slept very heavily for three hours before the women had come in, and now, on the hard floor, found it difficult to get back off, and so lay there inhaling her scent and listening to the faintest of snores. He found her utter, cold-blooded calmness just as compelling as her looks, and could not prevent himself from imagining *her* in the hands of the Gestapo. If she had no doubt that they could reduce him to a wreck in ten minutes, what would they do to all of that beauty? And surely she knew that by the law of averages it had to happen one day.

There was also the uncertainty, not all of it unpleasant, as to what the immediate future might hold. He seemed to have plunged into a world composed entirely of attractive women, without having the slightest idea whether they considered him as anything more than a colossal nuisance. Liane, by some distance the most attractive of them all, certainly seemed to.

Eventually he slept, to awake with a start, in broad daylight. All three women were up, fully dressed, and there were mouth-watering smells of hot croissants and coffee filling the apartment. Slowly he rose to his feet, every muscle stiffly painful.

'I was about to wake you,' Liane said, in English. 'Soon it will be time for you to leave.'

'In broad daylight?'

'This is the safest time. In those crumpled clothes you look like a labourer, a jobbing gardener, perhaps, seeking work.'

'Right. If I may have a spot of breakfast, and if you'll give me the time to shave—'

'Jobbing gardeners do not shave,' Liane said severely, as if she were addressing a small boy. 'But you may have some breakfast. You will take him, Severine.' She smiled at John. 'It is dangerous for *me* to be out in daylight. I am even more wanted than you, Mr Bayley, and the Gestapo already have a photograph of me.'

After breakfast Severine put on her coat and hat. 'Just walk beside me and look humble,' she said. 'And leave any talking to me.'

John shook hands with Nathalie and to his embarrassment was pulled into her arms for a hug and a kiss, on the mouth. He looked at Liane, hopefully, but she made no move towards him. 'You have my gratitude, Mademoiselle de Gruchy, all of you. You are very brave women.'

'We are fighting a war, monsieur. I shall see you again, if all goes well.'

'Oh, right.' Now that was promising. Jolinda would have to forgive the odd flirtation, if it would help to get him home. Titillatingly, he had a strong feeling that getting close to Liane de Gruchy would involve a lot more than a flirtation.

'Am I allowed to ask where we're going?' he asked Severine in a low voice, as they made their way through quite busy streets. There were soldiers about, but not obtrusively, and as Liane had prophesied, no one appeared the least interested in him, although various French people greeted Severine. But now they were on a deserted street.

'Why, to Madame Constance. Did not Mama explain it to you?'

'Ah . . .' he felt he needed to choose his words with care. 'She said something about a lady named Constance. Would that be her surname?'

'That is the name by which she and her house are known. You know what I mean?'

'Ah, yes. I think so . . . And you are taking me to this house?'

'You will be safe there until your removal can be arranged. There is an RAF officer there now.'

'Good Lord!'

'The route has been set up by Mademoiselle de Gruchy.'

'But she does not live there.'

'No, no. She lives, well, everywhere. Sometimes in Vichy, sometimes in the south. She only visits Paris from time to time to make sure there are no problems.'

'And when she is not here, this Madame Constance is in charge? There are no men involved?'

'Oh, yes. We have the men who will make you a new pass, and provide the rail tickets. They also act as couriers. But it is best to leave the hard work to us.' She giggled. 'We can do things, and go places where men would be forbidden or immediately suspected.'

'And you are never suspected?'

'We provide a service without which the Germans would find life intolerable. Madame Constance runs the best house in Paris.'

John stopped walking. 'You mean, Germans go to this house?'

'But of course. We accept only Germans. Only German officers at Madame Constance's. But the doors are not open for custom until two o'clock, so you will not encounter any of them in the morning. Now see, we have arrived.'

John felt he had entered an utterly surrealist world, and not only because of his situation. He had, as a young pilot, visited the occasional brothel, and in France during the six months his squadron had been posted there before May 1940. He had even visited one when on leave in Paris, but his taxi driver had not suggested Madame Constance's, presumably because the fellow had supposed she would be outside a young pilot's price range. His memory was of some squalor and of women over thirty pretending to be young girls. Now, as Severine, who *was* a young girl, pushed open a squealing gate set in a high wall situated on another deserted street, he found himself in a very large area which had clearly once been lawns and formal gardens, but which was now overgrown. The drive on which they stood was, however, well surfaced, and gave access to a large parking area at the foot of the steps. The steps themselves led up to the double front doors of a splendid mansion. The walls needed paint and the general appearance of the house was distinctly shabby, but when Severine rang the bell and the door was opened for them, John found himself in a high-ceilinged hall of some elegance, with a flight of curving stairs mounting one wall to a gallery, and open double doors on his right revealing another large room, tastefully furnished and with a bar counter running its length. On the shelves behind the counter was a considerable array of bottles.

The woman who had opened the door, dressed in a shapeless gown, was tall, heavily built in a raw-boned fashion, and had a face to match. However, she regarded Severine with more surprise than disfavour. 'What are you doing here at this hour? You should be sleeping. We are all sleeping.' She looked at John, eyebrows arched.

'Squadron Leader John Bayley,' Severine explained.

'Shit!' the woman commented. 'Another one?'

'He is special.'

The woman looked at John again. 'Shit!' she repeated. 'The one they are looking for.'

'Liane knows of it and has accepted him,' Severine assured her. 'She says to put him with the other one and send for Forbas. Arrangements will be made.' She turned to John. 'You have nothing to worry about now.'

John hoped she was right. 'Aren't you staying?'

'No, no. I will be back this afternoon.' She gave one of her giggles. 'But I will be working.' She squeezed his hand. 'I will try to see you again.'

The front door closed behind her and John looked at the woman. 'I am Marguerite,' she announced. 'Come.' She led him up the stairs to another hall, which seemed to extend the entire width of the building and off which there opened a dozen doors, six on each side. Then there was another staircase and another floor of bedrooms, then yet another staircase and he was at the entrance to a garret. Marguerite opened the door. 'Company,' she announced.

The little room was sparsely furnished with two cots, a table and two chairs. Seated at the table was a man in shabby clothes who wore a large moustache. He had been reading a book, which John saw was *The Complete Works of William Shakespeare*. The remnants of a breakfast were pushed to one side and there were two other books on the table: the Holy Bible and a French–English Dictionary and Phrase Book. The man stood up. 'Welcome. Jimmy Leadbeater, Flying Officer, 416 Squadron.'

'Wellingtons,' John commented. 'When did you come in?' He wondered if this chap could have gone down on the Amiens raid.

'Three days ago. And you?'

'Squadron Leader John Bayley, 833.'

Leadbeater sprang to attention. 'Sir! *The* John Bayley?'

'As far as I know, I'm the only one.'

They had been speaking English, and Marguerite, having listened uncomprehendingly, snorted and closed the door.

'She's always like that,' Leadbeater explained, 'but they say they can get us out, sir.'

'And I believe them.' John sat down. 'And drop the "sir" business. No ranks until we're home, Jimmy. What about the rest of your crew?'

Jimmy also sat down, shoulders drooping. 'They bought it.'

'Bad luck.'

'We heard you'd gone in, oh, must be nearly two weeks ago. No one over there has any idea what happened to you, save that you're still alive. You're the word around here. Did you really shoot a Jerry?'

'It was him or me.'

'If anyone had told me I'd be sharing a room with John Bayley . . . is it true you have thirty-six kills?'

'Thirty-eight, I believe. Doesn't seem very important right now. What's our relationship with our hostesses?'

Jimmy grinned. 'They are there and we are here. When they are awake they are entertaining German officers. When they are not entertaining German officers they are asleep. We couldn't afford their prices anyway. The only two we ever communicate with are Marguerite and Madame Constance.' He cocked his head as the landing outside the door creaked. 'I think you are about to meet the boss lady now.'

The door opened, and both men stood up. Madame Constance was certainly a striking figure, if entirely lacking Liane de Gruchy's petite poise and beauty. She was about six feet tall, with a voluptuous figure, coarsely handsome features, and, in this case resembling Liane's disguise, a mass of curling red hair, only hers was dyed rather than a wig. She made John think of the heroine of a rather substandard Hollywood historical epic. 'Squadron Leader Bayley,' she announced, to his relief speaking English. 'I will not say welcome. You are a danger to my house, and the route. But I am told that I must accommodate you until you can leave.'

'Thank you, madame. I shall endeavour not to be a nuisance.'

'You will not leave this room, except to bathe and use the toilet,' she said. 'There is a bathroom at the foot of the stairs. You will make no noise, and you will not smoke.'

'I do not smoke.'

She did not seem mollified. 'You will not approach any of my girls.'

'Do they come up here?' John asked innocently. 'I mean, who feeds us?'

'Marguerite does that. This floor is forbidden to the girls, but then, they are girls. Now you must be patient and rest as much as possible.'

'What about exercise?'

'I'm afraid that will not be possible, unless you can do it

130

quietly in this room. You cannot go out during the day, and at night the house is full of Germans. Broaden your mind. Improve your French.' She gestured toward the books and left.

'She's not quite the dragon she appears,' Jimmy said. 'Do you want the Shakespeare or the Gospel or the phrase book?'

'I'll take the Gospel.'

'Religious man?'

'I just happen to have read a lot of Shakespeare.'

The waiting was both tedious and frustrating, relieved only when a man arrived with photographic equipment and carefully erected his tripod. His official reason for being at the house was to photograph the girls as pin-ups for the Germans. His visit suggested progress, as did the appearance of a barber, who demolished Jimmy's moustache. The boy was almost in tears; it was only after the hair had been removed that John realized that he was indeed only a boy.

'I'm nineteen,' Jimmy said indignantly.

'Then you are one of the wonders of the world,' John told him. 'At nineteen I couldn't even raise a whisker.'

But Jimmy was one of those men who even had hair growing on his shoulders.

The frustration was increased by a complete lack of information as to what was happening in the outside world. Marguerite was totally uncommunicative. Constance visited them every couple of days, but had very little to say. When pressed, she shrugged. 'The Germans are winning the War. They are at the gates of Moscow.'

'And the British?' John asked.

This time there was no shrug. 'They bomb France.'

'I do not think that you like us,' Jimmy remarked, unwisely John thought.

'You ran away,' Constance pointed out.

'Is that really what they think of us?' Jimmy asked, after she'd left.

'The majority, yes, unfortunately,' John said.

'Yet she's risking her neck to help us.'

'As she said, she's acting under orders.'

'Who gives these orders?'

'You'd never believe it.'

'You almost sound as if you know who he is.'

'*She*.' John grinned.

Most frustrating of all was the day, a week later, when Constance appeared accompanied by a man, and carrying a valise. This she placed on the table and opened it. 'Here are your clothes, Mr Leadbeater, and your papers. You will go with Auguste. He is your cousin, as your papers indicate. You are going to visit your parents in Perpignan, but as you have a severe speech impediment, it is necessary for Auguste to accompany you, and he will of course do all the talking. You leave this afternoon.'

'That's tremendous,' Jimmy said, and looked at Auguste, who grinned and shook his hand.

'What about me?' John asked.

'It is being prepared, but it is taking time. The Boche, having your name, have obtained a photograph of you. Liane feels she must take you out herself.'

'Won't they by now have assumed that I am dead in a ditch somewhere?'

'We have no evidence of that. Anyway, it is what Liane wants. And she is the boss, eh? We will be back at two o'clock.' The door closed, but almost immediately Marguerite arrived with a better than usual lunch and a bottle of excellent wine.

'Would you know who this Liane person is?' Jimmy asked as they ate. 'Sounds like a female.'

'As I said,' John reminded him.

'And you know of her?'

'I know *her*.'

'A *femme formidable*,' Jimmy suggested.

'Very.'

'And you're her baby. Sounds like a bit of all right. Supposing I get home before you, is there anyone you'd like me to contact?'

'My father and my wife. Tell them I'm still alive and will be home eventually.'

'Do I mention this Liane?'

'No.'

Jimmy winked. 'No names, no pack drill, eh?'

'No names, no possibility of betrayal to the Germans,' John said. 'We'll have a drink together when I get home.'

Seven

The Route

'Oh, Max, Max . . .' Field Marshal Erhard Milch was a heavy man whose face seemed to be all jaw. It was an habitually stern face, but this morning it looked genuinely distressed. 'What are we going to do with you?'

Max sat, virtually to attention, before the desk, his cap on his lap. 'It was not my intention to let either you or the service down, Herr Field Marshal. I acted instinctively. Those thugs—'

Milch held up a finger to silence Max's outburst. 'Those members of an elite fighting force who receive their orders from General Himmler himself, as directed by the Fuehrer, and who were carrying out those orders. The Russians were taken with arms in their hands and they were about to execute a German officer.'

'We do not know that, sir. They took me to their camp and fed me. Their leader, the woman Galina, was quite willing to negotiate. I had offered her, all of them, their lives if they would guide me to the nearest German position, and she was on the point of agreeing when the SS arrived.'

'And she tried to run away.'

'Can you blame her? She had apparently encountered these *Einsatzgruppen* before.'

'Can you blame them for shooting her?'

'They wounded her, Herr Field Marshal, and brought her down. She was their prisoner. Then to drag her, still bleeding, to a tree and hang her without the slightest compunction for her condition, and needless to say without any semblance of a trial . . . that is barbarism.'

'War is organized barbarism, Max. And it is you we have to worry about, not some Russian guerrilla. I should point out that you had no authority to offer these people a safe conduct, to offer them anything. And now . . . Consider yourself, your career, from the point of view of an outsider – an admirer, even: Reichmarschal Goering, shall we say. You are an Englishman who chose to adopt the nationality of his mother's country, and fight for it. Admirable. You have made yourself into one of the two or three finest fighter pilots in the land, and that means the world. Even more admirable. You have been shortlisted for promotion to colonel and command of a group. All this at the age of twenty-one. You are spoken of as someone who may well become the youngest general in German history. Magnificent. But now let us look at the debit side of your ledger. Your wife was convicted of treason and executed. No one can possibly hold you responsible for that – except perhaps that you should not in the first place have married Heidi Stumpff, and certainly not confided your orders to her, even in the intimacy of the marriage bed. But the fact is that when you were told what had happened, you assaulted a senior Gestapo officer and put him in hospital. It does not matter that everyone knows Luttmann to be as unpleasant a character as it is possible to imagine; the fact is that you challenged the institution of the Gestapo. You survived that because of your record and the circumstances.

'But now you have assaulted an officer in the SS, while he was carrying out his orders and before his men. He also is in hospital. But that is less relevant than the fact that you have again challenged an institution of the State, and the SS is considerably more important than the Gestapo. It has become virtually the heart and soul of Nazi Germany, and is certainly the keeper of its conscience. Now, again because of your fighting record, you will not be punished, but the incident must go on your record and be accounted for. Officially, you have had a nervous breakdown due to having spent too many hours in combat in Russia, compounded by the sudden and inexplicable explosion of your machine in flight. Everyone –' he gave a brief smile – 'except possibly Captain Karlowitz, is very sympathetic. But it follows that an officer who has suffered a nervous collapse from too much combat has to be withdrawn from combat until he is adjudged to have fully recovered. It also follows that an officer who has suffered a nervous breakdown cannot be considered for command in an active theatre. You will go to Norway and take command of the Trondheim base.'

'Trondheim?' Max muttered. 'Would I be right, Herr Field Marshal, in assuming that is the equivalent of a Russian officer being banished to Siberia?'

'As regards weather, I'm afraid that is probably accurate. However, there is some activity. The British have started sending convoys to Russia by way of the North Cape and Murmansk. We have surface elements up there whose business it is to disrupt this traffic. The Luftwaffe is supporting them in this, and our bombers need protection. However, you are not to fly in combat yourself until specifically cleared to do so. I wish you to understand this, Max. For the foreseeable future it is very necessary for you to pay strict attention to orders and to carry out those orders without question. Your entire future depends on this. You can never afford to forget that you are now in the SS black book.'

'Yes, sir. May I ask who has taken command of Fighter Wing Five?'

'Captain Langholm, who has been promoted to Major. I hope you approve.'

'There is no finer pilot, or commander, in the Luftwaffe, sir.'

'Good. Well, then, I will wish you good fortune in your new posting.'

Max stood up. 'Thank you, sir. And for everything.' Max hesitated. 'Has there been any news of my brother?'

'I'm afraid that your brother would appear to be dead. It's over a month since he crashed, and after that first day nothing has been seen or heard of him, despite an extensive search. There can be no doubt that if by some miracle he had gained Vichy or Spain we would have heard. I'm sorry.'

'Thank you, sir. *Heil* Hitler.'

Norway, he thought as he went down the stairs. With winter coming on. And if he was grounded as regards combat, he was never going to make the magic hundred kills: the Russians were so clearly beaten the War would certainly be over by Christmas, and he didn't see the British fighting on alone for what could be a very long time.

Did he regret what had happened? He could not. He did not *know* that Galina would have taken him to safety, but he did know that he had promised her her life. As for the SS, if that organisation truly was now the 'heart and soul' of Nazi

Germany, what hope did any of them have of resuming a normal life?

And Johnnie appeared to be dead, after always having managed to survive being shot down in the past. Again he wondered how his father was taking the news. And John's wife. He wondered what she was like, this sister-in-law he had never met.

So, what was he going to do? Why, crawl into his Trondheim hole and keep out of trouble. But he had a few days' leave before heading for the Arctic. He went up to his room at the Albert Hotel and picked up the telephone.

The days after Jimmy Leadbeater's departure were utterly lonely. John was visited only by Marguerite, twice a day, and she was as uncommunicative as ever. He studied the French phrasebook hour after hour, and felt he was gaining quite a vocabulary, although he did not suppose that he would ever sound like a true Frenchman. For relaxation he read the Bible from cover to cover, and then had to revert to Shakespeare, a considerable contrast.

He also found himself increasingly aware of his surroundings. The house was clearly very old, and sound seeped upwards through the ancient timbers. There was very little during the day, but a great deal throughout the night. The sound had always been there, of course, but while sharing the room with Jimmy Leadbeater it had never seemed so immediate. Now, lying awake on his narrow cot, he could hear the shouts of drunken laughter, the occasional cry of anger, no doubt as two officers fell out, and now and then a sharp female shriek from the first floor, which created all manner of supposition as to what might be being done to the unfortunate girl.

He had to wonder if all the girls knew that he was upstairs and how it might be affecting their performance, as they also had to know that if he were suddenly to appear they would all be bound for a Gestapo torture cell. And at last there came the night when, having finally fallen into a deep sleep, he was awakened by the sound of his door opening.

The room was utterly dark. He had no idea what time it was, as Aimee Lafarge had insisted he leave his watch with his uniform: it was English-made and would be a dead giveaway. 'Who is it?' he whispered. No German officer would be moving with such stealth.

'It is Severine,' she replied, and now he could smell perfume as he heard the door close.

'What are you doing here?'

Material rustled as she came closer, but the darkness was so intense he couldn't make out more than a shadow. 'I have come to see how you are, and to say goodbye.'

'Goodbye?'

'You are to leave tomorrow.'

'Ah.' His heart leapt. 'Well, you will be pleased to see me go.'

Hands slid over the blanket, and he estimated that she was kneeling beside the cot. He stretched out his own hand to touch her shoulder, and encountered naked flesh; the rustle he had heard had been her removing her dress, and he did not suppose she wore underclothes when working. But then he felt other hands on his ankles, and had a most peculiar sensation. 'Just how many of you are there?'

'Only Louise and me. Louise wished to meet you.'

'Oh. Well, hello, Louise.'

'I like the feel of your feet, monsieur.'

The blanket had now been removed and Severine's hands were sliding over his hips to find what she wanted. His head was spinning. His situation, the fact that he had been entirely surrounded by women for the past month and that since his marriage to Jolinda and before his crash he had become used to sex at least twice a week, had left him feeling decidedly randy. Nor did he think either of these young women was in the mood to be put off. Joly flashed through his mind, but he dismissed the thought.

His protest was feeble. 'I cannot pay you.'

She giggled. 'This is on the house.'

'Will not Madame Constance be angry?'

Severine gave another tinkle of laughter. 'She says it is forbidden to fuck with you. But I will suck him, eh? That will be good for you. Louise.'

A pair of naked breasts was pressed against his arm.

'You play with Louise,' Severine ordered, now in complete command. 'Her tits are bigger than mine and she has a nice bottom, too.'

Well, he thought, if you can't beat them . . .

137

Never had he felt so relaxed as when he awoke to daylight. He almost felt as though it had been a dream, but his body told him it had been real enough; there were even a couple of small bite marks on his thighs where Severine, apparently in a state of high excitement after he had climaxed, had indulged in a few nibbles. While Louise . . . He wondered what she looked like; there had certainly been enough of her. Well, he thought, Jolinda never need know . . .

He felt quite reluctant to get up, until he remembered that they had claimed that they were actually bidding him goodbye. Then he sat up, just as there were footsteps on the landing outside. A moment later the door opened, and he looked at . . . he frowned. His instincts told him that it was Liane de Gruchy, but it looked more like her mother. The woman wore a straggly grey wig and a shabby dress with battered boots. Her face was grey and there were lines where he remembered only smooth white flesh. Her shoulders were bowed and she walked with a stick.

But she carried what looked like a heavy satchel as well as an equally heavy valise, without obvious discomfort. These bags she placed on the table. 'You are a late sleeper, Mr Bayley,' she remarked in her usual perfect English.

'Well, there's not much else to do.'

'Except leave this place.' She seized the blanket and jerked it off him, regarding him for some seconds, while he sat absolutely still. 'Who was it?' she asked.

'Eh?'

'You have had sex. Quite recently.'

'I beg your pardon?'

'Mr Bayley, from your expression and your eyes, I would say that you have only just woken up. You are also, I have been told and can see for myself, a very fit young man. Fit men, young or old, but certainly young, who have not had sex in a while, always awake with an erection.' Her tone left him in no doubt that she knew what she was talking about. 'This can be due to a full bladder, but you are as flaccid as an airless balloon. Or do you attend to yourself?'

'For God's sake, are you my mother?'

'As of this moment, yes.'

'What?'

'We are leaving Paris this morning, travelling as mother

and son. Now get up and get dressed. Your new clothes are in this valise.'

John got out of bed. 'Regarding your powers of deduction, I would not like to get anyone into trouble. They only came to say farewell.'

'They? You did do well. I imagine one was Severine. Do not worry, Mr Bayley, I will not tell Constance. I think every man should have sex on a regular basis, otherwise the brain gets clogged with desire, and for the foreseeable future you need your brain to be totally alert and concentrated on the business in hand. Now go and use the bathroom. Today you must shave, and time is passing.'

Once again her way of taking everything in her stride was breathtaking, as was the confirmation that they were going to travel together, even if she was disguised as an old woman. But there were so many surprising things about her, things he wanted to find out, like how she spoke such perfect English, how she had come to murder a German officer, what had happened to her family. She was certainly an aristocrat. And where was she taking him?

By the time he returned to the bedroom Marguerite had served breakfast and Liane was drinking coffee. 'Now,' she said, 'your papers are here. I'm sorry that you've had to spend so long in this room, but it was necessary to wait until the search for you had entirely died down.

'Now, you are Jean Le Maitre, and you are taking your poor old mother back to her home in Toulouse. You will speak as little as possible. I am a dominating old bitch and will interrupt everything you say, and more often than not will say it first. You are terrified of me, and cower every time I lift my stick. I may even beat your from time to time. You understand?'

'It sounds entrancing.'

She smiled. 'I will make it up to you.'

'I certainly look forward to that.'

'You appear to be insatiable. Are you not a happily married man? And a father? That is what Nathalie told me. Think of your wife, to whom you are now going. I will make it up to you by delivering you to my friends in Spain. Is that not what you most fervently wish?'

*　　*　　*

Once again, a nerve-racking walk across Paris, and another even more nerve-racking train journey, which lasted most of the day. But Liane de Gruchy was both totally confident and in total command of every situation. She was also a magnificent actress. She went into action at the Gare d'Austerlitz, where the German soldier standing beside the ticket collector inquired, 'You are returning to Limoges, monsieur? How long have you been in Paris?'

'I . . . ah . . .'

'He has been in Paris long enough to collect his poor old mother, you silly man,' Liane said aggressively. 'Collect me, mind you. Can you believe it? My husband says I must not travel alone, so he sends this halfwit to look after me. Me! Do you know, he has only been in the city three days, and he has had all his money stolen by some painted tart!'

'But that is very serious, madame,' the soldier said sympathetically. 'Have you reported this to the police, monsieur?'

'Him?' Liane demanded, before John could even get his mouth open. 'Of course he reported it to the police, but when they asked for a description of the girl he could not give it. Said it was too dark for him to see her face. Can you believe that of all the men in the world I had to be given him as a son?'

The soldier returned John's papers. 'It is a long way to Limoges,' he remarked, even more sympathetically

'We are going to Toulouse,' Liane pointed out scathingly. 'Can't you read the tickets?'

'Good luck,' the soldier said, more sympathetically yet.

They boarded the train and sat together at one end of the carriage. 'You are magnificent,' John whispered.

'Speak French,' she reminded him. 'At least until the carriage empties.'

This in fact slowly happened, as the train stopped it seemed every kilometre. At each station some people got on, but more got off, until in the middle of the afternoon they were alone, having lunched on bread and cheese and wine. 'Do you make this journey often?' John asked.

'I have made it often, before the War.' She smiled, reminiscently. 'But then I always travelled first-class.'

'Of course. Your parents grew wine in the Gironde.'

'That is one way of putting it. My family have grown grapes

outside Pauillac for ten generations, Mr Bayley, from which de Gruchy wine is made. Have you ever tasted it?'

'I don't think I have. I think my stepmother used to serve it at her dinner parties, but I was too young to partake.'

'Your stepmother is a woman of taste. It is the finest claret in the world.' A brief smile. 'And the most expensive. And can she no longer obtain it?'

'My stepmother is dead.'

'Oh, I am sorry. Was she killed in the Blitz?'

'No. She died of cancer in 1934. I should tell you that she was a German.'

For just a moment a sheet of ice clouded those magnificent blue eyes, then she shrugged. 'One cannot choose one's parents, much less one's step-parents.'

'She was not a Nazi. She left Germany when they came to power.'

'And she appreciated de Gruchy wine. I think I would have liked your stepmother.'

They rode in silence for a little while, but eventually he could not resist asking, 'This work you do, for the Resistance and helping us to evade capture, isn't it very dangerous?'

'Isn't war, by definition, dangerous?'

'But if you were to be captured by the Gestapo . . .'

'I would no doubt have to die, screaming.' Her smile was twisted. 'But at least I would know that I have lived.' She moved her finger to and fro to end the conversation as some people entered the carriage. 'We will soon be in Limoges.'

'And then how long to Toulouse?'

'Oh, several hours. But we will spend the night in Limoges.'

The entire train disembarked and they left the station in the midst of a crowd of people. Their passes had been checked an hour previously, at the border, and none of the Vichy police on duty seemed very interested in the arrivals. Liane led John down some dingy streets until they reached a bakery. 'Good evening, Celeste,' she said to the large woman behind the counter.

'Oh, mademoiselle,' Celeste cried, and came round the counter to embrace her, before looking apprehensively at John.

'We will be spending the night,' Liane explained.

'Oh, mademoiselle, but . . .'

Liane frowned. 'There is trouble? Where is Anatole?'

'I am here, mademoiselle.' In contrast to his wife, a rather small man emerged from the inner room.

'What is the problem?'

The baker looked at John. 'We have one here already.'

'I do not know of this.'

'He was brought here by Monsieur Pierre, two days ago.'

'Pierre is here?' For the first time since John had met her, Liane's voice was animated.

'No, no, mademoiselle. He was only here for an hour. But he said the cargo should wait here for you. He knew you would be coming by.'

'Oh.' Liane was suddenly deflated. 'Where is the cargo?'

'In the room. But there is only the one room.'

'Well, Jean here will have to share. I will sleep in your room.'

Damnation, John thought. He had been looking forward to spending the night with this entrancing creature, even if only conversationally, and he certainly did not wish to have to share her company for the rest of the journey.

'You wish to see the cargo?' Anatole asked.

'I will see him later,' Liane said. 'But there is a problem, unless he speaks fluent French. I cannot travel with two inarticulate men.'

'I think his French is very good,' Anatole remarked.

'Well, that is something. We will work it out. Now you must feed us. We are starving.'

'Of course, mademoiselle. Come in. Celeste, I will mind the shop.'

Celeste ushered them into an inner parlour and produced hot soup and some kind of goulash and, inevitably, bread and cheese and wine.

'This is going to go down a treat,' John said, sitting opposite Liane to watch her take off her wig and shake out her hair. 'Is this chap really going to be a problem?'

'Not if he can operate on his own. I am prepared to act as a guide, but he will have to follow us rather than be with us. Pierre does not always think very clearly.'

'Pierre being your husband?'

She gave a tinkle of laughter in between conveying spoonfuls of soup to her mouth. 'Pierre is my brother.'

'Oh, forgive me. But you do have a husband?'

She put down the soup spoon to pour some wine. 'Why should I have a husband?'

'Well, you're a beautiful woman, top class, accomplished, a brilliant linguist, obviously as brave as a lioness . . .'

'It is very sweet of you to pay me such compliments. What males you think that I am a brilliant linguist?'

'Well . . . you speak English as if it were your mother tongue.'

'It is.'

'Eh?'

'Half my mother tongue, at any rate. My mother is English, and I was educated in England. A place called Benenden. Have you heard of it?'

'I should think that everyone has heard of Benenden.'

'I was there with my sisters – not all at the same time, of course. I am the eldest.'

'And your brother?'

'Oh, he went to Eton.'

'I suppose that explains quite a lot. Are they all in the Resistance like you?'

A shadow crossed her face. 'Not all.'

John ate in silence for some minutes; obviously he had to be careful of probing too deeply into whatever tragedies lurked in her past. 'And you have actually killed a German officer?'

'Haven't you?'

'Well, yes. It was him or me.'

'Mine was even simpler. He had raped me.' She gazed at him for some seconds, then refilled their glasses. 'Or perhaps, being a man, you do not feel that rape warrants a death sentence?'

'I . . . actually, if I came across someone raping you I would have killed him myself, without hesitation.'

'Raping me or raping anyone? For instance, raping the old woman I pretend to be on occasion.'

'Well . . .' he could feel the heat in his cheeks.

She gave one of her enchanting tinkles of laughter. 'I am not criticising you. You are a man.' Her tone indicated that she might be sorry for his predicament. 'And I know I am beautiful. The good God gave me my looks, and I must presume he had a reason in mind.'

'Killing Germans?'

'That is as good a reason as any. But I think the reason was to use my beauty, and my other talents, to help defend my country – both my countries. But Germans . . .' she drank some wine. 'On May 10 last year, a girl friend of mine and I were in the north of France. We did not manage to escape the invasion. We were captured by six soldiers. They were actually deserters. But they held us prisoner for two days, and they raped us . . . I have forgotten how many times.'

John stared at her. The thought of this magnificent woman being gang-raped had the blood pounding through his arteries.

'Then they were taken by their own people, and we were set free.'

'And your ravagers got patted on the back?'

'No, no. They were hanged. But for desertion, not rape. But something like that puts one off men, you know. I had a flat in Paris . . .' her mouth twisted. 'I still do, even if I cannot use it. I returned there and soon after the Germans occupied the city I was visited by one of the Gestapo officers who had interrogated us after our rescue. He pretended that he wanted to see that I was all right, but what he really wanted was me. So, as I am a small woman and he was a large man, he took what he wanted. But I had resolved never to be raped again, so while he slept I cut his throat and left for the south. And my friends.' She finished her wine and stood up. 'There you have the confessions of a murderess.'

'What happened to your friend?'

'Oh, she had already left France. She was an American and she went home. Now we must go to bed; tomorrow will be a long day. Anatole will show you to your room. I hope our new travelling companion does not snore.'

John caught her hand. 'Mademoiselle – Liane – I would like you to know that I entirely support everything you have done, or may do in the future.'

She looked down at her hand, but did not immediately withdraw it. 'Then we will do well together.'

Her reaction encouraged him to venture. 'Even if, may I say, it is a catastrophe for the masculine sex that you should have come to hate all of us.'

'Not all, Mr Bayley. I admire my brother. And I have –' another twist of the lips – 'a lover. From time to time.'

'If he is not your lover all of the time he needs his head examined.'

Now she did withdraw her hand. 'He is a British officer, in Military Intelligence. We can only see each other occasionally. He is my controller. Goodnight, Mr Bayley.'

Anatole opened the door and raised the candle above his head. 'Company, monsieur.'

The man lying on one of the two beds sat up, and then stood. There was a candle already burning in the room and John discerned that he was very large, a couple of inches the taller, and more heavily built. 'I say,' he remarked.

'You travel together, eh?' Anatole said, and left.

'Squadron Leader William Overton,' the large man announced. '433.'

Another bomber squadron, although John did not approve of the readiness with which the information had been vouchsafed. He nodded. 'John Bayley.'

'Rank?'

John did not suppose there could be a single member of the RAF who had not heard of John Bayley. Or, judging by Jimmy Leadbeater's remarks, did not know of his clash with a German officer. On the other hand, he reflected, he probably just had a big head. 'Squadron Leader.'

'Ah. You can prove this?'

'Do I have to? Can you prove your rank?'

'Of course I cannot. Forgive me.' Overton held out his hand. 'We are to travel together, the baker said.'

John squeezed the offered fingers. 'Apparently.'

'But we are to have a guide. I came here with a guide, but he left me to await another.'

John took off his shoes, jacket and tie and lay down; for some reason he was suddenly reluctant to undress completely before this man. 'That would have been Pierre de Gruchy.'

Overton sat on his bed. 'You know him?'

'I have never met him. But I came here with his sister; she is to be our guide to the Spanish border.'

'Ah. That would be the famous Liane.'

'You mean you've heard of her?'

'Has not everyone heard of Liane de Gruchy, the leader of the Resistance?'

Judging by himself, John had not supposed anyone in

145

England, save for her mysterious controller-cum-lover and presumably his team, had heard of Liane. But no doubt he was simply out of touch, locked away as he had been for the past three years in the very enclosed world of the RAF. And no doubt Pierre had spoken to this man of his sister, undoubtedly with pride. 'I suppose you're right,' he agreed.

'Tell me, is she as beautiful and as sexually attractive as they say?'

Again John wondered. Pierre would hardly have spoken of his sister's sexual appeal to a complete stranger. 'You will have to judge for yourself when you meet her tomorrow. Now, old man, it's been a long and exhausting day. I would like to get some sleep.'

Overton blew out the candle and lay on the other bed. He seemed to go off immediately. To his annoyance, John found sleep elusive. Of course he was overtired, and his brain was teeming with the events of the past two days. For a month he had been existing in a limbo, both mentally and physically. For someone who had spent the previous year and more as a leader of men, making the decisions on which their lives – and even more – depended, finding himself totally at the mercy of others had been traumatic.

And those others had been entirely women, to whom he had clearly been no more than a thing, a rather obstructive object that had to be transported from place to place with a great deal of effort. All his adult life he had been a man who, when he entered a room, whether because of his name or his charisma, had caused heads to turn. Well, he supposed everyone needs to be deflated from time to time.

He had even managed to submerge his masculinity in his anxiety just to survive the passage of time until he could get home. And suddenly, almost at the very moment he had been told to stop existing and start living, his manhood had become important again. He did not suppose that either Severine or her friend had really considered him as anything more than a plaything, but they had certainly awakened his basic instincts. And then Liane! The epitome of womanhood. He did not doubt that everything she had told him of herself was true; she had revealed neither coyness nor embarrassment. Those things had happened, and she had taken them in her stride as no doubt she would eventually take capture and torture and execution by the Gestapo in her stride: 'I will at least know that I have lived!'

Had she really gone home with Severine that first night to share her bed? There was an intriguing thought. So now he wanted her, as he did not suppose he had ever wanted anyone before. It was not merely the sex, although he wanted that too. He wanted to know, to understand, to have her know him, to share, to protect and even to die for, especially as he knew that if it came to that she would be dying there beside him.

All this while on his way home to the most perfect woman in the world, his wife and the mother of his son. He really was a cad. But he couldn't help wondering how Joly would respond to being raped, by six men, one after the other, and then a seventh? He wondered how Liane's nameless friend had reacted. Unlike Liane, she had fled. But Liane had had nowhere to flee to.

And now this idyll, which had lasted precisely one day and had at most only a couple more to go – Liane was only committed to taking him as far as the Spanish frontier – was to be spoiled by the presence of a man he instinctively disliked. Why? Simply because Overton had not heard of the famous John Bayley? There was conceit!

At last he dozed off, only to awake with a start. Overton might not have heard of one of Fighter Command's most famous aces, but he had heard, and apparently a great deal, about Liane de Gruchy. Something to be investigated tomorrow morning . . .

When John awoke, Overton was already up and dressed. 'There's a bathroom at the end of the corridor,' he said helpfully.

John abluted and shaved, hoping for a glimpse of Liane, but without success. Overton had waited for him and watched him dress. 'Are you afraid?' he suddenly asked.

John considered. 'I don't think so. If anyone can get us out, Mademoiselle de Gruchy will do so.'

'And of course there's the reassuring thought that if we are, after all, captured, we'll merely be sent to a prison camp.'

John knotted his tie. 'I'm afraid that doesn't apply to me.'

'Why not?'

'I hate to spoil your morning, but you are travelling with a wanted criminal.'

'What are you saying?'

'Simply that I killed a German officer to avoid capture.'

Overton stared at him with his mouth open.

'So you see, if we are spotted, they're likely to shoot first and ask questions afterwards. I imagine that goes for the Vichy police as well; the business was fairly well publicized. I'm sorry you've got yourself involved in this, but there it is. I had no idea we were going to pick up anyone along the way.'

'Mademoiselle de Gruchy knows this?' Overton snapped his fingers. 'But of course: she is wanted for murder herself.'

John, about to open the door, checked. 'Her brother told you that, did he?'

'Ah . . . yes, of course.'

'He seems to have taken quite a shine to you. Shall we breakfast?'

Liane was already tucking into delicious, freshly baked croissants. 'Anatole is the best baker in Limoges,' she announced. 'And this is Squadron Leader Overton?'

Overton kissed her fingers. 'Mademoiselle de Gruchy, I seem to have waited all my life for this moment.'

'Another gallant Englishman? I am overwhelmed.' She smiled at John's expression. 'You have met my brother.'

'Squadron Leader Overton and your brother are great friends,' John remarked.

'How splendid. You mean you met him in England, before being shot down?'

'Ah . . .' Overton looked confused.

'After Dunkirk,' Liane reminded him. 'Pierre escaped with the allied armies. He only returned here this year after being trained by MI6.'

'Yes, of course. I met him that summer.'

'How did you meet?' John asked conversationally.

'We met in a pub. I was having a drink in the bar, and this Frenchman came in and we got to talking. I liked him immediately. He told me all about the family business, and about you, and about how one of your sisters married a German officer, oh, everything.'

Liane had been drinking coffee. Now she slowly put down the cup. 'I think it's nearly time to leave.' She stood up. 'I'll just go to the toilet. Mr Bayley, I think you should go as well.'

John stared at her in amazement, but she had already gone

148

to the foot of the stairs and was clearly waiting for him. 'Excuse us, old man,' he told Overton, and hurried behind her, following her up the stairs.

Liane led the way along the corridor to the bathroom and opened the door. 'Come in,' she said, 'and close the door.'

The suddenness of her invitation took his breath away. 'I thought this moment might never come,' he ventured, wondering if he should, or dared, take her in his arms.

She faced him. 'This man Overton, is he a friend of yours?'

'Good lord, no.'

'But you knew of him. He is in the same service.'

'It's a pretty big service, and he's in Bomber Command, while I'm a fighter pilot. I'd never heard of him until last night. But then,' he added thoughtfully, 'he had never heard of me.'

Liane had been watching his changing expression and listening to his change of tone. 'You do not trust him.'

'I wouldn't go that far. He seems a little odd, but if he's an old friend of your brother . . .'

'He is not a friend of my brother.'

'But . . . if they met in England . . .'

'They did not meet in England,' Liane said. 'Pierre certainly escaped at Dunkirk, and he spent several months being trained as an MI6 operative before returning to France. Overton is also right when he says that my sister, Madeleine, took the easy way out and married a German officer. But Pierre did not know that when he was in England. He only found out after his return to France.'

'Hmm. Couldn't Overton just be mistaken as to dates, and Pierre have told him about his sister while they were coming here?'

'My family does not talk about Madeleine.' Liane's voice was low but vehement, and John realized that if ever the sisters were to meet again there could well be another tragedy. 'And certainly not to strangers they have just met. Your Mr Overton is lying to us. He is a Gestapo agent.'

'Oh, come now. You don't know that. I'm sure he can explain . . .'

'As you say, Mr Bayley, I do not *know* that: what I do know is that the Gestapo have two great goals here in France. One is to lay their hands on me and the other is to infiltrate and destroy the escape route for which I am largely responsible. The lives, not only of me and my associates but of a good number of British agents as well as future evaders like yourself, depend on their being unable to achieve either of those goals. It is not something about which we can take any risks. I just wanted you to understand the situation.'

'You mean . . .' John licked his lips.

'Yes, Mr Bayley. I mean to kill him. You do not have to be involved, but I could not take the risk of you being stupidly patriotic and attempting to interfere. Now, you remain here until I call you.'

'I can't do that.' He gazed into her eyes and flushed. 'Don't get me wrong, mademoiselle, I believe you, and I understand what you feel you have to do. But shouldn't I help you? He's a big, strong man and looks as if he can take care of himself.'

'Have you ever killed a man, Mr Bayley? Oh, I know you have probably shot down a few German planes, but that was in the most impersonal of combats. And I know you shot that German officer. But as you said, it was him or you. I am talking about cold blood, an execution, not a fight. There is a very considerable difference. Anyway, Anatole will help me.' She gave a brief smile. 'He and Celeste will have to get rid of the body. But as no one except us four know that he is here, that will not be difficult.' She gazed at him, then suddenly stood on tiptoe to kiss him on the cheeks. 'You are a war hero, Mr Bayley. Stay that way. Do not come out until I call you.'

The train rumbled south. They sat opposite each other, Liane reading a newspaper. John had no idea what had happened, or how it had happened. By the time he had been allowed downstairs Overton had disappeared; presumably his body had been concealed somewhere. Liane had been her usual calm and composed self, as had Celeste, even if Anatole had seemed a little agitated.

And he had become an accessory to murder. He entirely understood Liane's reasoning, and he had to admire her total single-mindedness. It was akin to what a fighter pilot needed when in the air. But the man he had been setting out to kill had always been at least as well-armed as himself. It had always been a duel between equal adversaries. So would he have preferred to stand facing Overton, pistol in hand, at twenty paces? This was 1941, not 1814.

And yet, looked at in romantic terms, one would believe that the best man would win. He had won in the air, thirty-eight times, because he had always believed that he was the better man. On the one occasion he had come face to face, on equal terms, with a better man, he had been shot down. But of course that *was* incredibly romantic, schoolboy stuff. This was a country in a desperate state, for which only desperate measures would suffice.

His real problem was that not a shred of actual proof had been produced, or even sought, as to Overton's guilt or innocence. Blatchford had suggested that the Germans would attempt to infiltrate their own people into the escape pipeline, and were perhaps already doing so. Thus Liane had merely summed up the situation to her own satisfaction, deduced that a man who had lied had to be an enemy and thus a danger, and eliminated him without hesitation. So far as he knew, Overton had not even been charged or allowed to speak in his own defence. So it was done, and they could all breathe more easily. *But suppose she had been wrong?*

And despite everything, she continued to fascinate him. He knew he would never meet another like her. But perhaps that would be a stroke of luck, on more than one count.

She had put down her newspaper and was studying him, as was her habit, and now the carriage was momentarily empty. 'You should not brood on the past,' she said, 'even the immediate past. When one of your comrades is shot down, do you wander around holding your head in your hands or do you square your shoulders and get on with your duty?'

He did not think it would achieve anything to attempt to explain his feelings. 'May I ask a question?'

'Of course.'

'How many men have you killed?'

He had taken her by surprise; she had supposed he would want some details as to how Overton had died. 'I have no idea.'

'That is a remarkable statement.'

'To you, obviously. In your war everything is cut and dried

and recorded. How many enemy aircraft have you shot down?'

'Thirty-eight.'

'Thirty-eight! Then you are a genuine ace. How splendid. But surely not all were fighters? Some were bombers with a crew of several men.'

'That's true. But I don't think all the pilots and crews were killed. Quite a few managed to bale out.'

'But there was also the German officer outside Amiens. In any event, they were mostly one-to-one and thus you can remember them all. It's not like that in my war. I have killed, one-on-one, and I have been involved in a gun battle with the SS when I do not know how many, if any, of them I hit. It was fought in the dark. But I have also blown up a train, when I know a great many people died. But I cannot tell you the name of any one of them. Nor can I be sure they were all Germans. That is the nature of the war I fight.'

'And you never have nightmares?'

She regarded him for several; moments, then she said. 'Yes, Mr Bayley. I have nightmares.' She got up as the train slowed to enter Toulouse. 'We get off here.'

Another house, another welcome. As usual the people were apparently delighted to see Liane, and paid very little attention to John. 'How often do you make this trip?' he asked at dinner. She had removed both her wig and her make-up and was again the utter beauty he had first seen.

'Very seldom. I have more important things to do.'

'So why have I been so lucky?'

She poured wine, as she apparently liked to do when considering a question. 'It is not a case of luck. I was leaving Paris anyway, and you are a special case.'

'Why's that?'

She sipped. 'Because you killed a German officer, Mr Bayley, and are as wanted by the Gestapo as am I. Now, tomorrow begins the last stage of your journey, and perhaps the least comfortable. Jules will take you to a depot on the canal, and there you will join a barge as a member of the crew. This will take you down to Béziers. It is a matter of three or four days; the barges travel very slowly. It is also very hard work, because the Canal du Midi climbs very high, several hundred metres, and then of course it has to come

152

down again. This is done by means of locks, hundreds of locks. Sometimes there are several joined together, what they call an *escalier*. Going up, each lock has to be entered, the gates closed, and the chamber filled with water to raise it to the next level. Coming down, each one has to be emptied. The opening and closing of the gates, and the opening and closing of the sluices, all has to be done by hand. There is a keeper on each lock, or series of locks, but he requires the barge crew to do most of the work.'

'Sounds entrancing.'

'I am sure you will enjoy it, even if it rains. The food is good, and the company excellent.'

'I should think that three days floating down a canal with you would be very close to paradise.'

She wrinkled her nose, and that *was* entrancing. 'I will not be with you.'

'What?'

'I have other things to do. So we part company tomorrow morning.'

'Damn.'

'I can do nothing more for you.'

'I understand that. But . . . well . . . these last few days . . . you have got to be the most exciting woman I have ever met.'

'Despite . . .?'

'Yes, despite. Or maybe, because. Listen, I am going to make sure that you are known as a heroine. I'm going to tell—'

She frowned, and shook her head. 'You will tell no one, either about me or how you got out of France.'

'The people I tell—'

'No one, Mr Bayley, except the intelligence officers who will debrief you on you return to England. But there must be no one else – not even your wife and family. Please understand this. A single careless word could end my life, and those of my associates. The Germans are not fools, and as you have seen, they are getting closer every day. Will you swear to me that not a word of what has happened to you over the last month will be revealed to *anyone*, at least until the War is over?'

'Oh, well, if that is what you wish . . .'

'That is what I must have.'

'Then I swear.'

She smiled and rested her hand on his. 'Thank you. Now finish your coffee and come upstairs. I wish to say goodbye to you in a proper fashion. We shall not meet again after tomorrow.'

PART THREE

A Thousand Plus

'Thousands at his bidding speed
And post o'er Land and Ocean without rest:
They also serve who only stand and wait.'

'On His Blindness', John Milton

Eight

Romantic Matters

In the chill December drizzle Berlin was not the happy place Max remembered from even four months ago. One expected people to hurry in the rain, but not also to gather in small groups at street corners and mutter at each other. The news from Russia had clearly begun to filter through. The sand-bagged buildings, the cratered streets and occasional piles of rubble were reminders that the war with Great Britain was far from over, and was indeed coming closer.

Still, the mood of the city matched his own. Despite his magic interludes with Hildegarde, and in August with Erika, for the past year Max had been weighed down by the catastrophe of Heidi, and more recently the tragedy of Galina. Except for a few fleeting minutes he did not think he had really been happy since. And three months in Trondheim had not exactly been the most exciting period of his life, especially as he knew that, however unpleasant the strong winds and driving rain had been, they were only a harbinger of what lay ahead when he returned from this leave.

It could have been very different. His Flight Commander, Heinz Loestner, was a splendid fellow, and he and his pilots were clearly in awe of their famous Station Commander. Max did not know how much they knew about the reason he had suddenly been pulled out of the firing line, as it were, but no one had dared ask any questions.

They certainly had enough to do. Milch had been right about the British convoys using the passage up to and around the North Cape and into the Arctic Sea; the squadrons were called out almost every day. And there was sufficient RAF protection to make it exciting. But he had to stand on the tarmac and watch them go, and then wait for them to come back. Or not, as the case might be. The temptation to disobey orders and go up himself had been enormous.

Even more frustrating was to receive the news from Russia. If the weather was really as bad as it was reported, Gunther and the Wing must be having a terrible time. While again he was standing on a tarmac in complete safety. It had not been a difficult decision to take his leave in Berlin; he intended to seek an interview with Milch: surely sufficient time had elapsed to have his grounding overturned. Besides, the only alternative would have been Bitterman, and as Max von Bitterman would certainly have heard of his disgrace, that would have been unbearable. In any event, he was more likely to be able to get hold of Erika here than in the south. The memory of their last night together before his departure for Norway had been the only thing that had preserved his sanity. Not that he had told her where he was going or why; just left her with the impression that he had been recalled to Berlin, briefly, for a high-level conference.

'Colonel Bayley! It is good to see you,' gushed the reception clerk at the Albert. 'Will you be with us long?'

'A week, Johann. Have you a room?'

'Of course we have a room for you, sir. A week! How splendid.' He snapped his fingers and a bellboy hurried forward to take Max's bag and the key. 'Shall I book you a table for dinner, sir?'

'Thank you.'

'Ah . . . for one?'

'At the moment. But I may be joined.'

'Of course, sir.'

Max followed the bellboy up the stairs and along the wide, carpeted hall. Returning to the utterly civilized ambience of the Albert was always a pleasure, even if all the memories were not pleasant. It was in this hotel that he had first met Heidi, in the company of Erika, and it was in a bedroom in this hotel that he had proposed marriage. As all the bedrooms were virtually identical, the room to which he was now shown could have been the very one. On the other hand, if the Gestapo report was to be believed, it was in the bar downstairs, when, in his absence, she and Erika had been contentedly getting drunk together, that Heidi had made the acquaintance of that English spy and begun her journey to the gallows.

He tipped the boy, took off his tunic and tie and sat at the table and the telephone, his heart, as always, pounding pleasantly. He gave the number and waited.

'Hello.'

'Thank God you're here. Listen, I'm at the Albert. Join me for dinner.'

'Who is that? Max?'

'Well, of course it's Max. Who else could it be?' Even as he spoke the words he realized that was a ridiculous question, in view of Erika's lifestyle.

'It's good of you to call, Max. Are you on leave?'

Max stared at the phone. She might have been some casual acquaintance being polite. 'You are not alone?'

'Certainly I am alone. I am just dressing for the evening.'

'But you have a date. Well, break it. I have been waiting for this evening for three months.'

'I'm sorry, Max, but I won't be able to dine with you.'

'Shit! All right, I can wait until tomorrow.'

'I won't be available tomorrow. Please do not call again. Have a nice furlough.'

The phone went dead and again he stared at it, this time for several seconds, before replacing the receiver. She was ending their relationship, just like that! Because of another man? Or because . . . she had learned of his disgrace. Erika did not associate with unsuccessful men.

He had a tremendous urge to pull the telephone clear of its wires and hurl it across the room, was actually reaching for it when it jangled again. Relief rushed through his system: she had realized what a fool she'd been. He grabbed the receiver. 'Yes?'

'Oh, Colonel Bayley! I'm sorry to bother you.' It was the reception clerk.

The last straw would be if the dining room was fully booked. 'What is it?'

'It's just that there is a message for you. I should have given it to you when you checked in, but the fact is that it was delivered several days ago, and I'm afraid it got filed and overlooked. It said we should hold it in case you came to the hotel, but as we did not know when next you would be in town . . .'

'All right, all right,' Max interrupted the flow. 'Just give me the message.'

'The envelope is sealed, sir.'

'Then send it up.'

'Of course, sir. Right away.'

Max paced the room while he waited. There were not many people who knew he used the Albert as a base when in Berlin. Perhaps Gunther also had leave. That would be splendid. They could have dinner together and then drown their sorrows.

There was a tap on the door. 'Come.'

The bellboy entered with his silver tray. Max took the envelope, frowned at it. He did not recognize the handwriting. The boy withdrew and he slit the envelope.

Dearest Max,

I hope you will not consider this an imposition, but having a few days' leave, and remembering that you said you always use the Albert when in Berlin, I decided to call there and see if they had news of you; we have had nothing here save the information that you had been relieved of your command and returned to Germany. As you may imagine, speculation is rife, but as it is also rumoured that there is an SS connection with what happened, we have not been able to make any inquiries. But there is at least a chance that you have been given a desk job in Berlin. It would have been too much to hope that you are actually staying at the hotel, but they seemed to know your name and were sure you would visit them in the course of time. I am here for another week, and will be returning to Smolensk – brrr – on 8 December. I would so love to be able to see you again. My address is on the top of this note.

Hilde.

Max stared at the words for several moments. He had supposed he would never see her again. But she wanted to see him, and if she did not know exactly what had happened, she knew that he was being disciplined.

And she was actually here, in Berlin! Then his eyes flickered up to the calendar hanging on the wall. Today was Saturday 7 December. She was leaving tomorrow! He picked up the receiver, gave the number at the head of her notepaper, and waited, heart pounding.

'Who is it calling, please?'

'Colonel Max Bayley. I would like to speak with Captain Gruner.'

'Just one moment. Hildegarde!' the woman called. 'It's for you. A man!' She did not sound very approving.

'Yes?' Hildegarde also sounded a little breathless.

'Hilde! Thank God you're still here.'

'Max!' she cried. 'Where are you calling from?'

'I'm at the Albert. I only just got your note. Will you have dinner with me?'

'Oh, Max. I have an engagement. It is my last night in Berlin, you know.'

'I do know. That's why I want to see you.'

For a moment there was no response and his heart sank. Then she said, 'What time is dinner?'

'Now – as soon as you can make it.'

Another brief hesitation. 'I'll be with you in an hour.'

'And you'll stay?'

'Yes, Max, I'll stay. But I leave very early in the morning.'

They sipped wine, gazing at each other across the table. He had never seen her in civilian clothes before. Tonight she wore a low cut evening gown, and it had been all he could do not to take her upstairs the moment he saw her. But the whole night stretched ahead of them. Just one night, after so many nights of sheer emptiness. How had he ever supposed that Erika was beautiful?

But there were shadows behind her eyes. 'Would you like to know what happened?' he asked.

'If you would like to tell me.'

'I need to tell someone, someone I can trust. Can I trust you? It's not a pretty story.'

'I would like you to be sure that you can trust me, no matter what. As for stories, it's so long since I heard a pretty story I doubt I'm capable of appreciating one.'

'Is it so bad?' he asked.

Hildegarde shrugged. 'I suppose that depends on your interpretation of the word bad. Tell me yours first.'

He told her what had happened, watching her face as she ate. 'I think you're unlucky with women,' she remarked when he had finished.

'All women?'

'I hope not. Was she very beautiful, this Russian girl?'

161

'She was not a girl, and she was not in the least beautiful. She badly needed a bath. But I had given her my word.'

Hildegarde nodded. 'I understand. But to fall out with the SS . . .'

'I know. You are welcome to leave. That is what my other friends would do.' He was stretching a point, but he was also holding his breath as he waited for her reply.

She finished her dinner. 'I thought we were to spend the evening together?'

He squeezed her fingers. 'We'll have coffee and brandy in the lounge,' he told the waiter, and when they had settled themselves on a settee in a corner of the large, almost empty room, he said, 'Now it's your turn. I've heard that the population here in Germany are being called upon to give up all surplus warm clothing to be sent to the front.'

'That is true. There have been several cases of men being frozen to death. They're still in summer kit, you see. They do not have any winter kit.'

'That's terrible. Who is responsible for such a mistake?'

She made a moue. 'I think we all are. Don't you remember the early days? We were supposed to be in Moscow by September, and we gained so many huge victories, even that estimate seemed overcautious. Even when resistance stiffened as we penetrated further and further, it only seemed a matter of putting the date back a few weeks, into October. And then it began to rain. We had never seen such rain, Max. You know all those roads that were marked on our maps, paved super-highways leading into Red Square itself? They were all hardly more than cart tracks. This was only an irritation when they were dry, but in the rain they turned into rivers of mud. Nothing could move; everything slithered to and fro. If only we had started the campaign when we were supposed to, in mid-May, instead of being sidetracked into the Balkans . . .' she glanced right and left. 'I should not be saying this.'

'No one's listening to us. And I agree with you. If only OKW had not diverted those two Panzer divisions to the south . . . But it's not still raining, is it?'

'Oh, no. Everyone said the wet season in the autumn is brief. It'll soon be over. We'll only be a month late. But when the rain stopped, it started to get cold. It was so sudden. In one night the temperature dropped forty degrees.'

162

'But surely that made the roads passable again – certainly for the tanks?'

'Oh, yes. Supposing they could start their engines. It's so cold in Russia right now that the engine oil freezes in the sumps. The crews have to light fires under their tanks to warm up the oil before the engines will start.'

'What about the Luftwaffe?'

'They have to do the same before they can take off.'

'Jesus! Are you saying the campaign's a failure?'

'It's over for this year. Everyone is agreed it will continue next year, as soon as the thaw sets in. But that could be several months away. And in the meantime, our people sit and freeze. Apart from being virtually unbearable, it's ruining the morale of the front-line troops. Do you know that some of them actually got into Moscow? They claim to have seen the towers of the Kremlin. But they could get no further without tank or artillery support, and none could be got up to them. So they had to fall back.'

'But surely this weather affects the Russians as well?'

'Do you know, that's the really serious thing. It doesn't affect the Russians at all: this is their weather, they're used to it. They wear the warmest of uniforms. And they seem to have some new weapons as well. One in particular is a mortar, which delivers a shell that screams as it comes through the air. They called it the Katyusha. It terrifies our people.'

'But still,' Max said, as reassuringly as he could, 'as you say, it's just a matter of holding our positions until the weather thaws ... I mean, the Ivans have taken so many casualties this summer that they must be scraping the bottom of the barrel.'

Hildegarde started at him for several seconds. 'That is the most frightening thing of all.'

He frowned. 'What?'

'They seem to have as many men as ever. And ... this is top secret. We have received reports that increasing numbers of them are Siberians, Mongols and Tatars. The Russians are supposed to have some two million men in their Eastern Army.'

'Yes, but they need them there to combat the Japanese. The two countries have been at war, on and off and undeclared, for the past three years.'

'Suppose they have agreed a truce?'

'The Japanese cannot do that. They are our allies.'

'That's not actually true,' she said. 'They agree with many of our principles, and they've agreed to give us a free hand in Europe if we give them a free hand in Asia, but there has never been a formal alliance. They are quite capable of following their own agenda, without informing us. The point is, if the Russians now have the use of the better part of two million men, fresh troops, to throw against us, well ... will the War even be over next year?'

He finished his brandy and stood up, held her hands to raise her also. 'We both need cheering up. Let's go upstairs and fuck ourselves senseless.'

He supposed they had just about done that, as he watched her dressing in the half light of the December dawn. 'I wish you could stay, even for one more day.'

'I wish I could stay too, even for one more hour. But I really wouldn't like to wind up in a labour battalion for desertion.' She sat on the bed beside him. 'So ... until the next time. Will there be a next time, Max?'

'Listen! Marry me.'

She gazed at him, her face expressionless.

'Is that so impossible a thought?'

'That is the most wonderful thought I have ever known. But ...'

'I know. You have a train to catch. But if you'll say yes, we have something to look forward to. Leave the arrangements to me.' He smiled. 'I still have at least one friend left.'

She hesitated for a few seconds, while as always his heart began to pound. Then she leaned forward and kissed him. 'Yes.'

Max dressed, had breakfast and then telephoned the Air Ministry. 'Do you have an appointment?' the secretary asked.

'If I had an appointment already, I wouldn't be asking for one now,' Max pointed out.

'The Field Marshal's diary is entirely full.'

'Will you give him my name, and see if he can fit me in?'

'I do not think ...'

'I'll hold on,' Max said.

The secretary went off and returned a few minutes later. 'The Field Marshal will see you at two o'clock this afternoon.' He was clearly very surprised.

'Thank you,' Max said, and went back to bed: he had had

164

very little sleep. At two, he presented himself at the Air Ministry and was shown up to Milch's office.

'I can only give you ten minutes, Max. I have a meeting. Is all well?'

'If you mean is Trondheim still there, Herr Field Marshal, the answer would be yes.'

'But . . .?'

'I gather things are not going entirely according to plan in Russia.'

'Now, from where would you have gathered that?'

'I still have one or two friends left, sir. Apart from yourself.'

Milch considered the remark, then he nodded. 'We have not been able to maintain our schedule, yes. A combination of poor generalship and bad weather. However, generals can always be replaced, and the weather always improves. It is simply a matter of holding our positions until the spring.'

'Can we do that?'

Milch made a face. 'According to the generals, we cannot. They feel we should retreat. But as I say, defeatists can be replaced, and this is being done. Two days ago, the Fuehrer took over personal command of all our armies in the field. That means Russia.'

'The Fuehrer?' Max was aghast. 'But—'

Milch held up a finger. 'I know. They will say that he has no experience of commanding an army, has never even served on the General Staff. But he has a most remarkable grasp of military strategy, as he proved during the French campaign last year, and people forget that Napoleon had no experience of strategic command when he was appointed to lead the Army of Italy in 1797, and look what happened after that.'

Max decided it would be imprudent to remind the Field Marshal that it had been Hitler's 'grasp of military strategy' to withhold the Panzers from delivering the coup de grace to the BEF and had allowed the British to extricate their army from Dunkirk. Instead he reckoned it was time to go the whole sycophantic hog. 'I would be greatly honoured to be allowed to serve under the Fuehrer's personal command, sir.'

Milch regarded him sceptically; he knew his young protégé too well. 'That's very commendable of you, Max, but I do not think it would be acceptable at this moment. In any event, what do you wish to return to Russia for? Apart from being even colder than Norway, there's no combat; your planes cannot fly. And when they do . . . did you know that Molders is dead?'

'Molders? But . . .'

'Our greatest ace after Marseille.'

'He was shot down?'

'No. Like you, he suffered engine failure. And before you jump to conclusions, it seems to have been caused by the cold rather than any unexplained malfunction. Unlike you, he was unlucky. He had frozen to death before our people could get to him.'

'Shit!'

'Quite. That makes you our second most successful living pilot. I imagine you also do not know that Udet is dead.'

'What?'

Milch gave a grim smile. 'Also engine failure, officially. Actually, he committed suicide.'

Max stared at him in consternation.

'He couldn't stand the casualties we are suffering in Russia and the delays in bringing our new planes into production. I am taking over. So, with fortune, I may be able to help you. But I must hurry slowly. So, enjoy the rest of your leave and then return to your post. You are doing excellent work.'

'Thank you, sir. Have I your permission to get married?'

Milch raised his eyebrows. 'Do you need my permission to get married? You are your own commanding officer, although I would hope that you have chosen more wisely than the last time.'

'She will need the permission, sir. She's a serving officer with the Wehrmacht in Russia.'

'Good God! In what capacity?'

'She is General Clausen's secretary.'

'Would that be Rupert Clausen?'

'I think that is correct, sir.'

'Oh, Max, Max! You certainly can become involved in some peculiar attachments.'

'Sir?'

'What do you know of Clausen? Or of this . . .?'

'Captain Hildegarde Gruner, sir.'

'Hildegarde Gruner? Apart from her physical attractions, which I assume are considerable.'

'I know that she is the woman I would like to marry, sir.' Max spoke very slowly and evenly.

'And again, may I assume that you wish her to be able to join you in Trondheim, presuming she accepts your proposal?'

'She has already accepted my proposal, sir.'

'Are you aware that the Fuehrer, as the new supreme commander, has issued orders that there is to be no retreat, anywhere, on the Russian front? That our troops must hold their positions, to the last man if necessary, until we are in a position to resume our offensive?'

'That is surely madness.'

'Obviously I did not hear that comment,' Milch pointed out, 'or I would have to place you under arrest.'

'I apologize, sir. I spoke in haste. What I meant was that the order could not possibly apply to a non-combatant female who has never fired a shot in anger.'

'It applies to every member of the army. Your Captain Gruner may not be on the front line, but she is fulfilling a function . . .' he cleared his throat. 'If every non-combatant decided to end his participation in the campaign, whether it be to get married, to visit his sick mother, or just because he, or she, is fed up with the cold, where would we be? And permission cannot be granted to one and then refused to another. I would also suggest that you do not know this woman, or her situation, very well. I am going to be indelicate, and I would be very disappointed if you were to repeat what I am going to say to anyone. General Clausen has the reputation of being the greatest lecher in the Wehrmacht. Any female secretary of his is by definition also his mistress. Were you aware of this?'

Max could feel the heat in his cheeks, as he recalled Hildegarde telling him that the general liked to spank her; he had never thought to ask whether or not he took down her knickers to do this. 'Hilde has told me that he demands certain favours.'

'And you are prepared to accept this?'

'She is a grown woman, and it is the nature of the beast.'

'Do you also accept that she would almost certainly have known the implications of her posting before she accepted it?'

'She had not then met me, sir,' Max reminded him, stubbornly refusing to lose his cool: he knew that the Field Marshal only had his welfare at heart.

Milch sighed. 'Very well. I will see . . .' His head turned, sharply, as the door opened. 'I said that I did not wish to be interrupted.'

'But, sir . . .' the young officer was breathless. 'A communiqué . . .' he was waving a sheet of paper.

'Give it to me.' Milch took the paper and scanned it. 'Good God!'

'Sir?' Max sensed catastrophe.

Milch laid down the paper. 'At dawn this morning, their time, the Japanese air force attacked Pearl Harbor.'

'Sir?' the Lieutenant ventured.

Milch was continuing to stare at the paper, as if willing the words to go away. Now he waved his hand. 'Thank you, Odentz, that will be all.'

Odentz looked at Max, then clicked his heels and left the room.

'They have apparently destroyed the American Pacific Fleet,' Milch said, half to himself, 'and are also attacking Malaysia and the Philippines.'

'Did you not know this was going to happen?' Max asked.

'No, I did not know it was going to happen; no one knew it was going to happen.'

'But . . . the Japanese . . .' Max remembered his conversation with Hildegarde. 'I thought they were our friends?'

'They claim to be our friends, but they have never actually lifted a finger to help us. And they certainly have never shared any secrets with us. And now, this . . .'

'But surely, now they are fighting beside us . . . that has to be good news?'

'They are not fighting beside us, Max. They are following their own agenda.' He snapped his fingers, 'Of course!'

'Sir?'

'You wouldn't know this, because it is being kept secret, but we've been receiving disquieting reports that the Russians have been introducing fresh troops in their counter-attacks, and that there is considerable evidence that these troops are from their Siberian army.'

'Good lord!' Max said, as ingenuously as he could.

'It is a serious matter, because they are supposed to have more than two million men in that army. What has been puzzling us is how they dared take the risk of reducing their eastern forces, when they are well aware that the Japanese are basically on our side, and when in addition they have been fighting an undeclared war with Japan for three years. But now it becomes clear. They knew, and they have known for some time, that there was no risk of Japan resuming hostilities against them, because they intended to go in another direction.'

'Do you mean that Japan has betrayed us?'

'I cannot believe that, but the Russians must have a better spy system than we thought possible. That is a serious matter.'

Max considered. 'On the other hand, Herr Field Marshal, there is surely a bright side to the situation. If the Japanese are attacking Malaysia that must mean they are at war with Great Britain, and that must be a help to us.'

'As the only place we are consistently engaging the British is at sea and on a miniscule scale in North Africa, it's not likely to have an immediate impact on the British war effort.'

'Yes, but isn't the entire British war effort – and the Russian, come to think of it – being sustained by American aid, this Lend-Lease Agreement? If America is now engaged in a full-scale war with Japan they'll need all their resources for themselves, surely?'

Milch leaned back in his chair. 'Have you ever been to America, Max?'

'No, sir.'

'I have. And I remember the Great War. That was before you were born. The Americans are a frightening people. Because of their amazing mixture of nationalities, races and even religions, only tenuously held together by a very thin layer of British law and custom inherited from the colonial days, they have no common historical heritage or culture, custom and behaviour such as exists in most civilized countries. They claim to have no interest in other people's problems, in going to war on behalf of those problems; only in making money. But virtually their entire brief history has been devoted to violence. However much they may deny it, they worship the boys in blue, the gunfighter, the gangster, always with the proviso that the man in the white hat, the good guy, wins in the end.'

He paused and flushed, aware that Max was staring at him open-mouthed. Max had, in fact, not seen this talented man, who was his closest friend, so animated since June 1940, when Goering had turned down his plan for an immediate airborne invasion of England in the week after Dunkirk.

'What I am saying,' Milch continued in a lower voice, 'is that America is a vast ant heap, filled with biting, scratching, tearing insects. Left to themselves they will eventually consume themselves in their own frantic world. Be so careless as to poke them with a stick, and you stand the chance of being overwhelmed. Japan has now poked them with a stick. Well –' he sighed – 'as you say, at least it should keep them off our backs for a few years to come. We need to use the time well. I have an appointment with the Reichmarschal, and I'm sure we will have a lot to discuss. Enjoy the rest of your leave and then go back to Trondheim. Keep your nose clean and I'll see what I can do about you and your Captain Gruner. *Heil* Hitler.'

Max lay on his back on his bed and stared at the ceiling. He had done little else for the past four days, apart from eating well and drinking even better.

He had no idea why he was still here. For four months he had not flown any airplane, much less fired a shot in anger; he certainly had not needed a furlough. He had been left only with the memory of those last traumatic moments as his engine had burst into flames, and the even more traumatic moments that had followed. Everyone seemed agreed that he was just fortunate to have survived – both the flying mishap and his confrontation with the SS.

But no one had apparently been interested in his side of the story. He had not even been allowed the luxury of a court martial. That had undoubtedly been because his Luftwaffe superiors, headed by Milch himself, had been reluctant to take on the SS, and no doubt had felt that a guilty verdict was a foregone conclusion. But far more important, he had not been required to appear before a board of inquiry, to establish exactly what had happened to his engine, as it had happened to Horst Geiger's engine . . . as it had happened, he was beginning to suspect, to perhaps quite a few other pilots. And to Molders? That too, he had no doubt, had been a high level decision. As he had been reminded by Albrecht in Budapest, the Gustav was probably the finest fighter aircraft in the world at that moment. It was certainly a match for any other, even the new Spitfire Mark IV. That its engine occasionally exploded for some unexplained reason, and might cost a life or two, was surely of no relevance against the number of lives being lost every day in this war, while to raise the slightest doubt in the minds of the pilots who flew the machine, which might impair their confidence and thus their efficiency, would be criminal. But Molders! A hundred and fifteen kills, a general at the age of thirty, and now just a name in the history books. And Udet! Perhaps that was the more serious. A high-ranking officer, an ace in his own day with more than sixty kills, committing suicide? What deep-seated malaise did that truly cover?

While he had been ordered to crawl back into his frozen Norwegian hole and wait for something to turn up, and pray that Milch would be able to work a miracle and that it would be Hilde.

The telephone jangled. He got out of bed and crossed the room to the table. 'Yes?'

'Herr Major!' The clerk's voice was breathless. 'I have Field Marshal Milch on the line, to speak with you.'

Max stared at the receiver in consternation. Milch? Calling him? Here? 'Put him through.' Had the miracle after all happened, and so quickly? 'Herr Field Marshal?'

'Max? I have some news for you.'

Max could hardly believe his ears. But the Field Marshal's voice was sombre rather than animated. 'Sir?'

'The Fuehrer is addressing the nation on the wireless this evening. I suggest you get to a set and listen.'

'Yes, sir.' Now he was totally mystified.

'He is going to tell you, tell us all, that he has today declared war on the United States of America.'

Again Max stared at the receiver.

'Are you there?'

'Yes, sir. But . . . why? What does it mean?'

'As to the why, Max, I am not sure that even he knows. But it means, as a French general once said, at the Battle of Sedan when surrounded by our armies, that we are in a chamber pot and will shortly be covered in shit.'

* * *

The taxi halted before Hillside House and Joan Carling stepped down. She paid the fare and then turned to brace herself to receive the onslaught charging at her.

Mark Bayley's older sister, she was a big woman, attractive, with the strong Bayley features neatly rounded into softness and her yellow hair cut short, but while it was over a year since the apartment block in which she had lived in London had received a direct hit, and the broken bones caused by falling through several collapsing floors had knitted, it had taken a long time and she was inclined to resist even affectionate violence. Fortunately she had known Rufus for years, and he merely wished to lick her hand. 'You,' she remarked, 'are getting distinctly fat.'

The taxi driver had placed her small suitcase on the ground before driving off, and she picked it up to walk to the front door, the dog still trying to nuzzle her. She always loved coming to Hillside. She had lived here for nearly twenty years, firstly as friend and companion to Karolina and then as housekeeper to her brother after Karo's death. She still felt guilty at ever having left it, although Mark had been insistent that when she met a man she could love more than him she should grasp the chance of complete happiness.

And at least she could feel that he was in good hands. She had virtually hand-picked Helen as his second wife, and there she was; she had heard the taxi and beaten Clements to the front door. 'Joan, darling! I didn't expect you so early.'

'Amazingly, there were no delays and I made every connection.'

'And you're looking so well! Is Jim all right?'

Helen was gushing. Well, Joan remembered that Helen always gushed, but today the gush had a hidden meaning. 'Thank you, Jim is fine. Working hard. But I'm afraid there's nothing to tell you.'

'Oh.'

Helen, Joan remembered, had been almost as devastated as herself by the loss of the baby on that dreadful September day. For Helen it had been more immediate, as it had been for Jim and for Mark. She, the bereaved mother, had been in a semi-conscious state of shock for several days after she had been dug out of the wreckage of her home, and in fact she had not even been aware of her pregnancy until the doctor

172

had told her of the dead foetus; in the middle of a war there can be so many possible reasons for a couple of missed periods.

Marrying, as she had done, at the age of forty-four, she had never really expected to have children at all – not that she would have objected to the idea, as it would have arisen out of moments of passion with Jim. Those were always moments to be treasured. Her life had not been chaste. As a young woman in the Great War, working in a factory and for the first time earning sufficient money to be her own mistress, she had been, as she now recognized, a little too easy. She knew her rather strait-laced younger brother had never approved. But Karolina had changed all that, teaching her the truly important things in life without ever attempting to curtail that life. The mere presence of her example had been suffi-cient.

She supposed, had Karolina lived, she would never have got married at all. Because had Karolina lived, she would never have had to make that unforgettable journey to Germany in an attempt to regain Karolina's son; never have had the horrendous experience of being a prisoner of the Gestapo, and thus Jim Carling would never have had any reason to seek her out, in his capacity as a representative of the Ministry of Propaganda looking for first-hand examples of Nazi brutality.

The happiness of Karolina's world had been like an eider-down quilt, softly soothing. The happiness she had found with Jim was like running barefoot across a lawn – perhaps encoun-tering the odd pebble, but on the whole totally exhilarating. If she had refused to accept the possibility of her body reacting so positively, she had been delighted to be told that it had. Then to be told, in virtually the same breath, that the baby was dead . . .

So now she merely squeezed Helen's hand and led her into the house. 'Clements! How good to see you.'

'Miss Joan! May I say that you look as lovely as ever?'

'You may always tell lies like that.' She took off her coat and hat and handed them to him. 'There's a case . . .'

'I'll take it up to your room.'

'I'm sure you feel like a drink,' Helen suggested; it was time for her to remind everyone that *she* was now the mistress of the house. 'Pinkers?'

'That would be very nice.' Joan continued to lead the way,

through the drawing room and into the library. The house was heated, but there was also a roaring fire in the grate and she stripped off her gloves to hold her hands close to the flames for a moment. 'What do you think of the news? Isn't it tremendous?'

'Is it? America being absolutely wiped off the map?' Helen splashed Angostura bitters into two glasses and added gin.

Joan sipped appreciatively, sat down and crossed her knees. 'Oh, come now, America can't be beaten because of the loss of a few battleships – annoyed, yes, which is bad for the Japs. And now they're on our side, and against Germany too. That means we can't possibly lose.'

Helen also sat, glass held in both hands. 'That's what Mark says. I wish I could believe it.'

'Don't you think Mark knows what he's talking about? What does Jolinda think about it?'

'I think she's pleased, although with all this talk about Japan invading California, or at least bombing it – that's where her mother lives, you know. But with Joly . . . one never knows. I mean, she's very moody. Well, I suppose that's understandable . . .'

Joan finished her drink, got up and mixed herself another; they had reached the reason she was here. 'There's no news at all? I mean, we know he's alive, don't we?'

Helen held out her glass for a refill; it was always a waste of time trying to pull rank on her sister-in-law. 'We know he *was* alive. This man came to see us, a Flying Officer Leadbeater. He claimed to have met Johnnie when they were both hiding from the Gestapo or something.'

'Claimed?'

'Well, he wouldn't tell us anything more than that. He wouldn't even tell us *where* they'd met, or what they were doing. Said he wasn't allowed to. Well . . .'

'Did Mark see him?'

'Oh, yes.'

'And?'

'Oh, Mark believed him. But Mark *wanted* to believe him, don't you see? So did Joly. Mark said that he would have been forbidden to talk about how he got out, and who helped him, by some government department called MI-something-or-other, just in case word of it got back to the Germans and endangered other people trying to get out. This chap Leadbeater said he'd only come to see us because he had promised Johnnie that he would tell us he was alive and well. We drank champagne that night, I can tell you.'

'I should think so too!'

'But that was three months ago.' Helen almost wailed. 'And not a word since. I mean, if this chap could get out back in September, why didn't Johnnie come with him?'

'Well, obviously there has to be a reason.' Joan wished she could think of one. Then she snapped her fingers. 'It must be to do with that business of his having shot a German officer to escape capture.'

'Yes,' Helen agreed, shoulders hunched, 'that has to be it.'

Joan contemplated her again empty glass but decided that getting tight was not going to achieve anything. 'If the Germans had got hold of him, they would've said so. Loudly.'

'If he was killed resisting arrest . . .'

'They would have announced that too. I'm sure of it.'

'Yes, but he would have been in disguise. And he would have known that if he were captured he'd be shot or whatever. He might have been killed resisting arrest, and the Germans not known who he was.'

'Does Mark think that might have happened?'

'No, no. He's determinedly optimistic.'

'And Joly?'

'As I said, it's very difficult to make out what Joly thinks about things.'

'And how's the baby?'

'Oh, he's fine. He's out with Nanny right now, but he'll be back for lunch. You'll see him then.' She gave Joan a nervous glance. 'You do want to see him?'

'Of course I want to see him, silly,' Joan said. 'He's the very last Bayley.'

'Brass!' Cynthia Hapgood hissed, standing in the doorway.

Jolinda raised her head. 'Doing what?'

'Coming here.'

'What?' Jolinda instinctively tightened her tie knot and straightened her tunic.

'By himself,' Cynthia said, 'but the boss is watching.'

'Well, get on with your work,' Jolinda said, and again bent

over the papers she had been studying. Cynthia retired into the outer office.

Since her father's promotion and John's disappearance, Jolinda had felt increasingly isolated in her job, although she was still happier at the airfield than anywhere, save in the company of baby Mark. But even he was a constant reminder of the happiness that had been, and now, with every day, seemed less and less likely ever to be again. Work was a panacea, or a placebo – she was not quite sure which. Everyone was unfailingly polite, embarrassingly trying to hide their concern for her well-being under a carefully edited layer of 'normal' good humour and camaraderie. Wing Commander Browne stopped by the WAAF office every day for a chat, and more often than not Bob Newman did so as well.

Bob felt a special interest, of course. Not only had he been John's best friend, he had also been his best man. Now he gave every impression of feeling personally responsible for her. He had in fact repeatedly suggested she might like to go to the pub with him – 'and the lads', of course – for a drink. Thus far she had always declined, although the temptation was there, especially on evenings when she knew that Mark would be away on some conference or other and there would be only Helen at home. Helen was a very sweet person, always anxious to do the right thing, to make her feel entirely at home at Hillside, which in fact she did. But Helen had clearly made up her mind that Johnnie was dead. Even if she would never admit that, it was evident in her heavy sighs, the way she steered around the subject of his return. Or not.

Bob and the lads refused to contemplate the possibility that their Squadron Leader, as they still considered him although Newman had been promoted to take his place, would not be coming home. In their company she could be that certain too. But the certainty was diminishing day by day. She had not seen him since that fateful day, after the most memorable sex she had ever had, when she had driven to the station on the pillion of his Harley-Davidson and watched him climb into his Spitfire.

Four and half months ago! Perhaps it was not so very long, but it had seemed an eternity. The visit of that Leadbeater character had not actually helped. For that night and the next fortnight she had been on cloud nine. But Leadbeater had strongly suggested that John could not be more than a fortnight behind him. That had been three months ago.

This was where her father would have been such a comfort. Mark was always encouraging, but Mark, if still important in the aircraft industry, was no longer in the heart of the RAF. He did not know what was actually going on; Daddy did. But he had been posted to a command in the north, and had not been able to get down to see her for two months. Then he had been totally optimistic, and he remained so in his letters. But in his heart? And his head?

And now this man, who she had never met, coming towards her, unaccompanied by the WingCo . . . that had to have been his decision.

She felt quite sick as she heard the feet on the steps and listened to the scraping of a chair as Cynthia hastily stood to attention. 'Sir!'

'Air Commodore Poultrie.'

'Yes, sir!'

'I am looking for Section Officer Bayley.'

'Yes, sir.' Cynthia marched across the room and stood in the doorway. 'Excuse me, ma'am. Air Commodore Poultrie is here.'

'Oh! Please ask him to come in.' Jolinda stood to attention, saluted as the tall, somewhat sharp-featured man loomed in the doorway. 'Sir!'

'At ease, Section Officer.'

'Thank you, sir. That will be all, Miss Hapgood.'

'Yes, ma'am.' Cynthia went to the door.

'And close the door, would you, Miss . . . ah . . .'

'Hapgood,' Jolinda repeated. But this was the worst she could have expected.

Cynthia closed the door.

'Do sit down,' Poultrie invited. Jolinda sank into her chair and the Air Commodore placed the straight chair in front of the desk and also sat. 'I know your father. And your father-in-law,' he added, as if uncertain which was the more important reference.

Jolinda could think of nothing to say, except to ask the one question she dared not.

'I understand you have a son.'

'Yes, sir.'

'That must have been a great comfort to you, these past months.'

Why don't you come out and say it, you great oaf? Jolinda wondered. But she said, 'Yes, sir. He would be better with a father.'

'I'm told that you are an American.'

'I have dual nationality, sir.'

'But you've lived most of your life over there?'

'Yes, sir.'

'And I believe you served for a while with the Army Air Corps?'

Jolinda felt close to screaming; would he ever stop beating about the bush? 'I did, sir, yes.'

'So, how do you feel about this development?'

'I am delighted that the United States is now in the War, sir.'

'You don't feel that you should hurry back and rejoin your old outfit?'

'No, sir, I do not. I feel I am doing the best job I can right here. There is also the fact that I am married to an English officer and have an English son. As well as an English father.'

'Oh, quite. Absolutely. I imagine you know the facts surrounding your husband's mishap?'

At last. 'I know that he was alive when he reached the ground, sir.'

'Oh, indeed. Did you also know that he found it necessary to kill a German officer to avoid capture?'

'I know that is what the Germans claim, sir.'

'I'm afraid it's true. So you'll understand that because of all this it has taken some time to get him out.' Jolinda's heart leapt. 'The Spanish got in on the act and our people had a difficult time. The Spanish, as you may know, are fascists – or at least, they have a fascist government – and when they discovered that Squadron Leader Bayley was in their country, they wanted to put him under arrest and return him to Germany.'

'May I ask how they discovered that, sir?'

'I suppose some Spanish clerk at the embassy leaked it. Our people had to do a lot of diplomatic cajoling as well as arm-twisting to get him out.'

'But he is out, sir?'

178

'Oh, indeed. He's in London.'

For some moments Jolinda couldn't speak. All this pointless chat, when . . .

Poultrie was peering at her. 'Are you all right?'

Jolinda swallowed. 'Just . . . as you say, sir, it has been a long time. May I have leave?'

'To go up to town? I don't think that would be a good idea.'

Jolinda stared at him with her mouth open.

'You wouldn't be able to see him, you see.'

'Is . . . is he all right?'

'Oh, as far as I know he's physically sound. But he's being debriefed by MI9. That's all very hush-hush, but I gather he has a lot to tell them. He'll be free in about a week, and have leave. Then you'll be able to have some time off to be with him.'

'Thank you, sir.'

'Well . . .' the Air Commodore stood up. 'I thought you'd like to know. We are delighted to have him back, of course. I imagine you are, too.'

Jolinda had to suppose that he was suffering from acute embarrassment. 'Yes, sir.'

'There's just one thing: you must not ask him about his experiences during these last few months. I appreciate that you will want to know what happened and how he got on, but you see, he was rescued, and taken care off, and eventually smuggled out of France, by members of the French Underground, the Resistance. And, well, one careless word could endanger quite a few lives.' He glanced at her expression and gulped. 'Of course, I'm not suggesting that you would betray any confidences, but . . . well, we simply can't be too careful.'

'I understand, sir.'

'Yes. Well . . . good luck.'

'Thank you, sir.' Jolinda saluted.

Nine

Speed

John closed the bedroom door, leaned against it.

Jolinda, who had led him into the room, turned to face him. 'Should we have stayed down longer?'

'They understand that . . . well . . .'

'We have things to discuss – or not, as the case might be.'

There were so many things to discuss which could not be discussed. There were so many things to be done which he had, from time to time, doubted he would ever be able to do again. There were so many things to look at, to be seen, which he had doubted he would ever see again, things such as Jolinda slowly unbuttoning her tunic.

But overlaying them all, there were so many things that had to be forgotten. No, not so many things. Just the one. But that . . . Liane had told him that a virile man who did not have sex, at least occasionally, could have his brain so clogged with desire that his efficiency might be halved. But far from unclogging his brain, she had filled it up again, with a greater desire than he had ever known. And he could not be sure whether the desire was for the most beautiful and compelling of women, or for a beautiful woman who could kill, without passion or even, he felt, any animosity towards her victim, but simply because it had to be done. But now she was gone. 'I shall not see you again,' she had said.

Of course he knew that to her he was no more than an incident. He hoped he had been a memorable incident, but in a life so filled with incident as hers, so lived on a knife-edge far sharper than even that of a fighter pilot, he could not hope to be more than a brief memory. But for him . . . some poet had written, he recalled, 'see Naples and die'. He wondered if any poet would ever write 'hold Liane de Gruchy naked in your arms and cease caring whether you live or die'.

Jolinda laid her tunic across a chair and released her tie. 'Have I said the wrong thing?'

'Eh? No, of course not. I . . . ah . . ..the boy's looking fine.'

'He is fine. And he did recognize you – or more probably, I think, your voice. Would you like me to finish undressing?' Both voice and expression were a mixture of apprehension and defiance.

John crossed the room and took her in his arms. 'I feel as if this is our first night together.'

She kissed him. 'Snap. I feel quite virginal. And I'm told I can't even ask you how many women you had to sleep with to get out of France.' She felt his body stiffen even as a shadow crossed his face. 'Shit! Now I *have* said the wrong thing.'

'No,' he said fiercely, 'never the wrong thing.'

'But—'

He lifted her from the floor and carried her to the bed. 'No buts, either. I'm back. I'd like that to be all that matters.'

She kicked off her shoes. 'It is all that matters, Johnnie. To me.'

Yet there were certain things that could not be kept secret. To John's great relief there was no problem when he got to grips with Jolinda's body. But of course she had to come across the scar tissue on his leg and wanted to examine it. 'This looks like a professional job.'

'Do you mean the shooting or the mending?'

'Both, I'd say. I assume the shooting was done by that German officer. I mean, that's public knowledge, right. As for the mending, I suppose you can't talk about that.'

'I can tell you that she was a nurse.'

'You mean you got to a hospital without the Krauts finding out?'

'No, she did it in her own home.'

'So you weren't entirely bereft of female company.'

'She happened to be a widow, who was sixty-two years old. She had been a nurse in the Great War. Now, you know I can't tell you anything more than that.'

'I know. I'm being a very naughty girl.' She switched off the light. 'But you will be able to tell me about it one day, won't you?'

'When this is over.'

'Promise?'

'I promise.'

She snuggled against him. 'I'm glad she was sixty-two.'

The whole family was interested, and anxious, about what was going to happen next, although they controlled their curiosity for the next few days. They were glorious days, even if the weather was abominable. But to sit on the hearth rug and play with little Mark while Jolinda sat and watched them, her splendid legs always available for a stroke, was sheer heaven. Gradually the memory, first of all of Severine and then even of Liane, began to dissipate. She was a dream that had drifted across his consciousness, but he also knew that she, and her very existence, was very close to a nightmare. Even the long weeks he had spent hanging around Spain, the days he had spent in a Spanish cell not knowing if, or indeed when, he was going to be escorted back to the border to be handed over to the Gestapo, began to fade, even if his anger lingered. That near catastrophe had been caused by the anxiety of the Madrid Embassy not to risk offending the Franco regime. But at least it had ended well, as he had been virtually abducted by a couple of MI6 agents and smuggled across the border into Portugal.

And now he was home, and safe, and enjoying the gradual reduction in tension as each day went by. But even a week in paradise must come to an end.

'Is it back to the station?' Mark asked at breakfast.

Helen shuddered.

'Actually, not right away,' John said.

'Thank God for that,' Jolinda remarked. 'I think they should keep you on the ground for a while.'

'I seem to have been on the ground for a hell of a long time.'

'If you're not going straight back to flying,' Mark said, 'what are you going to do?' He believed in sticking to the point.

'I honestly have no idea. I'm supposed to be going up to a place called Hatfield, I think it's in Hertfordshire, for a meeting with a WingCo named Hoosen.'

'Did you say *Hatfield*?'

'Do you know it?'

'It's where de Havilland have their factory.'

'Don't tell me I'm being sent back to Tiger Moths?'

'They've been working on something very big,' Mark said, 'very hush-hush.'

'But you know what it is?'

'I'll be very interested to hear what they want you to do,' Mark said, enigmatically.

'This is called a Mosquito,' Wing Commander Hoosen explained. 'It is the most revolutionary combat aircraft ever built.'

He was a dapper little man who wore a moustache and exuded a tremendous air of enthusiasm, and John did his best to look impressed, although the twin-engined machine on the tarmac in front of him struck him as being rather old-fashioned, certainly in appearance.

'Have a closer look,' Hoosen invited.

John went up to the machine, nodded to the two mechanics waiting beside it, and peered into the cockpit. 'I flew a two-seater at the beginning of the War. But the gunner was situated in a separate cockpit behind the pilot.'

'That would have been a Boulton Paul Defiant.'

'Yes, sir.'

'How did you get on?'

'I was shot down the first time I encountered a 109. Jerry was about half again as fast, was better armed, turned and climbed far quicker, and frankly, having to leave the gunnery to someone else was cack-handed.'

'Absolutely. In this machine the pilot will do the shooting.'

John stooped to look underneath. 'What with?'

'Oh, this machine is unarmed. Strictly PR. It's a prototype, although we already have an operational squadron. A bomber, a fighter and a fighter-bomber version are all being developed.'

'Sounds interesting, although I wouldn't like to be drifting around taking photographs and have no firepower when a 109 turns up. Will the fighters also be two-seaters? I mean, I can understand two seats being necessary for photo reconnaissance, but I can't see the use in a fighter.'

'The co-pilot is your navigator.'

'I've never had a navigator. We don't use them in Spits.'

'What length of time was your average sortie?'

'Hour and a half, maybe.'

'During which time you might cover five hundred miles, there and back. Thus most of your flying time is over familiar territory and can be done on compass and speedo. This little fellow has a range of three times that.'

'You have to be joking – with respect, sir.'

'I never joke about the Mosquito.'

'But . . . fifteen hundred miles would take us to Berlin and back with fuel left in the tank.'

'There you've hit the nail exactly on the head. You will have bomber range with fighter speed and manoeuvrability.'

John gave a low whistle. 'Some concept – if it works.'

'It works. As I said, this machine is operational. We've been using it and its sisters for photo ops for the past three months. This baby has nipped down to Naples to photograph Italian dispositions there and come back for tea, all without refuelling.'

'And the Italian air force hasn't taken offence? Much less the Luftwaffe? I mean, no matter what kind of range it has, an unarmed aircraft has got to be a sitting duck.'

'Jerry doesn't know what's hit him – mainly, I suppose, because nothing *has* actually hit him, yet. He knows something's going on, but he has no idea what it is.'

'I'm sorry, sir. You've lost me.'

'Well, let's put it this way: what would you regard as a reasonable range from which you could bring down a German aircraft?'

'Well, obviously, the closer the better. I usually try to get up to within a hundred yards.'

'And over that? Say five hundred?'

John shrugged. 'It can happen, and sometimes it does. But the odds are against it.'

'But you can usually get within the required range. How do you do that?'

John frowned. Judging by both his rank and his medal ribbons this man was at least as experienced as himself. 'It's not difficult, as a rule. As you both want to get at the other, you generally close up pretty fast. Then it's a matter of looking for height advantage, or getting on his tail.'

'But the key to combat is what you have just said: you both want to get at the other. Supposing your opponent decided to decline combat and go home?'

'That's a pretty dicey thing to attempt, when in battle. It wouldn't make you very popular with your mates, either.'

'I said *decline* combat, not break off. What would happen if, the moment you sighted a flight of Messerschmitts, they turned and made off? Could you catch them?'

John considered. 'It would be difficult. I think we have the faster machines, but the difference is only a matter of ten or so miles an hour. Superiority in the air, when you have a general speed parity, depends more on speed of turn, rate of climb; in other words, manoeuvrability rather than sheer velocity.'

'Quite. I understand you have thirty-eight kills to your credit. I assume some of those were bombers. But do you think you would have been able to shoot down any enemy fighter if he'd made off the moment he saw you?'

'Of course not. But if he did that, he wouldn't be fulfilling his function, whether that be to attack one of our formation or defend his own. So why would he be up there at all?'

'He might be taking photographs.'

'Ah, I see what you're driving at. This is a PR job. But it would still be very dicey. I mean, taking photographs, of enemy installation or dispositions, by definition means penetrating enemy airspace, probably to some distance. If while you're doing this the alarm goes out, which it certainly would, you could find a squadron of interceptors waiting for you on your way home.'

'So what would you do?'

'I suppose, try to blast your way through them.'

'Suppose you were unarmed?'

John grinned. 'Your best bet would be to bale out before they shot you up.'

'Shouldn't you try to outrun them?'

'Wouldn't be practical, sir. There's no plane on earth can outrun a 109, if it happens to be between you and where you want to go. I suppose, if you spotted him early enough, you could go the other way. But then you'd run out of fuel over enemy territory, wouldn't you?'

'Not with fifteen hundred miles in your tank.'

John looked from him to the Mosquito. 'It's a point. But, to follow your hypothesis to a logical conclusion, sir, if you took evasive action by flying deeper into enemy airspace, they would merely call up more fighters and you'd have flak to contend with as well.'

'But supposing you were capable of flying too fast for any interceptor to catch, or any anti-aircraft gunner to hit, even allowing the maximum deflection?'

John looked at the machine again. 'That would have to be some speed.'

'How would four hundred and twenty plus grab you?'

'Are you serious, sir? This . . . four hundred and twenty? May I ask how that is achieved? Have we got a new engine?'

'There's no single answer to that, Bayley, as I'm sure you understand. There is no new engine. The Mosquito uses the good old Merlin, as does your Spitfire. It's a somewhat modified version, certainly, but the additional speed is obtained through a new exhaust system and various other refinements, such as additional streamlining together with reduced weight. Have a closer look at the fuselage. You won't find a single rivet head protruding above the surface. Do you remember how the Spitfire's speed was increased by about thirty mph when all the rivet heads were shaved off?'

'Ye-es . . .' John said.

'This plane actually doesn't have any rivets at all.'

'Sir? What holds it together?'

'Examine it.'

John frowned and went up to the machine, running his hand over the bodywork. 'My God! This is wood!'

'Right first time.'

'You seriously expect a plane made of wood to fly at more than four hundred miles an hour? It'd fall apart!'

'This machine has flown at over four hundred miles an hour on several sorties, including that one to Naples and back. It's still in one piece.'

'But how?'

'The secret is lamination.'

'That's glue, isn't it? You mean it's just glued together? Jesus!'

'We're not talking about ordinary glue, Bayley. This fuselage is created in a mould. The various sections are dovetailed together just like a piece of furniture, with glue, and then subjected to enormous heat and pressure, the glue as well, until what emerges is a solid shell that is as hard as steel only half as heavy, and half as expensive too – at least in terms of material cost. And it saves steel, which is always in short supply. The process itself is of course expensive. I know it sounds pretty well unbelievable, but it works. Now, would you like to take her up? I'll fly co-pilot.'

'I'd love to take her up, sir. But . . . why me?'

'Because we'd like you to fly one. Operationally.'

'Well?' Hoosen asked, as they walked away from the aircraft. 'What do you think?'

John stopped and turned back to look at the machine. 'That is the most fabulous experience I've ever had, sir.'

'Oh, good show. I hoped you'd say that. Come inside.' He ushered John into an office, cosily warm after the chill outside. 'Julie, this is Squadron Leader Bayley. You may have heard the name.'

The young woman was plain, but had a pleasant smile. 'Indeed I have, sir. Will you be joining us, Squadron Leader?'

'Ah . . .'

'I think we could all do with a cup of coffee,' Hoosen suggested. 'Do sit down, Bayley.' He sat himself, behind the desk, while the secretary did things with a small hob in the corner. 'You have to volunteer.' He gave a brief smile. 'It's not everyone's cup of tea. But if you enjoy flying it . . .'

'I did enjoy it, sir. But frankly, photo reconnaissance is not really my scene. And I assume it would mean leaving 833?'

'It would mean leaving 833. I assume you know that, in view of your long absence, you've been replaced as Squadron Leader?'

John accepted a cup of coffee from Julie. 'Thank you. Yes, I do know that, sir. By Bob Newman. He's the ideal chap for the job. But I would still hope to be posted to a fighter squadron.'

'You would be flying a fighter – the best fighter in the world.'

'But . . . you said—'

'That the fighter version is still being developed. However, we're only talking about a few months, now. You'll need that time to get to know your machine. You will also have to train for night fighting. Ever done any night flying?'

'Not intentionally.'

'So you'll need the time. It'll also mean a leg up.'

'Sir?'

'WingCo. Oh, you won't have a wing to command, but you'll be joining an elite group. Which is where you belong, in view of your record. So . . .?'

Thoughts chased each other through John's mind. His only real fear during the long four months that he had been out of action had been that of being grounded because some idiot might suppose he was no longer flying fit. It had occurred to him that the pill might be sugar-coated in the form of another stripe, but he had not felt that even promotion would make up for not being allowed to fly in combat. But here he was being offered both the stripe and . . . the best interceptor in the world, with the suggestion that he would no longer be flying in an essentially defensive role. It sounded like a dream. But it would mean turning his back on the machines, and the men, with whom he had lived and fought for what seemed an eternity, even if it was only eighteen months . . .

It was a decision such as he had made once before, when he had broken his engagement to Avril Pope in order to pursue Jolinda Hargreaves. He still felt guilty about that from time to time, although there had been other, no less compelling reasons for not going through with what would probably have been a disastrous marriage. But he had never regretted the decision. So now . . . Hoosen was watching him somewhat anxiously. 'I would like to volunteer to fly Mosquitoes, sir.'

'You must tell us all about it,' Helen said at dinner.

'I'm sorry. I'm forbidden to talk about it. It's top secret.'

'Oh!' Helen looked at her husband.

'I'm afraid he's right, darling. This is a very hush-hush business, and must remain so until these new aircraft are fully operational and in the public eye, as it were.'

'But *you* know all about it.'

'I've been shown the machine, yes. But I'm in the business.'

'Well, really!'

'Let's concentrate on what really matters,' Jolinda suggested.

'I suppose you know all about this new airplane?' Helen remarked, now in a thorough huff.

'No, I do not,' Jolinda said, 'but I do know that Johnnie is to be a WingCo.'

'John,' Mark said. 'you never told me!'

'Well, it's not actually confirmed yet. I gather I get the rank when I qualify for the new job.'

'Do you have any doubt about that?'

'No.'

'Well, then . . . Clements! Bollinger!'

Max found it difficult to decide whether February in Trondheim was worse than January; the ice on the harbour was certainly thicker. But he supposed he was better off here than in Russia, where the Luftwaffe was hanging on to its positions by the skin of its chattering teeth. Poor Gunther and Horst!

As for Hildegarde . . . she wrote to him every week, but as all mail was subject to the censors she had to be very guarded in what she said. Thus she always appeared cheerful and upbeat, but he could read between the lines with sufficient clarity to be certain that she was feeling more than just her separation from him. The only doubts she expressed about the future concerned the likelihood of a delay in their wedding, but that in itself was a giveaway.

Meanwhile, he supposed, life had to go on. He stood at the window of his office and watched a Gustav slither down the iced-over runway before coming to a halt precariously close to the perimeter fence. It was a tribute to his pilots that there had only been one landing accident so far.

The machine was instantly surrounded by the ground crew, while the waiting fire engine returned slowly to its station. Max went into the dispersal room to greet the pilot. He had in fact been sent up an hour earlier in response to a call from Oslo Command to check out an unidentified aircraft coming up the coast, almost certainly on photo reconnaissance. 'Well?' he asked. 'That took you a while. Did you get him?'

'No, Herr Colonel. I did not.' The young man seemed thoroughly out of sorts.

'Well,' Max said soothingly, 'picking up a lone machine in all that cloud has to be tricky.'

'It's quite clear above three thousand metres, sir. I picked him up all right. The coordinates were spot on, and I was actually in front of him when I saw him.'

'But he saw you and made off?'

'That's one way of putting it, sir.'

Max frowned. 'How would you put it, Lieutenant Weber?'

'Well, sir, he didn't see me for several minutes. I got behind him and was closing, and I was within a thousand yards and getting ready to open fire, when someone on board the enemy machine noticed me.'

'You man this was a bomber? Flying alone?'

'I don't think it was a bomber, sir. It wasn't big enough. But I'm sure it had more than one person on board. And when whoever it was spotted me, it just went off.'

'Went off? Before you could fire?'

'I did fire, sir, as soon as I saw it moving away from me. But the range was too great.'

'You say you saw it moving away from you. What was your speed?'

'I was attacking, sir. Five hundred and seventy kph.'

'And it moved away from you? That's impossible! How fast was it moving?'

'Well, sir, when I realized what was happening, I closed down my vents and got up to six hundred. I could only sustain that for a few minutes, of course, before my engine started to overheat and seize. But the enemy still moved away from me, very comfortably. It was going at least seven hundred kph.'

'Weber,' Max said, 'are you sure you weren't hallucinating? It's very easy to do, alone up there. You know as well as I that the fastest Spitfire in the RAF has a top speed of three hundred and seventy mph. That's just under six hundred kph. There's no aircraft in the world capable of flying a hundred kph faster than that!'

'It flew away from me, sir. When my speed was six hundred.'

There could be no doubt that he was telling the truth, as he saw it. And Max knew that the Luftwaffe was experimenting with an aircraft to be powered by jet propulsion, which it was claimed would fly at a thousand kph. Therefore it was reasonable to suppose that the RAF would be doing the same. But the key word was *experimenting*; so far as he knew no such machine had yet taken to the air. Could the British have stolen so enormous an advantage as to have such a machine in service?

'Sit down, Weber, and describe this machine to me.'

'Well, sir, as I said, I am sure there were two men on board.

I only had a brief glance, but it struck me that they were seated beside each other, like pilot and co-pilot, instead of one behind the other, as one would have expected in a fast, small plane.'

'You say small. How small?'

'Oh, it was bigger than my 109, but not by so much. I'd say it was about the size of a 110. Yes, of course, it had twin engines too. Do you think the British have developed their own version of the 110?'

'The 110, Weber, is significantly slower than the 109, and equally, much slower than a Spitfire. They were a complete failure during the Battle of Britain two years ago. I can't imagine the RAF seeking to replicate them at this stage. And two engines . . . that's the reason the 110 is slower: the additional weight; yet you claim this monstrosity outpaced you.'

'Sir?' The young man bristled.

'Relax. I'm not calling you a liar. But if I am to report this to headquarters, as I must, I wish to make sure they are not going to call *me* a liar. So tell me this, and think very carefully before replying: did you observe any additional means of propulsion?'

'Sir?' He was clearly mystified by the question.

'What I'm thinking of would be a couple of large exhausts, below and behind the engines.'

'I saw nothing like that, sir.'

'Very good. Now, what sort of armament did it carry?'

'I saw no weapons, sir.'

'Weber, be reasonable. You claim to have encountered a machine that is a hundred kph faster than a Gustav, flying unaccompanied and unescorted in our airspace, and that it was unarmed? Defenceless?'

'I saw no evidence of any guns, sir. And although, with that speed, it surely would have had the advantage in combat, certainly one-to-one, it made no attempt to engage me.'

'Very good, Weber. Go and have a glass of schnapps and a rest. On the basis of what you've told me, we'll make up a report for GHQ. I will require you to sign the report.'

'Yes, sir.'

The door closed and Max looked at Senior Lieutenant Kuypers, who had been taking notes. 'Battle fatigue, Herr Colonel?'

'Hardly likely. He's only been commissioned three months.

He hasn't any kills, as yet. That's why I gave him this chance to bag one.'

'Well, then, sir, that's probably it: inexperience.'

'You don't need a whole lot of experience to watch an aircraft of which you are supposed to be at least the equal, getting away from you in a straight line.'

'The Englander could have been a coward.' Max gazed at him and he flushed. 'There must be some explanation, sir.'

'Even if he was intent only on getting away,' Max said, 'that he could do it simply by opening his throttle is a very disturbing factor. Maybe he was unarmed – this time. What happens if the next time he *is* armed, and there happens to be a squadron of them?'

Kuypers scratched his head.

'You make up that report and let me see it. The sooner we get it off the better.'

'Yes, sir. You don't think it could have been an American machine, do you? I know they don't have roundels, but the colour is the same, and if Weber only caught a glimpse . . .'

'That,' Max said, 'is the most disturbing thing of all.'

Over the next few days Max spent a lot of time looking at the sky. It was a tremendous temptation to go up himself, regardless of his orders. But there were no further reports of this phantom machine invading his airspace. It was the following week that Kuypers appeared in the doorway of his office, looking breathless. 'Message just in, sir.'

'Yes?'

'Field Marshal Milch will be landing here in half an hour.'

'All right, don't panic. He's not likely to bite – you, at any rate. Turn out a guard of honour and make sure that Weber is available.'

Kuypers hurried off and Max straightened his tie, made sure his various crosses were properly aligned, and put on his cap. As he had not heard from Milch since their December meeting, such a sudden appearance at this remote station could only be related to his report. He knew he would have to brace himself for some very searching questions, as would Weber. But the ultimate responsibility would be his.

'The plane is overhead now, sir,' Kuypers said from the doorway.

'Very good. Turn out the guard.'

Max went outside, inspected the forty men hastily assembling on the apron, then looked up at the sky. Milch always flew a 110, and there it was, dropping out of the clouds to approach the field. He recalled flying over the Dunkirk battlefield, not quite two years ago, with the Field Marshal in a 110; was this the same machine?

The Messerschmitt circled the field, receiving instructions concerning wind speed and direction and runway conditions, but as it was the middle of the day there was no ice and the wind was light. As it came lower Max could see into the cockpit, and he frowned. The Field Marshal was piloting, but behind him . . . his heart gave a great leap. The passenger wore a flying helmet, but he was sure he could see yellow hair peeping out from beneath it, and a moment later her face came into view as she looked down at the assembled men.

He almost ran forward, but made himself advance only the two steps necessary to place himself in front of his men. The aircraft touched down and rolled to a halt. Milch threw back the canopy and stepped on to the wing, saluting the two mechanics who had hurried forward. He said something to them, then stepped down and turned back to face the machine. Max was now advancing again, but he checked in turn as he saw the fluttering uniform skirt and the long legs coming over the cockpit side; getting out of a small airplane was definitely not a recipe for female modesty, certainly when her hands were occupied with carrying a briefcase. But a moment later she was on the ground, smoothing her skirt before pulling off her helmet, handing it to a mechanic and replacing it with her side cap, which she had been carrying beneath her shoulder strap.

Max stood in front of them, determined to keep his face straight and his voice even. 'Welcome to Trondheim, Herr Field Marshal.'

'It's good to see you, Max.' Milch shook hands. 'I believe you know Captain Gruner?'

Max gazed at Hildegarde, who gazed back. Her face was also impassive, but her eyes were dancing.

'It is, of course, highly improper for two German officers, in uniform and in public, to kiss each other,' Milch pointed out, 'but you may shake her hand.'

Max took Hildegarde's hand and she gave his fingers a quick squeeze.

'Now,' Milch said, 'let us get the formalities out of the way and get in out of this cold. We have a lot to discuss.'

Max escorted him round the guard of honour, while Hildegarde stood to attention at one side. Thus far she had not spoken a word. But she was here, and with the man who held their fates in the palm of his hand. Max wasn't sure whether or not he was dreaming.

But at last the inspection was over and he was ushering the visitors into his office, past a row of saluting officers.

'Close the door,' Milch said, and he sat behind Max's desk. Max closed the door. 'Now,' Milch said, 'you may kiss your fiancée.'

Max hesitated only a moment, then took Hildegarde into his arms. 'Is this really happening?' he whispered.

'Oh, yes,' she murmured. 'Oh, yes.'

'I'm sure you both need to breathe,' Milch suggested, after a few moments. 'Sit down.' Max glanced at Hildegarde. 'Both of you.'

Max placed two straight chairs before the desk and they sat together, rather as if we were two delinquent schoolchildren before the principal, Max thought.

'I should tell you,' Milch said, 'that the only way I could extricate Captain Gruner from Russia was by having her transferred to my office as my private secretary. I should also say that General Clausen was not very happy about it. But what's the use of having rank if one does not occasionally pull it, eh?'

'Indeed, sir. And thank you. May I ask what the situation in Russia is? We get very few reports up here.'

'The situation in Russia is behind God's back. But our people have, in the main, been able to hold their positions against waves of fresh troops. Those Siberians. Available because of this Japanese adventure. However, the thaw is expected any day now, and we will be able to resume our advance. The Fuehrer is determined not to be distracted this year and to have the campaign completed by the end of the summer.'

'And Five Wing?'

'They're all still there – those of them who haven't come down with frostbite. Because of the weather, there's been little action in the air. They too will get moving again this summer.

What is annoying, and a little bit disturbing, is that the Russians appear to be obtaining increasing amounts of materiel from the West, despite the situation in the Pacific. You know that Singapore has fallen?'

'Yes, sir.'

'That means that the British and the Dutch have been entirely eliminated from south-east Asia, and the American army in the Philippines has been shattered. When you add to that the fact that both the British and American Pacific fleets have been destroyed – the Japanese are claiming to have sunk even one of the aircraft carriers that escaped Pearl Harbor – one would have to say that the democracies are in very deep trouble. Yet they continue to pour material into Russia. It is incredible – and disturbing.'

'Back in December, sir, you told me that America was like an ants' nest, and that one stirred it at one's peril.'

'I did. And I still believe that, but I also said that the Japanese attack should keep them occupied for a year or two. Now it looks as if it might be much longer than that, and yet they seem to have capacity to spare. But I wish to talk about the situation here in the west. Captain—'

Hildegarde opened her briefcase and took out a file, which she placed on the desk. Milch opened it. 'This includes your report on this mysterious aircraft your pilot encountered.'

'Yes, sir. I know it sounds fantastic, but young Weber has always been a conscientious and level-headed officer. I am forced to believe that *something* odd happened up there, even if I cannot accept it all.'

'You may accept it, Colonel.'

'Sir?'

Milch tapped the file. 'There are seven reports in here, from both pilots and observers on the ground, of a very fast twin-engined machine being used by the RAF. They can't all be figments of the imagination. But your man seems to have got closer than any other observer. I note he says the plane was not armed.'

'He did not see any obvious gun muzzles, sir. But he only had a good view for a few seconds.'

'Agreed. But this aircraft made no effort to attack him, although he was alone and unsupported. This also ties in with the other reports. Not one of these machines has ever engaged in combat. They appear to be being used only for reconnaissance. However, as you mention in your report, that is not to say that they cannot be armed, and that could be a serious development. Now, of the seven sightings I have on file, two were in the Mediterranean and one up here. The other four have been over north-western France and Belgium. It's almost unbelievable, but one of the sightings took place over Cologne. That's a long way for an unarmed aircraft to penetrate our space and then leave again unscathed. Flak was useless, both because of its speed and its altitude. Two fighter squadrons were scrambled, but neither could get near it. Max, I want one of those machines brought down so that we can look at it.'

'Yes, sir.' Max's heart began to pound.

'You know that poor Marseille went in?'

'Yes, sir. In the desert, I understand. Do we know what brought him down?'

'Yes, we do. His engine blew up and he did not have time to bale out.'

The two men stared at each other. 'Jesus!' Max whispered.

'I agree with you.'

'But—'

'Max, we've been through this before. The Gustav has now been in production for just on a year. There are well over a thousand of them in service and they have proved a most successful aircraft. Sadly, six of them have developed this unfortunate engine failure. Six, out of a thousand plus. And we are in the middle of a war. It is not possible to even consider grounding the fleet to look for some elusive fault. Marseille was, and is, a hero of the Third Reich. He will always be remembered. My point is that you are his natural successor.'

'Marseille had more than a hundred and fifty kills,' Max muttered.

'And you have eighty. I think it's time you began to add to that number.'

'Yes, *sir*.'

Beside him, Hildegarde stirred restlessly.

'Beginning with one of these mysterious machines. It is my conviction that you are the pilot most capable of bringing one down. Now, as I have explained, they are most active over

France. Therefore I am transferring you back to your old station at Ostend.'

Max could hardly believe his ears. Hildegarde's hand crept into his.

'You will command the station, but you will have carte blanche as to what missions you undertake. You and I will know that your principal mission is to bring down one of these planes.'

'Yes, sir.'

'Excellent. Now, I would like some lunch, then I will take my leave. I wish you to be in Ostend by the end of this week.'

'Yes, sir. Ah . . .'

Milch grinned. 'The really important matter, eh? I think you are senior enough to employ a female secretary. However, if you intend to sleep with her, I would like you to be married. We do not want any more Clausen-type scandals. In any event, you are not yet a general, although if you succeed in this task you may well be one, very shortly. Now, I assume this place has a town hall?'

'Yes, sir.'

'Well, time is passing. I wish to be in Oslo by this evening, so send someone over there right away to obtain a special licence. Then whoever performs the ceremonies can come over here and get it done before lunch. Does that suit you?'

Max looked at Hildegarde.

'That suits me very well, Herr Field Marshal,' she said.

The officers and men gave Milch three cheers as he boarded his 110. As he had a long flight ahead of him, he was actually the most sober man on the station. When his aircraft had left the ground, they crowded round the newlyweds to offer more congratulations.

'I feel quite battered,' Hildegarde gasped, as at last they were allowed to get upstairs to Max's quarters.

'You realize there is only the one bed.'

'Whatever would we do with two? Oh—'

Heinrich waited in the doorway. 'Herr Colonel, Frau Bayley.'

'Heinrich looks after me,' Max explained. 'And now, us.'

'Hello, Heinrich.'

'Frau Bayley.' Heinrich bent over her hand and then left the room, carefully closing the door behind him.

'Frau Bayley,' Hildegarde mused. 'It's not something I thought I'd ever hear.'

'Don't you like it?' Max asked. 'Because it's English?'

'I love it. But . . . what am I, officially? Frau Bayley? Captain Bayley? Or Frau Captain Bayley? Or perhaps Captain Frau Bayley?'

'You are Frau Bayley when out of uniform, Captain Bayley when in uniform.'

'I am in uniform now.'

'But you are about to take the uniform off, I hope.'

She undressed slowly.

'It's been all but six months,' he said, 'but for that one night in the Albert.'

'And that was two month ago,' she reminded him, carefully laying her tunic and then her skirt across a chair. 'I'm sorry about the woollen underwear. This weather is hard on the fundament when you're wearing a skirt.'

'I've spent almost every night of those six months dreaming about those legs,' he said, as she slipped down her thick stockings.

She slid beneath the blanket. 'You mean there've been no blonde and buxom Norwegian *frauleins*?'

He undressed in turn, rapidly. 'Not one. What is the situation with generals?'

'Generals,' she said, 'are history. And he never did fuck me, you know. He was one of those peculiar men who believe that as long as you don't actually penetrate, you aren't committing a sexual act. Thus you can put your hand on your heart and swear to your wife that you've never committed adultery.'

'And the wives believe it?'

'Some do, apparently – or at least they pretend to. But I would like to bury Clausen for ever. Will you help me do that, Max?'

'One should always oblige a lady.'

When they'd got their breath back, she said, 'I thought Berlin was the best I'd ever had, but that was better.

'Max, do you think you can bring down one of these phantoms?'

'I'm going to try.'

She shivered against him. 'Suppose it turns out to be armed after all?'

'No matter how fast he is, he has to get within range to hit me. That means he'll be within my range as well.'

'You're always so sure. Max, if anything was to happen to you . . .'

'But he isn't armed,' Max said, 'or he would have shot down young Weber. So sleep easy, my dearest girl.'

'So there she is,' Hoosen said. 'The de Havilland F11.'

John gazed at the machine. Superficially, it looked no different to the aircraft in which he had trained for the past two months. But the difference was immense.

In the very nose, surrounding the camera, there were four .300 machine guns, and mounted under the wings were four twenty millimetre cannon. All of that, he thought, and 400 plus miles an hour . . .

'There will also be four five-hundred-pound bombs in your fuselage when you're operational,' Hoosen pointed out.

'Which will be . . .?'

Hoosen grinned. 'Soon enough, Wing Commander. You have to select your crew.'

'Hmm.' During his training he had had six different navigators, and had been told from the start that he would have to make a selection. The trouble was that he had liked them all, while he'd felt that they'd all been thrilled at the idea of flying with such a famous fighter ace. Nor had he been able to detect any great difference in knowledge or efficiency between them. But that had all been in training. 'You do realize that it's a blind selection?'

'Not so blind,' Hoosen suggested. 'Two have been navigators in Wellingtons, over Germany, and two more have done some PR work in Spits. Admittedly the other two have no combat experience, but they are regarded as highly promising.'

'I entirely agree. I couldn't ask for a more enthusiastic bunch. I suppose sensibly one should go for either Langley or Belden.'

'Because of their Wellington experience?'

'Because of their experience under fire.'

'Sound thinking. Of course, if your first choice lets you down, you have the right to replace him.'

'And utterly ruin both his morale and his confidence.'

'Didn't you ever have this problem in 833?'

'Not quite in the same way. There were eighteen of us, at

full strength, and the idea was to put up twelve at a time. If someone was slow getting off the ground – or worse, slow getting into combat when the squadron engaged – he was exposed to all the other members of the squadron and he quickly got the message that he either had to pull his socks up or ask for a transfer. Equally, of course, one man letting the squadron down did not necessarily mean disaster. But I never had to tell one of my people that he was being axed; the couple who dropped out realized on their own that they didn't have what it took. Here we are in a one-to-one situation, when a mistake could be fatal.'

'I take your point. But—'

'And I take yours: the decision has to be made. Langley.'

'I couldn't agree with you more.'

'OK. Now tell me when we're operational.'

'We have to wait on the brass for that. But it'll be soon. There's something very big in the air, and you will be part of it.'

Ten

Millennium

'S ingle baby entering Box Six,' the voice on the telephone said. 'It's moving very fast.'

'That's the one,' Max commented.

'Shall I scramble, sir?' asked the dispatcher. 'We'll be next.'

Max regarded the wall map of northern France and Belgium. The Luftwaffe had, over the eighteen months since the Battle of Britain and the increasingly regular incursions into continental airspace by the RAF Bomber Command, devised a very sophisticated system of defences, named the Kammhuber Line, based on a series of 'boxes' into which the entire area was divided. Each box was defended by a separate interceptor wing, and the whole was linked by radar stations to a central headquarters that passed continual information to the various local stations. Thus the commander of each wing could scramble all his available machines whenever an intruder, or group of intruders, entered his box, secure in the knowledge that he would find the enemy, and equally that the engagement would be short and sharp from his point of view, and that as soon as the surviving enemy had reached the limit of his box, he could recall his planes to base to refuel and rearm, knowing that the next box would be waiting to take over the battle.

'Five minutes,' he decided. 'And only one squadron will go up. Hold the rest back.' He winked at the dispatcher. 'Our friend has got to come back again, and we don't know how soon he may decide to do that. I'll take the first.'

He went outside to where his pilots waited. 'Fifty-three will come with me,' he said. 'Fifty-four will await orders. Now remember,' he told the eager young men, 'conventional tactics will not work with this fellow; if you get on his tail he'll simply leave you standing. On the other hand, he's unarmed,

201

so we attack from in front, all of us, together. We want this baby.'

They certainly looked keen enough. He went to his plane, casting a single glance back to the window of his office, where Hildegarde waited. She raised her hand. He climbed into his cockpit. The engine was already running, and he was airborne a moment later. 'Eight thousand metres,' he said, and climbed as steeply as he could. There had been patchy spring cloud over the coast, but at 6,000 metres the sky was absolutely clear. It was still early in the morning, and he knew he, and his squadron, would be almost impossible to spot against the glow of the rising sun.

He swung just south of west, and a moment later his wing man, Joachim Elst, said, 'I see him. One o'clock.'

Max peered into the brightness and made out the speck, coming virtually straight for him, and perhaps a thousand metres beneath him. A sitting duck, it had to be.

'Line abreast,' he commanded, and the squadron fanned out.

The enemy aircraft was already close enough for its twin engines to be discerned. It looked innocuous enough, and in its head-on approach it was difficult to estimate its speed, beyond the rapidity with which it was closing. Max freed the firing button for both his guns and his cannon; he intended to give it everything he possessed, and he assumed that his squadron were preparing to do the same.

It was 1,000 yards away, 500 . . . if it really was unarmed, the British aircraft seemed intent on ramming him. His hand closed on the firing button, and suddenly the approaching plane disappeared. He realized immediately that it had dived, and went into a diving roll himself, turning with such momentum that he blacked out. When he could see again, the enemy was already several thousand yards away and disappearing fast.

Around him his pilots were chattering in a mixture of anger and consternation; he supposed it was a miracle none of them had collided. 'Do we go after him, Herr Colonel?' someone asked.

The invader was already lost in the sun. 'No,' Max said. 'Maybe Four Box will have more luck.'

'What are we going to do?' Hildegarde asked that night in bed.

Max still refused to be discouraged, although he had to recognize the enormity of what had happened. 'First of all, we are going to thank God that they don't seem to have sufficient of these machines to come over in squadrons.'

'But if they're unarmed . . .'

'They're going to be armed soon enough.'

'And then?'

'As I said, however fast he is, if he wants to hit me, he has to come close enough for me to hit him.'

She shuddered, and hugged him.

Air Commodore Poultrie surveyed the faces in front of him. No tyros here; every man was an experienced combat pilot. That they were all now flying the ultimate combat aircraft merely meant that they had closer bonds than ever. But today there was an air of tension and the pilots were more interested in one of the several senior officers who were seated to either side of the Air Commodore. This man, positioned beside Poultrie, wore the insignia of an Air Marshal. He was short and somewhat rotund, with a moustache decorating very rounded features. He looked positively benevolent, but those of the assembly who recognized him knew his reputation.

'Good morning, gentlemen,' Poultrie said. 'I know that you, and your machines, have been operational for the last fortnight and have been frustrated at not being let off the leash, as it were. But of course there was a reason for this. Your debut as a fighting force has been delayed so as to make the maximum impact, on an occasion that will be one of the decisive moments of the War. Air Marshal Sir Arthur Harris has come here today to put you in the picture. Sir Arthur.'

The head of Bomber Command stood up. 'What I am going to say to you is top secret and is not to be discussed outside this room. As I cannot give you a precise date on which your mission will take place, I understand that keeping the project under wraps may prove difficult. However, I am informed that you have all been trained to fly a top secret machine over the past few months, and as far as is known, no word of the Mosquito has so far been leaked. So I say to you, keep up the good work.

'Now, I am here today, as Air Commodore Poultrie has said, to put you in the picture. This is because I always believe

203

in having my people know exactly what they are required to do, what are their objectives, and, so far as I am able, what they are likely to encounter. I am addressing you as *my* people. I know you are officially serving under Fighter Command, but for the next fortnight you have been seconded to Bomber Command.

'Now, as I'm sure you know, the bomber has two basic roles in warfare. Tactical bombing is, as the name indicates, the business of attacking specific enemy military formations or installations, with the aim of rendering them unable to carry out their intended tasks. Strategic bombing follows exactly the same principal, only the attack is delivered against an entire nation, with the same idea; preventing it from carrying out *its* intended task, of waging war. I don't think anyone can doubt that where a nation's railway system is entirely disrupted or destroyed by bombing; where its factories are flattened; where its civilian population has its morale lowered by attack after attack, its will to wage war, and eventually its capacity to do so, is deeply, and hopefully fatally, weakened. Hitherto in this war, circumstances have dictated that we have been limited to tactical bombing of enemy dockyards and naval bases on the coast of Western Europe. Oh, we have carried out raids on selected targets inside Germany – we have even raided Berlin, on several occasions. But even these come under the heading of tactical bombing, undertaken to test the German defences and, to be perfectly honest, in the case of Berlin, propaganda purposes. Despite what the newspapers may have printed, not one of them has produced any significant military result. We are now at last in a position to abandon tactical bombing in favour of a strategic offensive.

'Now, I am sure you appreciate that this is an immense undertaking. Equally, you must understand that it will inevitably cause civilian casualties, perhaps on a very large scale. Let me make it perfectly clear that I do not look for civilian casualties. I abhor the idea. But as I say, given the location of most factories in the centre of cities or areas of population intensity, these are inevitable. The risk is increased by the fact that at this moment, bombing from any reasonable – that is, safe – height, is a sadly inaccurate business. Again, forget what you read in the newspapers. The fact is that only five per cent of all the bombs dropped since the War began have actually struck the intended target.

'However, we also need to bear in mind the casualties inflicted upon our own people, and especially those of London, during the Blitz, which was still in operation down to last spring. We need not fear any guilt for returning this devastation upon the enemy, with knobs on. But I want to talk to you about the Blitz. I imagine several of you, if not all, took part in the Battle of Britain, and so you know the awesome feeling that is experienced when you see several hundred enemy aircraft approaching or overhead. Do any of you have any idea of what was the maximum force the Luftwaffe sent against us in any one raid?'

He paused to look around their faces, and someone suggested, 'Three hundred?'

'On 15 September 1940,' Harris said, 'the enemy sent five hundred bombers over London at the same time. That is the greatest air raid in history. The biggest raid we have ever managed to mount in retaliation is two hundred and fifty. Well, gentlemen, it is our intention now to put all such raids into the shade. It is my intention to send one thousand bombers over the selected target. Now, obviously, I am not going to tell you what that target is at this time, but I can tell you that the operation is being code-named "Millennium".

'Now, I'm sure it'll be clear to you that this is no easy undertaking. It will require the employment of every single heavy bomber we possess that can be made serviceable on the night. This includes those currently being used for training ... and their crews. There are those who will, and in fact already do, call it a risk greater than any possible gain. Such negative thinking does not win wars. The gains will be three fold. Firstly, we know that the Nazi defensive system, this so-called Kammhuber Line, which has been responsible for so many of our casualties since its introduction, can only adequately cope with a limited number of bombers at a time, which is all they have so far had to deal with. My concept is that more than six hundred bombers passing through each of their so called "boxes" in an hour – what I would like to call a bomber stream – will entirely wreck their system. Secondly, a blow of this strength and power should just about eliminate the designated target. Thirdly, the propaganda value of such an exercise will be enormous. It is certain that the

Luftwaffe, heavily committed as it is in Russia, will be unable to retaliate, and this raid, the message that it carries, will strike fear into the hearts of everyone living in Germany: which city will be the next target for a thousand British bombers?

'Now I will come to the question that I know you will by now be asking yourselves: where do you, and your fast fighter-bombers – strafers, one might say, rather than blockbusters– fit into this scheme? I am going to tell you. There are obviously going to be some casualties on such a raid. Our intention is to minimize these casualties as far as possible. Thus, on the night of the raid, your squadron, together with a force of fast light bombers, are going to mount a diversionary attack on Belgium and Holland. This will take place before the main bombing force leaves England. I'm not going to allot specific targets. Your objective will be to bomb and strafe everything you come across. Your aim is both to occupy and distract the German radar stations which form the core of the Kammhuber Line and, more importantly, to draw up and engage the very consider-able interceptor forces that the enemy has in those areas. The timings will be given you on the night, but our intention will be to complete your raid, hopefully leaving the enemy both exhausted and distracted, wiping his brow and heaving a sigh of relief that the attack is over, his fighters on the ground being refuelled and rearmed, at the very moment the massive bomber stream appears overhead.

'It will be the greatest night in the history of the Royal Air Force. But I'm afraid there is one small caveat: we intend to launch the attack during the period of the next full moon, 25 to 30 May. That is to say, next week. We cannot be more precise than that because obviously the reason for waiting for the full moon is to obtain maximum visibility, and if the night of our first choice happens to be totally overcast, the attack will have to be postponed. However, in view of what I've told you, I hope you will understand when I now tell you that all leave is cancelled until after the raid. As I have said, this will not be for longer than a week.

'Thank you, gentlemen. I will wish you good hunting.'

'Some show,' remarked Squadron Leader Evans, as they sat in the rear of the van driving them back to the station.

'Are you referring to the speech or the plan?' asked Wing Commander Boston.

'Well, both, I suppose.'

'What he didn't tell you,' Hoosen said, 'is that he's trying to ensure the survival of Bomber Command just as much as he wants to bash Jerry.'

'I'm not with you, sir,' Evans said.

'The fact is, Bomber Command has been getting a lot of stick recently. As he more or less admitted, it really hasn't accomplished anything worthwhile since the start of the War, and now the Yanks have been given airfields for the purposes of their own strategic bombing offensive, we can expect them to be over here in ever increasing numbers with B-17s and B-25s. So there have been mutterings at the top as to whether or not Bomber Command should not be split up into several smaller, purely tactical units. That would put the old boy out of a job – or at least out of the job he wants, which happens to be the job he's got.'

'How do you know all this?' Boston asked.

Hoosen winked. 'I have friends in high places. So he's staking his reputation, and his future, on a really big propaganda coup which will prove to the world, and more importantly, the Chiefs of Staff, that Bomber Command is, and will continue to be, a vital part of the war effort.'

'You mean all that stuff about destroying the enemy's capability or will to wage war by bombing him was just flannel?'

'Not at all. He genuinely believes that it can and it will, if sustained long enough.'

'And meanwhile he's turning us into mass murderers of civilians.'

'That's one point of view. But I'm bound to say that I agree with the old boy. What do you think, John? Does Jerry have it coming, whether he's in uniform or not?'

John remembered Aunt Joan, the most innocent and unwarlike of women, living within not a mile of any military target, but blown up nonetheless. And then he also remembered Warsaw, and Rotterdam, and places closer to home, like Coventry. 'I reckon he has it coming,' he said.

The other officers were silent for a few minutes; they all had a healthy respect for John's record as a fighter pilot. Then Evans asked, 'But can he really do it? Can he raise the planes? I mean, what's our current front-line bomber strength?'

Hoosen considered. 'I would say about four hundred.'

'Then . . .'

'Well, as he said, he can probably raise the same again by using second-line and training machines.'

'With second-line and training crews,' Boston suggested.

'They'll never get better training than on an actual mission.'

The van pulled into the station forecourt.

'Well,' Hoosen said, 'as we're confined to barracks like a bunch of rankers, I suggest we spend the evening in the mess. Johnnie?'

'Seems like a good idea to me. I just need to make a phone call first.'

The Rolls came to a halt before the front steps and Rufus bounded forward. Jim Bearman hurried around the car to open the door for his friend and employer and at the same time field the dog. Mark ruffled the hair on the huge shaggy head. 'Bitten any good burglars today?'

Rufus panted contentedly.

Mark looked around the forecourt and frowned.

'No Harley,' Bearman remarked.

'I was sure he said he was coming in tonight. Hmm . . .'

Clements had opened the front door.

'Evening, Clements. Anyone home?'

'Indeed, sir. They're in the library.'

Mark nodded, gave Rufus a last stroke and limped through the drawing room. Jolinda was in the library doorway. 'Dad!'

Mark frowned. It was unlike his daughter-in-law to be visibly agitated, even if, remembering the night John had been reported missing, he knew that she could be very agitated indeed, under the surface. 'Trouble?'

'I don't know. Johnnie telephoned.'

Mark kissed her forehead. 'So he'll be late.'

'He's not coming.'

'Eh? Why?'

'He wouldn't say, just that he was tied up and that he would be for another week, at least.'

'Damn. He's just not lucky with birthday celebrations.'

'It really is too bad of him,' Helen remarked, as they entered the library. 'I mean, he missed his baby's actual birthday because he was practising with those new machines. But to do it twice . . . I thought the training was completed?'

208

'It is completed. I would say it's too bad of the service,' Jolinda suggested. 'But for a whole week, at least . . .' She watched Mark go to the sideboard and pour himself a whisky. 'You wouldn't know anything about it, would you, Dad?'

'How can I know anything about what's going on in the RAF?'

'You do know, don't you? Come on, Dad.'

Mark drank, deeply, and gave a satisfied grunt. 'It's only a rumour, but apparently Harris is scouring the country for planes and aircrew.'

'Hasn't he got enough already?'

'Apparently he wants more. And now: every last one. We've had a Lancaster in our hangar for the past month, trying out a new bombsight. We've been having a few problems with the exact siting. Today we received orders that the machine was to be returned to its squadron immediately, with or without bombsight.'

'So what's the flap? Don't tell me we're about to invade Europe?'

'I don't think that's possible. There's been no corresponding agitation in the Army or Navy. Anyway, we simply don't have the resources to mount an invasion of the continent on our own. We have to wait for the Yanks – I beg your pardon, Joly, I meant to say, our American friends – to get their act together. No, this seems to be a strictly RAF commotion. What I don't quite follow is where Johnnie comes into it. This calling in of every available heavy bomber is Harris's show, but the Mosquito squadrons are Fighter Command.'

'They carry bombs, don't they?'

'They're equipped to do so, certainly, but they hardly come into the category of heavy bombers. Anyway, they're too fast to form part of a bombing group. Hmm . . .'

'Well,' Helen said, 'as Johnnie's definitely not coming, are we going to celebrate baby Mark's birthday plus a month or not?'

Mark looked at Jolinda, who shrugged. 'I'm sure it's what Johnnie would wish us to do.'

'Right. Clements?'

'I have it here, sir.' Clements placed the ice bucket on the sideboard.

* * *

Max stood to attention as the now familiar Messerschmitt 110 dropped out of the heavy cloud cover and touched down on the Ostend airstrip. If he usually enjoyed his meetings with the Field Marshal, he was not actually looking forward to this one.

Milch acknowledged the salutes of the waiting ground crew and came towards him. 'Max! How are you finding married life?'

'This married life is perfection, Herr Field Marshal, as I hope you will observe for yourself. You will stay for lunch?'

'I think I can do that, yes. But first, we need to talk – privately.'

'Of course, sir.' Max ushered the Field Marshal into his office and closed the door. 'I'm afraid that I have no successes to offer you.'

Milch took off his cap and sat at the desk, laying his baton in front of him. 'You have had no sightings?'

'We have had several sightings. And once I felt certain we had an engagement in prospect. We were twelve to one. But the bastard simply got away from us.'

'Without firing a shot?'

'That's correct, sir.'

'Well, as long as they confine themselves to reconnaissance rather than combat, they're a nuisance rather than a threat. I am here on a more important matter.'

Max raised his eyebrows. He had not supposed there was a more important matter at this moment.

'Tell me what you know of the word "Millennium".'

'Ah . . . I believe, if any of us are still alive in sixty years' time, we will just have celebrated one.'

'You have not heard the word used in any current context?'

'No, sir.' Max was thoroughly mystified. 'I can see no reason why it should be.'

'Millennium means a thousand.'

'A thousand years, yes, sir.'

'But it can be applied to other matters referring to the figure one thousand?'

'Ye-es, sir . . .'

'We're getting reports from our agents in England of considerable aircraft movement within the country, of squadrons being secretly assembled on stations in the east. And with these movements is associated the word Millennium. This is obviously a code name for some operation the English are planning. The point is, does it refer to the place, or places, to which the plan is directed, or to the plan itself, perhaps its composition, having regard to the meaning of the word? Or is it just a name coming off the top of someone's head?'

Max frowned. 'It's difficult to relate it to any current situation.'

'Well, let us run through the possibilities. It definitely seems to involve the RAF. So, can it be their one thousandth raid?'

'Surely not?'

'I agree with you. They haven't yet achieved anything near that figure. Well, then, a thousandth city or target? But again, they've surely not reached that figure. A raid involving a thousand planes?'

The two men stared at each other. 'Is that possible?' Max asked.

'Based on the information currently available, I would have said not. As far as we know, Bomber Command only possesses about four hundred heavy bombers serviceable at any one time. But these reports of aircraft assemblies are worrying.'

'A thousand bombers,' Max said thoughtfully. 'That would certainly be a massive demonstration of strength. On the other hand, sir, it would surely only amount to a propaganda exercise. So they send over a thousand bombers all together. They could probably cover from Bordeaux to the Frisians.'

'That would swamp our boxes.'

'It would, but I would still think we could bring down a large number of them. It hardly seems worth it. Unless . . . can it be a preliminary to an invasion?'

'That would certainly seem the most logical explanation. Except that our most recent reports indicate that Great Britain does not have the resources to land on the continent, at least in any force. In addition, there are no reports of any concentrations of the Royal Navy, which would certainly be necessary to enable an invasion.'

'Then I would say again, sir, that if these reports are true it sounds like a massive and irrelevant propaganda exercise.'

'Yes. Yes, it would seem so.' Milch stood up. 'Let us go and have lunch with your beautiful wife.' He put on his cap, went to the door, then turned back. 'Suppose, just suppose, they do manage to scrape up a thousand bombers, and launched them all against a single target . . .'

'Sir, what target could possibly be sufficiently important to warrant such an outlay?'

'There's the point. One would suppose Berlin in the obvious answer. But would England dare send every bomber it possesses right across Germany at the same time? The casualties would be astronomical.'

Max grinned. 'We could wipe out the entire Bomber Command in one night.'

'But of course, they know that. It would have to be a target far closer to their bases, one covered by their radio direction-finding beams. Think of one, Max. A major target within reasonable range of England.'

'Well, in their various assaults on German targets, they've always gone for ports. The reason is obvious: ports, whether they are on the sea or on rivers, are easier to find and identify than inland cities. So, I would say . . . Hamburg.'

'Excellent. If they intend to raid Hamburg, they will have to pass over you here.'

'Yes,' Max agreed. 'I would look forward to that.'

Milch nodded thoughtfully. 'You do realize, Max, that if a thousand bombers were to get through and drop their loads on any city, it would be the end of that city? It would be wiped off the map.'

'I understand that, sir,' Max acknowledged. 'They will not get through here.'

'The squadron will stand by,' Dispersal announced.

'Golly!' Evans remarked. '*Der tag*, what?'

Hoosen was looking out of the window. 'The old boy must know something we don't. That's bloody thick.'

John could tell that nerves were beginning to fray, which he supposed was natural and inevitable, when they had been cooped up on the station for a week. He had just been lucky that he'd got in that phone call to Jolinda before security really clamped down and cut them off altogether. He certainly hoped it was tonight, 27 May. The first day of the full moon. But he agreed with Hoosen: the clouds were thick and low and very heavy. He did not suppose it would affect their operation greatly, as they would virtually be flying blind even if it was as bright as day. But for the bomber crews, so many of them totally inexperienced, to find a target in this murk would be an impossible task.

The Mosquito pilots went back to playing poker, the more frustrating because, being on stand by, they couldn't even have a beer.

The next two days were grim, as the total overcast continued, and the squadron was relieved only by the sensational news received on the 29th. Two days before, on the day of their first standby, Reinhard Heydrich, widely known as Hitler's Hangman, had been assassinated in Prague, where he had been appointed Reich 'Protector' of Czechoslovakia. But it was difficult for the British pilots to relate that incident to their own dilemma, even if they could recognize that the consequences for Czechoslovakia would be incalculable and probably horrendous.

On the morning of 30 May the cloud was broken, although still heavy. It was that afternoon when they were summoned to a conference with the Group Captain.

'You mark my words,' Hoosen said gloomily, 'the whole thing is going to be cancelled. We've spent ten days sitting on our asses to no purpose.'

But Spencer was smiling at them. 'Gentlemen,' he announced, 'we're going tonight.'

Several heads turned to look out of the window.

'I know,' Spencer said. 'It's not perfect, but the Met boys say that there's a chance of several breaks in the cloud this evening, and Air Marshal Harris has made the decision that the raid should take place. The fact is that if we don't go tonight we may not go at all. This is the last night with sufficient moon for a month, and who can tell what changes in the overall situation may take place in a month.'

Hoosen nudged John; they were sharing the same reflection: that while the Prime Minister and the War Cabinet had sanctioned this project, they were well aware that tying up the entire Bomber Command in a single enterprise was a very high risk strategy, and if given another four weeks to think about it, they could well change their minds.

'I can now also tell you,' Spencer went on, 'that the target has been decided. It was recognized from the start that even using a radio beam for navigation it had to be somewhere easy to find, in view of the comparative inexperience of so many of the navigators being employed. That meant somewhere on a river, which could be found and followed to the destination. It also, of course, had to be a place large enough and significant enough to be worth destroying. The choice was therefore narrowed down to one of two places, Hamburg or Cologne. Bomber Command has considered each alternative in detail and has opted for Cologne.

'Now, this choice in no way interferes with our task, which is to distract the German defences, both on the ground and in the air, by a diversionary raid on the Low Countries. The programme is as follows: Operation Millennium will commence at midnight, when the bombers will take off from their various airfields, rendezvous, and head across northern France for the Rhine. You will take off at 2200 and drop your bombs on your designated target areas. These are listed on the board. Having dropped your bombs you will remain in the area to act as back-up and to protect the light bombers who will be following you half an hour later. You will obviously maintain sufficient altitude to be out of the range of Jerry's flak, except when, if necessary, actually engaging an enemy machine. It is estimated that the bombers will have completed their mission and returned to base by 2330. You will follow them home. Questions?'

'We are to be airborne for a maximum of two hours, sir,' Hoosen said. 'We have much greater capacity than that. Should we not, on the completion of our mission, nip across to Cologne and lend a hand?'

'Definitely not,' Spencer told him, 'for two reasons. One is that you will not have a hand to lend, as you will have expended your bombs over Belgium and Holland—'

'We'll still have our cannon and machine guns, and we won't have sorted out *all* the enemy fighter strength.'

'The other reason, Wing Commander, is that you would get in the way. There are going to be a thousand-plus bombers over the one target, concentrating on dropping their cargoes. And it will be dark. The last thing they need is a bunch of Mosquitoes buzzing in and out and around. You would, in fact, stand a very good chance of collision, and certainly of being shot at by our own people. Bomber Command accepts that, however successful your diversionary raid may be, there will be interceptors left to engage them, and they are prepared to cope with that, principally by firing on any fighter that comes within range. This is a team effort, gentlemen. You are each required to do a specific job of work. Yours is perhaps the most difficult of the night, but you will do it with your customary and acknowledged skill and devotion.

'Good hunting.'

The pilots and their crews dined together. All were serious enough, although John reflected that this could possibly be because, unusually, no alcohol was served with the meal. 'How are you feeling?' he asked Langley. They had now been teamed for several weeks and he felt that he knew the sergeant as well as it was possible, given their different backgrounds. He also knew that Langley was a veteran of several raids over Germany, in his capacity of navigator in Wellingtons. But they had never been in combat together.

'Tense, sir,' the sergeant replied. 'But I have always been tense just before a mission. It goes once I'm airborne. I don't suppose you feel anything at all.'

'What makes you say that?'

'Well, sir, a man of your experience, with so many kills . . .'

'The tension is always there, Sergeant. In fact, if you weren't tense just before a mission, you'd be no bloody good. Tension gets the adrenaline flowing, and the adrenaline stokes up the brain, makes one more alert, quickens the reactions. You need all of those things to survive in aerial combat, much less triumph. Don't ever be ashamed of being tense.'

'Thank you, sir. May I say that it's a privilege to fly with you.'

John grinned. 'I hope you'll say that again, when we come back.'

Spencer gave them their targets just before take off. 'John, your Red Section will be first in: you're to take out Ostend. You will, of course, not attack the city; your target is the considerable base just outside. You will drop your bombs there, doing the maximum damage, and then strafe it. If the Luftwaffe come up, get as many as you can. Then follow the rest of the squadron to Brussels and on to Maastricht. After the Ostend attack, maintain twenty thousand feet and keep an eye open for the bombers. When they go home, so do we. Understood?'

215

'Affirmative, sir.'

He joined Langley, who was waiting by the aircraft with three ground crew. 'Couldn't ask for a better night, sir,' the sergeant said.

John looked up. There was quite a lot of cloud, but it was sufficiently broken to allow patches of brilliant moonlight to flood the airfield. 'If it's as bright as this over Cologne, those chaps'll be laughing,' he remarked, studying his instruments as he buckled his belts.

Langley was watching the time. 'Three minutes.'

John pushed his head out of the cockpit. 'Start her up, Corporal.'

The engines started and Langley commenced his checks, reading off the dials for John to say, 'Affirmative.' Then the battery starter was towed away and he could report to the tower, 'FF706, all checked.'

'FF706, you are cleared for take off.'

Spencer was already airborne, followed by Hoosen. John was next, and they circled the field while the rest of the squadron assumed their places.

'Take your positions,' Spencer said, and they climbed to 25,000 feet before setting course to the east. In only a few minutes they were across the Channel.

'Follow me, Red Section,' John said, and he went into a steep dive.

Below him the water sparkled in the moonlight. The sea port itself was blacked out, but it was still easy to discern; it was very nearly as light as day, and the docks made a perfect target.

'Left three,' Langley said, his voice quiet. 'Height eight thousand.'

John made the course adjustment, and now he could see the airfield, with its rows of parked machines. At the same time several puffs of black cloud appeared. 'They seem to be awake,' Langley remarked. But the gunners on the ground were not fast enough to deal with the Mosquitoes.

'Bombs ready,' Langley said, as quietly as ever.

Max and Hildegarde dined in Ostend, as they did almost every Saturday night. They had a favourite fish restaurant close to the docks, where they could enjoy everything from mussels to lobster, washed down with a good hock brought in from Germany. The waiters were servile and attentive, which Max, with his English upbringing, found irritating, although Hildegarde took it as their due; they were, after all, the conquerors.

'It will be thawing in Russia,' she remarked, as she ate her peach Melba. 'The campaign will be beginning again.'

'You sound as if you'd like to be there.'

'The only place I'd like to be is where I am, with you. But I do remember last summer, when every day brought a fresh victory, a fresh advance. Gunther and your Wing will be flying again now.'

'It is his Wing now,' Max pointed out.

'Do you resent that?'

'No. He's a first-class pilot as well as being my best friend. I wish him every joy of it. Besides, I know that nothing remains the same for ever.' He reached across the table to squeeze her hand. 'Except, I hope, you and me.'

She gazed at him for several seconds. 'Not even us, Max.'

It was his turn to stare. Like his father, or his brother, or his Aunt Joan, he had an in-built fear of a woman who could, so calmly, announce that she had only a few months to live. But lightning could surely never strike twice in the same place.

She gave a quick smile. 'Don't look so alarmed. I don't think they will shoot an army officer who becomes pregnant – at least, not if she is married.'

Now his jaw dropped. 'My God! Hilde!'

'Shh,' she begged. 'People are looking at us.'

'But . . . is it true? Can it be true?'

'Scheitel confirmed it this morning. I was waiting for the right moment to tell you. I'll have to resign my commission.'

'They'll have to give you maternity leave. *I* will give you maternity leave. But . . . I cannot believe it!'

She raised her eyebrows. 'Do you mean that you doubt your own virility? I've never seen any evidence of that.'

'Well, I've never been a father before.'

'I don't think you ever had the right woman before,' she suggested.

'Excellent point. We must have champagne.'

'Tomorrow,' she decided. 'We've had sufficient for tonight,

and I'm not sure baby would like to be involved in a car smash at this early stage in his life. We should get home.'

'Of course. Albert!'

He paid the bill and escorted her outside to the waiting command car. She looked out at the moonlight streaming across the sea outside the harbour. 'What a magnificent night. It is a night for – shit!'

The wail of the air raid siren cut cross the darkness. They both looked up but could see nothing. 'Listen,' Max snapped, 'you stay in town.'

'Of course I'm not staying in town,' she retorted.

'I have to get to the station.'

'*We* have got to get to the station.' She was already getting into the car.

Max scrambled behind the wheel, started the engine and raced out of the town, horn blaring to warn people to get out of his way. Now they heard the explosion of the anti-aircraft guns, but they still couldn't see any planes above them.

'Are they attacking here?' Hildegarde gasped, hanging on to the door as Max took a corner on two wheels.

'I shouldn't think so.'

'But they must be low if the guns are firing.'

'Yes,' he said. Hamburg, he thought. They must be on their way to Hamburg. But ... a thousand planes? Surely they would be heard, no matter how high they were. And these were apparently low enough to make the ack-ack gunners feel they could be reached.

'Are you going up?' she asked.

'I hope the squadron is already up, my darling. I'll have to catch them up.'

She bit her lip and then gasped. 'What's that?'

In front of them there was a sudden sheet of flame, and a moment later they heard the boom of the explosion, the shock waves causing the car to tremble and swerve to and fro.

'Max!' Hildegarde screamed.

'I have it,' he snapped, regaining control.

'What's the explosion?'

'Our fuel tanks. They're strafing the airfield.' His shoulders hunched over the wheel as he increased speed.

* * *

In the brilliant moonlight the field stood out as if illuminated. The three Mosquitoes swarmed down on it, reducing speed as they approached to make sure their bombs hit their targets.

'Two on the parked aircraft, one on the buildings and the last on that fuel tank,' John told Langley. 'But we need some altitude for that. I'll tell you when.'

'Understood.' Langley was concentrating. 'Two miles, six thousand . . . One mile, five thousand . . . Target, four thousand . . . One away . . . Level flight, two away.'

The noise of the explosions rose even above the roar of the engines, and the blast shook the aircraft.

'Three away.'

'Climbing,' John said.

'Six thousand.'

'Round we go.' He cast a glance to left and right. Behind him the night was brightened by the fires on the ground, but the other two planes were on station, untouched by the desultory ack-ack fire.

'Target one mile,' Langley said. 'Eight thousand.'

'That'll have to do. Your call, Sergeant.'

There was a moment's silence, then the quiet voice said, 'Four.'

John immediately opened full throttle, at the same time pulling back the stick. The whoompf came about three seconds later, and the night turned bright as day. The machine was carried upwards by the blast like a leaf in a strong wind.

'I reckon we just made that,' Langley remarked, 'but it was a hit.'

John again made sure that the other machines were still there. 'Let's do some work,' he said, and swung back towards the field.

Several planes were on fire, and some others had been tossed, either turned upside down or on to one side, their wings snapped. But three were off the ground and climbing. 'One each,' John said, and switched, as he liked to do, to the German wavelength.

The chatter was excited, and for a moment too fast for him to pick up, proficient as he was in German. Then a voice said, 'The Colonel! The Colonel! Where is the Colonel?'

'Colonel Bayley is dining in Ostend with his wife,' a calmer voice said; clearly that was ground control. 'He will be here.'

Max! John thought. A colonel! And obviously in command of the field. And he has a wife? He shook his head to banish the conflicting emotions welling up inside him.

The first machine was still climbing desperately. Now the pilot saw the approaching Mosquito and turned toward it. But John was far too fast for him, had completed his turn to get him in his sights, and fired a preliminary machine-gun burst. The German attempted to dive, but John comfortably kept him both in his sights and within range. He fired both his cannon, and the Messerschmitt exploded with such violence that the pilot was hurled from his cockpit to go whirling through the air.

'Like shooting fish in a barrel,' Langley commented.

John watched the parachute open, but his mind was still occupied with what he had just heard. He wondered where Max was now. Still in Ostend? Somewhere on the road? Or in that holocaust beneath him? How he wished Max could have been airborne, so that they could have met for what would have been the last time.

But there was still a job to be done. 'One strafing run,' he said, 'then we go on to Brussels.'

The Mosquitoes dived again.

Max stood on the apron and surveyed the glowing wreckage; amazingly, few of the buildings seemed to have been hit. Hildegarde remained by the car. 'They came in so fast,' Senior Lieutenant Fischer explained. 'We saw the flight approaching on radar and scrambled immediately, but they were on us before we could take off. Three got up and they were shot down in seconds.'

'How many of the enemy were there?'

'Three.'

'*Three*?'

'There were some more above but they did not come down.'

'There should have been a thousand.'

Fischer scratched his head.

Lieutenant Schiffers pushed his head out of the office window. 'There are some more coming now, Herr Colonel, but these are not so fast.'

'How many?'

'Estimated twenty-four, sir.'

'And I have no planes,' Max growled. 'Get Aachen on the

phone. Tell them what has happened here and tell them that I need planes *now*.' He returned to the car. 'It looks as if our quarters are undamaged. You'd better get to bed. I doubt they'll come back here.'

'But you are going up?'

'Just as soon as I can find something to go up in. There's something wrong. This was supposed to be a massive raid, not a few planes.' He looked up at the now empty sky. 'Where the hell are they?'

'What a show!' The Mosquito pilots might all be senior and experienced officers, but they were as excited as young recruits. 'And we didn't lose a plane!'

'A couple of the bombers went in,' Hoosen reminded them.

'But how did the big show go?'

It was just dawn, and few of them had slept at all. John stood at the window to look out at the morning; presumably they would be stood down in a few hours and he would be able to get home to Joly and the boy. But like his fellows, if for a different reason, his mind was still lost in the night's operation. For the third time since their estrangement, he and Max had been within a few hundred yards of each other. The first time, when they had both been tyros, in those early days of May 1940, Max had had him in his sights but had not fired, presumably because he had known it was his brother. By the second time, last autumn, they were both changed men, both by their experiences in combat and, in Max's case, certainly, by domestic catastrophe. Then Max had fully intended to kill him. This time . . . would the boot have been on the other foot? Could John really have shot his own brother down? But Max had never even got off the ground.

Spencer joined them. 'Signal from Bomber Command. The raid was a complete success. Cologne no longer exists – at least, that's what the crews are claiming.'

'Casualties?' Hoosen asked.

'On the ground, incalculable, at least at the moment. We lost a few, but not as many as had been anticipated. Now, as I was saying, while everyone is agreed that the target was obliterated, Air Marshal Harris wants proof. We're sending over four aircraft on PR duty, but as Jerry's still in a bit of a buzz it's felt that these should be armed. I'd like some volunteers.'

221

All the pilots stepped forward.

'Thank you, gentlemen. If you're up to it, Johnnie, and you, Joe, and . . .'

'I'm sorry to drag you out again,' John told Langley.

'No problem, sir. But *is* there a problem?'

'Only that his nibs wants evidence of what was done. So it's a quick in, take a few snaps, and then out again.'

'No combat, sir? If we bag another one, won't it be your fortieth?'

'Don't tell me you've been keeping count?'

'Well, sir . . .' Langley flushed.

'You're absolutely right. However, this is not a combat mission. Strictly PR. We'll be back for lunch.'

'Cologne,' Milch said over the telephone. 'They struck Cologne just after midnight. And there were more than a thousand of them.'

'Damnation!' Max exclaimed. 'Was it bad?'

'At the moment, we can't get in to find out, but that in itself suggests that it was very bad indeed. Now tell me what happened to you.'

'We were strafed, sir, but that was at ten o'clock. Our lot must have been a diversionary force.'

'So it would appear. Casualties?'

'Fifteen planes lost.'

'*Fifteen*?'

'Only three in the air. The other twelve were on the ground.'

'How many did you get up?'

'Three.'

There was a moment's silence. Then the Field Marshal said, 'You mean everything you got up was shot down.'

'Yes, sir. The enemy were faster and better armed.'

Another brief silence. 'This is a serious matter,' Milch said. 'But you say there were only three of them?'

'Only three attacked us, sir. I think there were more overhead.'

'Hmm. And you are all right?'

'I never even got off the ground.'

'And Hildegarde?'

'She's all right. A little shaken. Well, we all are.'

'But you will fly again?'

'Of course, sir. As soon as the replacement planes I have requisitioned arrive, and –' he looked out of the office window – 'they're coming in now. I intend to devise the necessary tactics for dealing with these enemy machines and instruct my pilots accordingly.'

'Good man. I look forward to hearing from you.'

Max hung up and went outside to watch the flights of Gustavs coming in. 'Now we have a squadron again, Herr Colonel,' said Senior Lieutenant Wexler.

'Indeed we do,' Max agreed. 'And the first thing . . .'

Both men turned as the Dispatcher hurried up to them. 'A signal from Central Control, Herr Colonel. There's a flight of enemy aircraft, moving very quickly, approaching from the west.'

'A flight? One flight?'

'Only four planes are reported, sir.'

'Reconnaissance,' Wexler suggested.

'Obviously, but we still want them. Which boxes have been alerted, Staedtler?'

'The boxes are still disorganized, Herr Colonel. Last night's raid left them all in a mess.'

'Very good. Tell Central Control we'll handle it, but I want accurate data as to the enemy speed and course, as quickly as possible, and a constant update of their position. Wexler, have these new machines fuelled and armed immediately.'

'Can we get up in time to catch them, sir?'

'No,' Max said, 'but this time we're going to stop them coming back. I want every machine we have serviceable in the air the moment we get a position.'

'Do you see what I see, sir?' Langley asked.

'Yes,' John said. 'What a mess.'

Actually, they could see nothing at all. In front of them, where their navigation told them Cologne had to be – or had been – there was nothing but an enormous pall of black smoke, several miles high and spreading over a huge area.

'Well,' Spencer's voice came over the mike, 'I don't think we're going to accomplish much here. Once we fly into that muck we won't see a thing. We'll photograph the smoke and go home. Follow me.'

The four Mosquitoes circled the cloud. Langley took several photos. 'Like the man said, sir, I don't know what these are going to prove.'

'They'll certainly suggest that there can't be too much left under there. So, home for lunch.' And Hillside this afternoon, he thought.

For some minutes they flew in silence. He suspected everyone was suffering a sense of anticlimax. Then Hoosen said, quietly, 'Bandits, ten o'clock.'

'And quite a few,' John muttered.

'More than twenty,' Langley said, 'two squadrons.'

'What do you reckon, sir?' Hoosen asked. He was speaking for all of them.

The hesitation was brief: despite the original orders of no combat, Spencer was feeling as frustrated as any of them. 'We'll take them. But no dogfighting. We shoot our way through and go home. But see if you can pick up number forty, Johnnie.'

'I certainly intend to try, sir.'

Johnnie! He was there! And flying one of these damned new machines! He could even have been one of those who had strafed Ostend last night. And now he was seeking his fortieth kill. And as always, *he* was out in front of his squadron. Without hesitation, Max made up his mind. 'Well, Johnnie,' he said, in English, 'you will be my eighty-first. Waggle your wings.'

For a moment there was no response; the English pilots had been taken by surprise, and the distance was closing very fast. Then the starboard machine did waggle its wings.

'He's all yours, Johnnie,' a voice said, and the other machines turned away to plunge into the midst of the main German body.

Shrugging off a fleeting memory from their shared childhood, Johnny set his jaw, ready for action.

Max had already set his firing button. He remembered from the last time he had encountered one of these that it had suddenly taken amazingly fast evasive action. But that machine had been unarmed. Now ... he fired both his cannon and mentally cursed: he had made the error committed by so many of his antagonists over the past two years, and fired too soon.

Then John was gone, diving beneath him. To get away? He couldn't believe that.

Angrily he twisted his head and saw the Mosquito, having passed beneath him and turned virtually in its own length, on his tail, its centrally grouped machine guns spitting red. Desperately he pulled the stick back and went into a steep climb, uncertain whether he'd been hit or not. He rolled, firing as he did so as the enemy plane passed across his vision, but he didn't suppose he'd hit anything. Now he dived. If he could get the bugger in his sights, just for a moment . . .

The Messerschmitt seemed to leap into the air as the cannon shells struck it. 'Shit!' Max shouted. Then he smelt smoke at the same instant as flames licked out of his engine. He was done. He pushed back the canopy and fell out into the bright morning.

A moment later his parachute opened and he was floating over the French countryside. And like that, it was over. Johnny had more guts than Max had credited him with. And there was the Mosquito dropping down beside him, and John raising his glove in a salute, before soaring away to rejoin his comrades.

'You're alive, and that's all that matters,' Hildegarde said.

'She's right.' Milch agreed.

'I've never been shot down before,' Max said, still miserable, 'by another plane.'

'It was bound to happen some time. There will be other battles, and these will be won. You will have your hundred kills.'

'Against those machines, sir?'

'Well,' Milch said, 'we'll have to develop some new machines of our own. In fact, we're already doing so. Now I must be going. I congratulate you, I congratulate you both, on your domestic bliss.'

He left them holding hands.

'The Bollinger, sir,' Clements said, placing the tray on the sideboard.

'You'll join us?' Mark said.

'What exactly are we celebrating?' John asked.

'Your fortieth kill?' Mark suggested.

'The success of the Mosquito in battle?' Air Vice Marshal Hargreaves said.

'Your shooting down Max?' Jolinda put in.

'I had the better plane,' Johnny interjected, still uncertain as to how he felt about his supposed victory over Max. What if he hadn't baled in time? At that moment, in the heat of battle, Johnny had seriously wanted to kill him, but now, in the cold light of day . . .

'You were the better man, on the day,' his father insisted.

'And there'll be other days,' Hargreaves said. 'The Cologne raid was not quite the success the newspapers are claiming.'

All their heads turned.

'Oh, the town is very badly damaged. They say more than fifty thousand people are homeless, but only about five hundred were killed.'

'Well, surely that has to be a good thing,' his daughter remarked.

'Perhaps, but there's no evidence that German morale has been damaged. So Harris is planning another.'

'Another thousand?' Mark was horrified. 'Will he get the go-ahead?'

'He has it. Whitehall is over the moon – more at the propaganda value than any actual damage. Britain, supposed to be in extremis, can still put up twice as many bombers as the mighty Luftwaffe. He has his eye on Hamburg, and this time he means business. Over half the bomb load is going to be incendiaries.'

'But,' John said, 'if he's going to blanket bomb with incendiaries . . .'

'Yes,' Hargreaves agreed. 'He means to burn the city to the ground.'

'And the people in it,' Mark said sombrely.

Jolinda shivered.

AUTHOR'S NOTE

The full life and career of Liane de Gruchy can be found in the four Resistance novels, also published by Severn House.

Resistance
The Game of Treachery
Legacy of Hate
The Brightest Day